Sex on the Move
A Wicked Words short-story collection

Look out for other themed Wicked Words Collections

Sex on the Move

A Wicked Words short-story collection

Edited by Adam L. G. Nevill

BLACK LACE

Wicked Words stories contain sexual fantasies.
In real life, always practise safe sex.

This edition published in 2006 by
Black Lace
Thames Wharf Studios
Rainville Road
London W6 9HA

Rush Hour	© Cal Jago
Missionary Impossible	© Maya Hess
Pumps	© Monica Belle
Are We There Yet?	© Portia Da Costa
Life Boat	© Virginia St George
Silent as the Grave	© Fiona Locke
The Brinks Job	© Sophie Mouette
Beauty and the Bull	© Heather Towne
Après-Ski	© Candy Wong
The Wildest Thing	© Teresa Noelle Roberts
Stretched	© Severin Rosetti
On Tour	© Andrea Dale
Pickup Girl	© A. D. R. Forte
Stage Four	© Maddie Mackeown
CC and her Riding Machine	© A Colorado Woman
Cockfosters	© Nuala Deuel

Typeset by SetSystems Limited, Saffron Walden, Essex
Printed and bound by Mackays of Chatham PLC

ISBN 0 352 34034 7
ISBN 9 780352 340344

Contents

Introduction and Newsletter

Ladies and gentlemen, this is the editor speaking. Fasten your seatbelts. There are no emergency exits.

Just the sounds of a train passing in the night, the sight of a plane passing overhead, the energy of an international airport or the briefest scent of the sea can set our imaginations alight. And who has not fantasised about the person in the seat opposite, the face in the crowd of passengers that turned our way or the beautiful eyes that stunned us, momentarily, behind a passing windscreen?

There is just something so damn exciting about transport. Maybe we associate planes, trains, ships and automobiles with the breaking free of routine and responsibility. Or escaping the predictability of existence and the same old faces, watching us, judging us. It could be the rediscovery of who we really are, and what we really want. Or, in turn, we are provided with an opportunity to be someone else, entirely, to play a role. And it can be the actual act of travel, and the means of transport, or the accoutrements of being in transit, rather than the destination, that so powerfully contain this excitement, this passion, this reminder of how intense life can be again. Of how many sensual opportunities exist, out there.

So, when we set the challenge for authors new and old to write imaginative, erotic stories about being on the move, we were caught in a blizzard of submissions. It was so, so hard to make a shortlist. But the successful applicants were chosen because they really captured the spirit of the venture – they distilled the desire to seduce and be seduced that comes with being on the move.

And we were amazed at the sheer range of ideas that touched down here. Maya Hess reminds us that 'In space, no one can hear you scream' in her wonderfully imaginative tale, *Missionary Impossible*. The exquisitely kinky Fiona Locke returns to Wicked Words and teaches us that even a hearse can be sexy in *Silent as the Grave*. In Monica Belle's *Pumps*, the narrator finds it hard even to get her journey started due to a predilection for vibrating hoses on garage forecourts. Portia Da Costa can do things with blindfolds and mystery journeys in cars that can make even the most insensitive skin shiver, pleasurably. Getting to work on a packed train will never be the same again after reading Cal Jago's delightful *Rush Hour*. And there's a real touch of Polanksi and forbidden love in Virginia St George's *Life Boat*. It's a veritable traffic jam of sex. As you turn the pages be prepared for group sex on ferries, naughty girls in ski lifts, domination in limousines, homoerotica in armoured cars and slave girls on tour buses. And, even after all that, we're still not down to fumes and there's no excess baggage. So let's go.

Adam L. G. Nevill, Editor, Autumn 2005

Want to write for Wicked Words?

We are publishing more themed collections, 2006 – made in response to our readers' most popular fantasies. *Sex and Music* and *Sex and Shopping* are the next two collections for 2006. The deadline for both collections has now passed, but if you want to submit a sizzling, beautifully written story for *Sex in Public* (deadline for submissions July 06), *Sex with Strangers* (deadline for submissions October 06), or *Sex with Celebrities* – fictional characters only! – (deadline January 07), please read the following. And keep checking our website for information on future editions.

- Your short story should be 4,000–6,000 words long and not published anywhere in the world – websites excepted.
- Thematically, it should be written with the Black Lace guidelines in mind.
- Ideally there should be a 'sting in the tale' and an element of dramatic tension, with oodles of erotic build-up.
- The story should be about more than 'some people having sex' – we want great characterisation too.
- Keep the explicit anatomical stuff to an absolute minimum.

We are obliged to select stories that are technically fault-less and vibrant and original – as well as fitting in with the tone of the series: upbeat, dynamic, accent on pleasure etc. Our anthologies are a flagship for the series. We pride ourselves on selecting only the best-written erotica from the UK and USA. The key words are: diversity, surprises and faultless writing.

Competition rules will apply to short stories: you will hear back from us about your story <u>only</u> if it has been successful. We cannot give individual feedback on short stories as we receive far too many for this to be possible.

For future collections check the Black Lace website.

If you want to find out more about Black Lace, check our website, where you will find our author guidelines and more information about short stories. It's at <u>www.blacklace-books.co.uk</u>

Alternatively, send a large SAE with a first-class British stamp to:

Black Lace Guidelines
Virgin Books Ltd
Thames Wharf Studios
Rainville Road
London W6 9HA

Rush Hour Cal Jago

I scanned the platform and took a step backwards, turning my head away from the sudden rush of air as the train roared into the station. The tube slowed to a standstill, a set of doors stopping directly in front of me. The carriage was almost empty. I picked up my briefcase and moved to the edge of the platform, pausing as a familiar sensation fluttered in my chest. The doors whooshed open and I strode along beside the train, passing two more sets of doors before I found the right one. Commuters were crammed into the tight space, squashed against the glass, tucked into the curves of the doorways, pressed up against one another. The perfect carriage. The perfect playground.

As the alarm sounded, signalling the imminent closure of the doors, I placed an impossibly high-heeled shoe on to the train, forcing my way into the heaving crowd. If there's one thing I've learned in almost ten years of commuting, it's that there's always room for one more – when that one more is me, obviously.

My last-minute entry meant that, as the train lurched into action, I was totally unprepared. The sudden movement flung me off-balance and straight into a fellow commuter. Not very dignified, but, as I looked up and saw my buffer, I realised that my being propelled into a stranger was something of a blessing. He was just right.

He was in his thirties, fair-haired with beautiful cheekbones. I smiled at him as I straightened myself up. 'I'm so sorry.'

He smiled back and looked a little embarrassed, the

way people do on public transport when someone forces them into communication. 'No problem.'

I continued holding his gaze until his eyes flicked to my left and then down towards the floor. Except he wasn't looking at the floor.

'If I will insist on wearing silly shoes . . .' I continued lightly, shuffling a pointed toe in his direction.

He looked up and I noticed his face redden slightly.

A shy one. How sweet. How absolutely perfect.

I smiled again and then turned around so that my back was towards him, quickly scanning the area immediately surrounding me. A man who looked far too hot in far too many layers of clothing was fanning himself with a copy of *The Times* to my left. Beside me, on my right, a studenty-looking girl was staring into space tapping her fingers in time with whatever was playing on her iPod. Directly in front of me, with barely an inch of space between us, a middle-aged man was engrossed in a Sudoku puzzle, a phenomenon that had frankly passed me by. There are much more exciting things to do on train journeys than number-crunch. Believe me, I know. And, just for your information, before I'd crashed into him, my man had been reading a book – a John Grisham novel. Not very original, but strangely reassuring. Safe men read courtroom dramas, don't they? Psychos don't, I was sure.

As we raced into a tunnel, I very slowly and deliberately bent down, placing my briefcase on the floor. I moved from my waist, keeping my legs and knees absolutely straight – terrible for the back, I know, but, sometimes, needs must – and, as I busied myself with pointlessly positioning and repositioning my bag, I slung my weight onto my left hip.

Bingo. The weight shift had done it. My arse had swung slightly to the left and edged back a little, so, as I forced myself to lean lower still and made a show of hunting for something in my bag, I felt my buttocks brush against Grisham.

He cleared his throat and I felt him move. Whether he was trying to escape the physical contact or increase it, I couldn't tell, as I quickly straightened up. I stood in front of him, much closer than was necessary, even in spite of the fullness of the carriage. My behind was still touching him but the contact was barely perceptible. I felt his breath, hot and heavy, on the back of my neck. This looked promising.

We slowed down and jolted to a stop at the next station. Sudoku was on the move. Perfect. We all edged a little away from him, giving him space to manoeuvre. There was only one direction I was going to move in: backwards. The doors opened, we created a pathway for his exit, and he was gone. I stood pressed closely against Grisham, feeling the rise and fall of his chest against my shoulder blades and the nudging of his toes on the back of my heels. And there was no mistaking what else I could feel stirring against my arse.

I edged my right leg behind me and pressed the back of my thigh firmly against his hardening cock. I shifted my weight again, slowly grinding against his crotch, and felt a burst of hot breath blast against my neck. Game on.

I bent down again, lingering to scratch a nonexistent itch on my shin, and swayed my hips from side to side, just enough movement to cause the friction I wanted. His breathing was shallow now and my knickers were distinctly damp. I straightened up and was surprised to suddenly feel his hand on my hip. His fingertips pressed into my skin, pulling me harder on to his cock. I continued to rock against him but was finding it difficult to remain discreet.

Determined though I was to keep control of myself, there was something I could not resist any longer. I eased my body away from his and felt his grip on my hip tighten. I reached back and gently rubbed the palm of my hand over the front of his trousers.

His fingers trailed along the curve of my hip, then grazed my arse, fluttering across the material of my tailored trousers. He began to caress more insistently, rubbing and squeezing my flesh, and then he drove his fingers between my legs in an effort to force my thighs apart. How easy it would have been to allow him to touch me there. But that wasn't part of the game. I twisted my lower body away from him.

I heard a low groan and quickly reached back, keeping the rest of my body at a safe distance. I closed my fingers around him, feeling his heat as I gripped his hardness, and I squeezed along his length, imagining the sight of him, his cock straining for release. I sensed the tension in every muscle in his body as he tried to keep his composure. He was struggling. He was not the kind of man who let strangers grope him on the train and he certainly wasn't the sort of man to make an exhibition of himself. And yet here we were. Even through the fabric of his trousers, I began to feel his cock pulse and twitch. He was going to come.

Perfect timing. As he tried desperately to hold on, we screeched into the next station. The doors opened and in a lightning moment I had released him, picked up my bag, barged past the student and exited the train.

I didn't look back, though I'd have liked to see the state I'd worked him into. I was curious as to whether the vision of his cock through his trousers was as impressive as the sensation of it in my hands. There was no doubt in my mind that it would have been. And I'd have liked to see the expression of sheer bloody disbelief on his face. It was an expression I'd seen so many times before – because sometimes I did look back – and it was one that sent an electric spasm between my thighs every time. How totally broken apart and lost they looked and how exhilarating to have been the cause of such undoing.

But, seconds later, my thoughts took a darker turn, as they often did. He would undoubtedly be pissed off. Would he really let me get away with it? Or would he follow me? Stalk me along the platform, shadow me through the exit barriers and track my movements on the streets above? Would he catch up with me, whisper angry words in my ear and demand to claim what had been promised? In short, would he be so desperate that he'd hunt me down and fuck me? And would I be so desperate for my own release that I would let him?

Needless to say, he didn't. He wouldn't. He would feel frustrated. Enraged, probably. He would think the word 'bitch', say it aloud even, a hiss of bitterness under his breath. But, ultimately, he wouldn't want to make a scene.

I always enjoyed the rush of those first couple of minutes afterwards. Because no matter how many times I'd done it, or how confidently I strode, or how much absolute trust I had in my intuitive ability to choose my playmate for the journey, there was always, always, the very real possibility that I could fuck it all up. There was always a chance that I'd pick the wrong man.

The cacophony of voices, traffic and general city noise brought some clarity to my frenzied mind as I exited the underground and made my way along the busy street above. But, still, my body was buzzing as I walked the familiar route to work.

There had been countless Grishams. My first hit was accidental, so I suppose it doesn't really count as a hit, but that was what started it all off, so I feel I should mention it. I had left work later than usual and was in a panic because I was sure I was going to miss my train, which in turn would have led me to be late for a dinner date with my then boyfriend. I'd sprinted down the platform, my heart sinking as I saw that the train was packed. A seat was out of the question, but would there be standing room for one more? Well, of course there was, but only just. It was the tightest of squeezes. I forced my way into a vestibule area at the back of the train just as the guard blew his whistle and the door was slammed shut behind me. There were so many of us in that tiny area, all standing in far closer proximity than we would have in any other circumstance. As the train rumbled along we all rocked together, bumping into one another a little, stumbling slightly and reaching out instinctively to keep our balance. I was pressed against a businessman: tall, broad, fortyish. We stood facing each other, my cheek almost touching his shoulder. We were a few minutes into the journey when I finally realised exactly where my hand had ended up when I'd tried to grab something to prevent toppling over. I felt myself blush but, as I went to remove my hand, the man took hold of my wrist, keeping me in position. All things considered, I guess he was a bit of a pervert. But, judging by the immediate drenching of my underwear, I guess I was too.

Trains had always, in my mind, been a great location for crotch watching. One of my favourite commuting pastimes up until that point had been sitting staring – discreetly, of course – at all the sights that met my eyeline You know how it is when sometimes you just want something? Well, Pervy Businessman made me realise just how easy it was to get it.

My first deliberate hit was just a few days after my liaison with Pervy. I hadn't managed to get it out of my head: his sheer audacity making me touch him like that in a crowded carriage. More than that, though, I couldn't get over how much it had turned me on. So one morning I found myself standing near the luggage hold during rush hour. A man was standing opposite me, quiet, unassuming. He looked respectable. Safe. Just as we arrived at the final station stop, we both gathered our belongings ready to move off the train. I had a quick look over my shoulder to check that no one was immediately behind us, then I took a deep breath, reached out and touched him. He turned to me sharply and opened his mouth as though to speak but he remained silent. I rubbed just a little and then squeezed his cock firmly, and then I was gone, speeding along the platform, heart thumping wildly and with a huge grin on my face. It had lasted no more than a few seconds but I couldn't believe I had done it or that I'd got away with it. And I knew then that I was addicted.

You're probably thinking that the leaving part is cruel, and I suppose, if I'm honest, it is. But I enjoy the power of it. Not that it always ends that way. Sometimes they get to come. Unfortunately for Grisham, he was simply a victim of timing. Early-morning meetings really could play havoc with a girl's social life.

My office building was one of those ultra-modern marvels – all open-plan work areas and glass-walled meeting rooms. It was a hive of creativity, containing everything required to produce some of the biggest magazine titles in the country. As the managing editor of the glossy women's monthly, I had an office in the middle of the main editorial area, but that wasn't where I headed straightaway.

I swiped my security pass in the main reception area, took the lift to the third floor and ignored the coffee cart, which was usually my first port of call. I headed straight to the staff toilets, swung a cubicle door open with far more force than I had intended, then locked it behind me and stood with my back to it. I slid one hand down inside the front of my trousers and then hooked a couple of fingers under the cloth of my underwear. I smiled with relief as my fingers began their exploration. There were certainly worse ways to start a Monday morning.

'Kate?' It was Natalie, my PA. 'Is that you?'

For fuck's sake! My hand froze, hovering inside my knickers. I leaned my head back against the door and closed my eyes.

'Kate?'

'Yep,' I said as cheerily as I could. 'It's me.'

'Thought so. Look, I thought I'd better warn you: I've just done the latest cover report and we seem to have forty grand unaccounted for.'

'Unaccounted for?' I sighed and repositioned my clothing, then flushed the loo. Well, thousands of pounds going missing does tend to quash one's ardour – as does having your PA standing with her ear almost up against the door when you're trying to come. I emerged from the cubicle.

'Morning,' Natalie beamed and then quickly became serious again. 'Yes, as in "missing". As in "we've clearly spent it but fuck knows how, where or why".'

I sighed again as I squirted soap onto my hands. It smelled of peaches. How very 80s.

'Also...' I looked at her warily and she smiled apologetically. 'Lindsay Sharman is kicking up a stink about her contract. As in she says we're in breach of it.'

I raised my eyebrows in alarm.

'Personally,' Natalie said conspiratorially, 'I think she's after a bit more money because her column's just won an award. I've dug her contract out and left it on your desk.'

'Thanks. In the meantime, send her some flowers and invite her out for lunch, will you? Sometime next week. I'm sure we can't be in the wrong with this, but I want to keep hold of her.'

I shook my hands over the basin and turned around to find Natalie in front of me holding out a paper towel. 'And also...' she began.

'Are you serious?'

''Fraid so.'

I snatched the towel from her and began to dab at my hands.

'Have you seen the papers this morning?' she asked.

I faltered. 'No. I was working on the train,' I lied.

'Working? On the tube as well?' She pulled a face. 'I don't know how you can. I hate the tube – why don't you just let me arrange for a car to pick you up in the mornings? Much more civilised.'

'As I've told you before, I'm doing my bit for the environment,' I said doing my best not to look shifty.

'Well, I think you're mad. Anyway, the papers. Maya Singleton has been outed in all the tabloids. There are photos of her and her girlfriend looking all lovey-dovey, which doesn't in any way reflect the content of our interview with her.'

I groaned. Maya Singleton was the hottest British property in Hollywood and we had bagged an exclusive with her a few weeks before.

'So, basically, that's October's cover and main inter-view feature shot to shit,' Natalie concluded. 'And, if you're wondering why I've accosted you in the loo, it's because Alex is waiting for you in your office so I thought I'd better prepare you.'

As if I didn't have enough to deal with without the publishing director pouncing on me as soon as I get through the door.

I smiled weakly. 'Thanks, Nat. And, when you've got a minute, would you mind . . .'

'There's a latte on your desk.'

Sometimes, I thank God for Natalie.

Miraculously, the day actually panned out far more posi-tively than the frantic exchange in the loo had led me to expect. A bit of creative thinking and a whole lot of charm meant that, by the time I left the office at 9 p.m., all crises had been pretty much averted.

I slumped, exhausted, into a window seat and willed the train to go faster. The day had presented one major challenge after another and I was looking forward to a soak in the bath and a glass or three of Shiraz. That didn't, however, stop somebody from catching my eye: a boot-shod woman sitting across the aisle. She was very attractive, petite but curvy with dark hair and dark eyes.

A small smile played at the corners of her mouth, which, together with her smart though somewhat rumpled appearance, gave her a just-shagged look, which I found rather appealing. There were a number of factors working against me here, of course. First, I barely had the strength to blink. Secondly, we were both sitting down. In my experience, standing was much better – easier access, easier to make any physical contact look accidental, easier to move position and conceal any sauciness, and easier to escape should a kerfuffle ensue. The final obstacle was, of course, that she was a woman.

It's not that I didn't want to play with women – I most definitely did and, on occasion, I had. It's just that they were tricky. If choosing a male playmate was a risky business, picking a woman was a million times more so. Fundamentally, the crux of the matter was this: no man had ever turned me down. OK, some were up for more than others, some played for a little while, then left rather hastily, some looked quite appalled with themselves – and probably with me too. But not one of them had told me 'no' or pushed me away. Are they just not fussed? Will they take anything going? Perhaps they simply have less to lose and, if some woman wants to grab their dick on their way to work, yippee. Women, I like to think, are far more complex creatures. Anyway, whether my Great Gender Theory was right or not, I remain convinced that a woman is far more likely to reject me so I'm always cautious.

That said, one of my favourite hits of all time was a woman. I had known I wanted her as soon as I had spotted her on the platform but I'd deliberated for ages because she looked so straight. Also, we were waiting for an overground train; the first stop wasn't for half an hour, so, if I made a move and she didn't want to play, I wouldn't be able to escape. But we entered the same coach and both stood at the end of the carriage, so I steeled myself and approached her. I had my hand up her skirt in a matter of seconds and had never felt a woman so wet. I buried my fingers deep inside her and fucked her deliciously slowly as we sped through the Thames Valley, her eyes locked with mine all the time as she stared in surprise while her muscles contracted around me. So determined was I to make her come that I flew past my stop and ended up alighting at Slough. Sometimes, alighting at Slough is worth it.

I turned away from the Booted One. Attracted to her though I was, it just wasn't going to happen. Sometimes, the desire to sleep is just too great.

The remainder of the week past quickly: more meetings, more financial headaches and plenty more train journeys to keep me occupied. Although, I have to confess, I had been very well behaved during my travels since Grisham – until the morning I found myself standing next to Issey Miyake on the tube. Well, a man wearing his aftershave, anyway.

He had caught my eye and smiled and I'd smiled back. He was good-looking and impeccably dressed. His suit looked expensive, though he stood in his shirtsleeves with his jacket slung casually over his shoulder. I felt drawn to him and found myself pressed against him in no time. I was going to enjoy this.

'I've seen you before,' he said suddenly, his mouth close to my ear.

I felt momentarily unsettled, unaccustomed to having to make conversation in such circumstances, but his voice was warm and my unease quickly dissipated. A voyeur who liked what he saw and has waited patiently for his turn – I liked that.

'Really?' I asked, in my lightest, most flirtatious voice. 'And what did you see?' I pushed out my bottom slightly so that it nudged at his crotch.

'You,' he said, gently caressing the back of my thigh.

I smiled. 'Yes?' I reached back to touch him, but, as I did so, found my wrist caught in his hand.

'Being a prick-tease,' he continued, tightening his grip on my wrist.

I gasped in surprise as he continued to squeeze my flesh. Without thinking, I tried to turn and flung my other arm back in an attempt to free myself, a move he was obviously anticipating because he immediately ensnared that wrist too.

A quick risk assessment told me that the situation was obviously not good: I had been grabbed by a stranger with a somewhat threatening demeanour and was unsure how I was going to escape. My heart rate quickened as fear combined with something just as potent; I felt inexplicably weak-kneed with lust and I was appalled at myself. I continued to twist a little in an attempt to break free but he held me firm.

Perhaps, I thought suddenly, this had been the point of the game all along: to find a player as equally skilled as I was. In which case, surely I had to step up now. To call out for help or catch someone's eye so that they rushed to my aid or even to struggle until he released me would all mean the end of the game. And, although people would take my side and he could end up in a whole heap of trouble, ultimately, I couldn't help thinking that I would have lost. And I was a sore loser. Something told me he realised that. Something also told me he wasn't intent on making trouble. He was just out to play. At least, I hoped so.

When we arrived at the next station, I was not surprised to be shoved forward. We made our way through the throng of commuters on the platform, he walking slightly behind me so he could keep me close without anyone being able to see how he was holding me. I assumed we were heading for the exit but, as I followed the crowd in that direction, he steered me another way.

We ducked under a chain sporting a NO ENTRY sign and headed down a steep stairwell. It was difficult keeping my footing with my hands pulled behind me, but, for some reason, I trusted him not to let me fall. I looked around. There was nothing there, just a small area with a barred gate leading to a narrow underground corridor.

He positioned me in front of the gate and stood behind me, retaining his one-handed grip on me. Then I felt movement and heard the rustle of clothing and panicked momentarily – this was all happening too fast. But within seconds his grip on my wrists slackened and I felt the coolness of silk snaking its way across my skin. He fastened his tie securely around both my wrists. It wasn't tight enough to hurt, but it was firm enough to immobilise me.

'Just so we're clear,' he said, '*I'm* playing with *you* now, not the other way around.'

I felt my face flush and my skin prickle as I considered the notion of simply being his toy, passive and vulnerable. The thought was not one that appealed. I couldn't suppress a sigh as I contemplated the fact that I thought I'd given up unsatisfactory sex years ago. What was the point in this?

His hands delicately traced their way across the small of my back and over my hips before coming together to meet on the swell of my buttocks. Then they skimmed downwards until they came to rest on the back of my thighs. He stroked across the fabric of my skirt and then ventured lower. I felt his fingers glide across my stockinged legs as he dived under my skirt, his touch gentle but insistent. I frowned, hating the fact that he was touching me while I couldn't touch him and knowing that there was nothing I could do about it. My skirt hitched as his hand pushed higher, locating the very tops of my stockings. He lingered there, rubbing his fingertips across the coarseness of the lace trim. An unmistakable sigh escaped from his lips as he touched the bare skin of my thighs. Perhaps I had overestimated his control. A smile twitched at the corners of my mouth. This would be easier than I had expected.

'You like that?' I teased and I leaned back a little so that my bound hands just about made contact with his crotch.

He moved back at once. 'Do you like this?' he asked and tugged the tie, making my upper body jerk backwards.

I cried out in surprise and felt ashamed of myself for reacting so pitifully. But then the silk fell away from my wrists and I turned to face him, smiling triumphantly. I had known that he wouldn't be able to hold out on me for long.

He flashed a broad smile, which caught me off-guard, and the next thing I knew he'd grasped my hands again and was tying them in front of me.

'You can't be trusted, I see,' he said, raising my hands slightly so that my arms were outstretched. He stepped forward, turning my body as he moved so that I was facing the gate again, and then he reached forward and deftly fastened the end of the tie to the rails. I went to speak – to object – but then thought better of it. The last thing I wanted was for him to think he had ruffled me. So I stood with my head resting on my hands against the railings, determined not to give anything away.

His hand moved up my legs and then hovered between my thighs. Despite my good intentions to stay in control, I was aroused and, when his fingers at last made contact with the place that yearned for it most, it took an unbelievable amount of effort to remain silent. I bit down on my lip as his fingers began to tease; back and forth they slid across the soft cotton, and then I felt cool air rush across my skin as my knickers were eased down and pooled at my feet. I took a deep breath. This hadn't been what I'd intended when I'd set off for work but I couldn't deny that I was excited.

'You like that?' he asked.

I shrugged, determined not to reveal the unexpected effect he was having on me.

He chuckled. 'You don't want to answer me?'

I cleared my throat and then shook my head.

The shock of his flattened palm making contact with my bare arse threw me off-balance and I momentarily swung a little on the short length of tie that was slackly holding me to the rail. I managed to steady myself quickly but the turn of events had taken me completely by surprise. Apart from anything else, I was shocked by his confidence, his boldness.

A second smack followed, and then another. He barely paused between smacks and I shut my eyes tight, my ears ringing with the sounds of skin-to-skin contact. I gasped with the suddenness each time – the sound, the force, the way it made my body jolt – and I determined to focus on the pain that was spreading across my arse. Well, not so much pain as heat. And, between my legs, fire raged.

I felt him move behind me, then his hands gently held my bottom. His breath cooled my burning skin and my body froze as I stood exposed. Seconds later, his tongue pressed against my tender flesh, tracing along the marks I imagined he must have left on my body. The sensation was excruciatingly sublime as the wetness from his mouth sent chills through my hot skin. My head swirled. Part of my brain still willed me not to give in but my body hummed and all I could think about was how much I wanted to come. I needed to. I hadn't been this desperate for months. But I just couldn't let myself.

'Stop it,' I whispered, breathless. I closed my eyes. 'You have to stop.'

His hands remained on my arse and when he spoke, his lips brushed against my sensitive flesh. 'You want me to stop?' he asked, and then the tip of his tongue zigzagged down my lower back before coming to a stop at the cleft between my buttocks.

I held my breath.

'Are you sure you want me to stop?'

I murmured an indecipherable sound and his tongue returned to my body, gliding its wetness along my centre, making me shiver. Before I knew what I was doing I had instinctively leaned further forward, exposing myself to him completely. He didn't waste a second. He held my thighs wider apart and then pushed his face between them. I moaned as his tongue lapped at my entrance and bent lower allowing him to tickle my clit with the softest motions. I gripped the railings as my thighs began to tremble and he pressed his whole mouth against me, stimulating me with his chin, nose, mouth, everything. I squirmed against him as my orgasm built. And then, nothing, his presence between my legs, gone.

'No,' I whispered, turning around to look at him over my shoulder. He was standing upright now, grinning at me.

'I decided you were right,' he said. 'You know, when you said about stopping.'

I stared at him in amazement. The muscles in my arms, I now realised, were burning having been held up for so long, and my arse was sore from the spanking. But my pussy was pounding. 'Is this payback?' I asked at last.

'I thought you needed teaching a lesson,' he said, stepping closer. 'How not to be a bad girl to men on trains.' He smiled. 'But you obviously can't take it ...'

'Of course I can take it,' I said indignantly. Although, of course, I couldn't.

'Really?' He stood directly behind me and reached for my clit. I gasped despite myself and writhed against his hand as he teased and rubbed for a few brief moments before stopping again.

'Please,' I said in frustration.

'Please what?' He stood so closely to me that I could

feel his breath on my skin. And for the first time, I felt his rock-hard cock straining against my leg.

I bit down on my lip. God, I was desperate.

'Hmm?' He dipped a finger inside me, coating it with my wetness, and groaned as he began to slowly finger-fuck me. 'Please what?' My muscles tightened around him drawing him deeper. 'If your pussy is anything to go by,' he said slowly, 'I'd say you were losing your resolve.'

I couldn't help but smile then. 'And you're not?' I asked as another finger pushed deep inside me. 'Because some-thing tells me this wasn't meant to happen.' I pushed my leg back slightly, nudging his hardness. 'I think you brought me down here to tease me a bit and then leave me wanting. But you haven't left,' I said feeling suddenly bold. He began to thrust his fingers harder. 'Oh.' I tried to concentrate on what I was saying. 'And you haven't left,' I said, bucking slightly to meet his thrust, 'because you want to fuck me.'

'I want to fuck you?' He withdrew my fingers and I panicked for a moment until I felt his fingers circling my clit.

I closed my eyes. I was so close but, now I'd said it, I wanted it so badly. 'Yes,' I hissed.

'Is that what you think?'

'Mmm.' I was starting to feel light-headed.

'And is that what you want?' I heard his zip ease down.

'Yes,' I whispered. 'God, please, fuck me.'

His whole length was inside me in an instant. He grabbed my left hip with one hand as he drove into me with long, smooth strokes and his other hand returned to my clit. My bound hands gripped the rail until the knuck-les faded to white and I pushed myself back forcefully against him, meeting every one of his powerful thrusts. I couldn't remember the last time I had felt so positively taken. He slammed into me harder, all the while rubbing and pinching my clit until it felt ready to burst. I could feel his muscles quivering and his breathing quickened as he began to thrust more rapidly. Then he reached forward and covered my hand with his, an action that, along with his fingers on my clit and his hardness inside me, pushed me over the edge. I came hard, my legs suddenly weak, my wrists shaking against the silk that held me in place; and, shortly afterwards, he climaxed too, burying himself deeper inside me and shouting out close to my ear.

I leaned heavily against the gate and closed my eyes as I waited for my breathing to steady. I could hear him adjusting his clothes and smelled a waft of his scent as he moved closer to me. My wrists began to tingle and I realised that they had been untied. I slowly straightened up and let my arms drop heavily to my sides. They ached and I stretched while clenching and unclenching my fingers in an attempt to loosen them up.

'They've gone a bit numb,' I said, but I knew as I said the words that they were unnecessary. And sure enough, when I turned around, he had gone.

Missionary Impossible
Maya Hess

Nadia Kasparova read the brief. Her eyes moved slowly, incredulously, across the screen as if they were revolving freely in their sockets, as weightless and relaxed as her dangling limbs. She pulled down the hem of her T-shirt, tucking it into the waistband of her sweatpants, and closed her eyes. Wiping away droplets of sweat that had beaded on her recently exercised body, Nadia recalled her years of training. She fast-forwarded everything that she had worked for, replaying it through her mind in order to focus on the latest and highly unusual set of experiments to be carried out on the World Space Station *Ventura*.

'Two hundred and eighty-three days and it has not entered my mind.' Nadia opened her eyes and exhaled heavily. Later, she would be drinking her breath in the form of recycled air. Water was precious three hundred miles above the Earth. 'Up here, I feel barely human. Why do they think I would want to act like one?' She read the brief again, just to make sure: 'Operation EROSS – Experimental Reproduction in Orbiting Space Station ... preparation for sexual reproduction during long-term space missions by husband–wife teams ... possible approaches to sexual relations in the zero-G environment ...'

Nadia switched screens to monitor her other experiments and smiled. She felt comfortable with the tables and graphs that presented strings of numerical information relating to her beloved seedlings. Studying the effect of microgravity on fast-growing plants was the first step to becoming self-sufficient in space during manned missions to Mars and beyond. Not only would the specimens eventually provide a supply of food, but they would also assist with reconditioning waste water and stale air.

How could they possibly expect her to divert her attention to *this* ridiculous new experiment?

'Pfah! I will not do it. My contract states my work and this –' Nadia flicked the monitor with her clipped fingernails '– this is what I am paid to do.' She left the cramped work space and retreated weightlessly to her tiny cabin, making use of the anchor points along the way. She began to mutter in Russian while she unfastened her comfort pack and withdrew a limited number of wet wipes. Unable to rid her usually clear and focused mind of the new brief from Mission Control, Nadia stripped naked and began to vigorously rub the sweat from her body before it could bead and escape into the cabin. She used tooth powder and dry shampoo and applied a smear of moisturiser – her only luxury – before dressing in that week's allocated clean clothing.

'Brig, I'm turning in. Is everything OK your end?' Nadia used the intercom to speak to Commander Robert Brigson.

'I'm just sending reports downstairs for tomorrow's docking procedures. Things are looking good for a clean swap and, boy, I can't wait for something different to eat.'

Nadia smiled, although wouldn't have done if she was speaking with the commander face to face. Robert was easy to get along with, as professional as they came yet strangely casual about falling around the Earth at eighteen thousand miles per hour. By 'downstairs', he meant Mission Control in Florida.

'And we'll have a new friend.' Nadia cleared her throat of whatever was caught there – perhaps the thought of a new crew member sent specifically to assist with the radical experiments, or perhaps just the tooth powder. You couldn't spit in space. Swallowing was imperative.

'Drew? You'll love him. We were in the Air Force

together in the nineties. Nadia, take a look out of your window.'

The intercom went silent for a moment as Nadia turned to the blackness outside. A small but brilliant spangle fizzed over Asia and within seconds had reared up over the planet, spreading its dazzling fingers around the edge of the Earth, making it look like a giant diamond solitaire ring. But only for a few moments, and then the invasive rays of the sun drenched the interior of the space station in annoying heat and light.

'That was nice. I'm tired. Good night, Brig.' Nadia strapped herself into the sleeping bag, which in turn was strapped to a bulkhead, and snapped a mask over her eyes to seal out the light. She sighed. In eighteen hours, the delivery spacecraft *Evolution* would deposit Mission Specialist Captain Drew Masters along with supplies of food, clean clothing and equipment for the laboratory. She struggled to get comfortable as the sunlight filtered through her mask. 'Damned sunrise happens every ninety minutes anyway.' Nadia squirmed onto her side and slipped angrily into her allotted eight hours of sleep. Her fitful dreams were filled with feeble excuses why she wouldn't conduct the ridiculous experiments and the new crew member forcing himself upon her in the name of science. Finally, she slept.

Nadia was woken by piped classical music, courtesy of Mission Control.

'Good morning, Miss Kasparova. Another beautiful day.'

Nadia recognised the voice as Brigitte's, assistant controller in Florida. It was comforting to know that every breath she inhaled, every experiment she undertook and every piece of food she ate was monitored and logged by scores of trained professionals back on Earth. Nadia was convinced that they could read her thoughts too – and she wouldn't have minded, either. Her brain was so honed and sharpened for life in space that there was nothing she wouldn't share with any of the staff back at base. Being an astronaut wasn't simply a job: it was her life.

'Hello, Brigitte. You have sunshine today?' Nadia pushed the mask up into her glossy blonde hair, cropped into a boyish style, and peeled apart the webbing that had held her in place. There was a lag before Brigitte's crackled reply beeped into the cabin.

'Still eighty-four degrees and the sun's going down. Now listen, Nadia, we've been working with your commander for the last few hours but he's resting now in readiness for the docking. All is on schedule and in T minus nine hours forty minutes you're going to have yourself a new buddy.' More static.

Nadia swallowed, remembering yesterday's unexpected brief. 'Buddy?'

Brigitte came back. 'Yeah, you know, like friend, pal . . . er, mate?'

'I know what buddy means.' Nadia was sensitive about her English, aware that her accent tolled with the harsh, almost manly, tones of her native Russian. She was jolted by a sudden wave of terror – something she hadn't experienced since her last solo space walk. 'Mate?' She knew the word meant friend as well as sexual partner, neither of which she wanted.

'You'll love him. And besides, you've got chocolate and gum coming. It's your lucky day, Miss Kasparova.'

Usually, Nadia enjoyed Brigitte's jovial company. Men made up the majority of the team in Florida, so conversing with Brigitte fulfilled a small requirement in her psyche for female company. She was precise and strict about satisfying basic requisites during a mission but resisted the more obvious and urgent human desires. Nadia considered herself as polished and intricate as the equipment that maintained their orbit. She was a faultless machine.

'I don't eat candy and I don't need company when I'm working.' Nadia retrieved her trainers from a locker and put on her crew zip-up jacket, every languorous movement a fight against freedom, a struggle against the precision of Nadia's mind. Her body wanted to drift aimlessly around the cabin while her brain was eager to get to work.

Brigitte briefed Nadia on various routine duties before tentatively mentioning Operation EROSS. 'It really is your lucky day, then, don't you think?'

Nadia recognised the overzealous banter for what it was. In her head, she thought in Russian but, when she spoke, her words were clipped and brisk English.

'My contract does not state that I must copulate with fellow crew members. I object strongly to the nature of this experiment.' Nadia waited impatiently beside the communication panel. She wanted to get to the lab.

'I don't think you're expected to copulate, Nadia. It's merely a simulation and apparatus evaluation for future missions. In years to come, as the space station grows and develops, married couples will live up there for months at a time. We can hardly expect them to, well, abstain.' More static interfered with the transmission. Nadia sighed, preventing herself from floating upside down in relation to the panel by gripping a strap. 'Nadia, are you still there?'

As mission specialist in charge of the laboratory, Nadia knew she would have to comply with orders. As she mentally scanned the fine print of her contract, she realised that several clauses bound her to fulfil her duties unless severe psychological deficiencies made such work impossible. For Nadia, the admission that she was not mentally fit for her work was worse than having to test the sexual apparatus with the newcomer.

'I'm still here.' She paused again, suddenly aware of the language and culture barrier as she attempted to put her feelings into words. 'I would have preferred to know this several weeks ago, so that I can prepare myself for this sexual activity.'

'Nadia, *no*, repeat, *no*.' The stern voice of the chief mission controller suddenly resounded through the beeps and static. 'Your orders do not include sexual intercourse. Repeat, do not have sexual intercourse aboard *Ventura*.'

'Yes, sir,' Nadia replied, dazed by the notion that anyone would consider her capable of such an activity. She couldn't recall the chief ever being so fervent, except when she successfully fixed one of the solar panels that hung like giant wasp wings from *Ventura*'s cylindrical body. 'Kasparova out.'

She left the cabin and steered her weightless, unusually irrepressible body to the laboratory. For the first time ever, Nadia wasn't sure that she was entirely in control of her actions. For the first time ever, Nadia's thoughts weren't completely focused on work.

Captain Drew Masters emerged from the transfer compartment of the axial docking port at 04.00 hours Florida time. The *Evolution* spacecraft had executed a flawless deposit of food supplies, clothing, technical equipment and one or two personal supplies, the last of which Nadia had not requested. Comfort, she believed, was for life on Earth.

'Welcome.' Commander Brigson assisted Masters as he emerged through the hatch. The two men attempted a brief embrace but settled for a handshake when their bodies refused to combine in the weightless surroundings. Nadia smiled. She didn't expect Operation EROSS to get much further than their clumsy attempts at bodily contact.

'Captain Masters.' Nadia nodded as she was introduced to the American. 'I hope you will find your time aboard pleasurable and productive.' The two men grinned and exchanged lewd glances.

'I don't envy you, Drew. You have a heavy schedule, I believe.' Commander Brigson studied his associate. 'Although, having read your mission brief last month, I gather that several enjoyable activities will ensue.' Brigson allowed himself a laugh, even though he knew Nadia would disapprove. It was tough working alongside the most perfect human being in the universe.

Nadia gasped. 'You knew?' She forced her hand to connect with her mouth, something that should have taken place with a short, precise movement but lost its impact with a slow-motion attempt at surprise. 'You knew that I would be testing this ... this ... apparatus with a stranger and you didn't warn me?' Eyes as deep as space bored into Commander Brigson. He raised his hands slowly in defence.

'The chief and I thought it best not to tell you too soon. We knew you'd fret. It's a very unusual experiment and highly classified. The world must not know about these investigations.' He paused for a moment, reading the Russian woman's stunning, angular features. He wouldn't have minded a go at trying out the apparatus with her himself, although couldn't imagine what contraptions the scientists back in Florida had come up with. 'It's not like you really have to *do* it, Nadia. You can keep your clothes on.'

'You two do it, then,' she snapped. 'If it's that casual, then be my guest and experiment until your heart is of the content.'

'Heart's content,' Drew Masters chipped in, bemused by Nadia's reluctance. 'We say heart's content where I come from.'

Nadia resisted informing the newcomer that they were nowhere near where he came from so she could use whatever turn of phrase she wished and, in her usual calm and professional manner, she breathed deeply and took a heart-slowing look at the giant blue ball that six and a half billion people called home. Nadia wasn't sure if she did any more. The sight of it reduced everything to its correct proportions. Within the frame of the porthole was the soup of all life, human or otherwise, bubbling and burning, simmering and steaming, loving and hating, breathing and dying – and reproducing, she thought, every single one of them. Suddenly, she felt godlike, as if she would be serving mankind by conducting the experiments.

A thin line of smile, as much as she could bear to allow, seeped from Nadia's lips as she realised the implications. 'I'll do it,' Nadia said quietly. 'All in the name of science, you understand, and my continued commitment to *Ventura*.'

The two men nodded and commenced stowing the fresh supplies. Nadia wondered whether they had ever really doubted her dedication, assuming that because she was a woman she would comply with whatever orders were issued. To a certain extent, that was true, but only Nadia herself knew how tough she was and how much she would oppose anything that went against her morals. Trained and sharpened to the limits of human capabilities, Nadia's mind was as tight and lean and finely bound as the muscles that wrapped around her long bones.

Later, Commander Brigson suggested that they eat beef goulash and peas followed by butterscotch pudding in celebration of the new astronaut's arrival. Drew watched as Nadia typed the meal request into the computer to locate the correct stowage locker. In the cramped galley, she skilfully manoeuvred herself from the food compartments to the small oven, opening and arranging the foil packets. Drew admired her self-control. He admired, too, the way her mind obviously latched on to every task, whether it be simple food preparation or an intricate experiment. Nadia's cool reputation reverberated around Mission Control like an ice-hockey puck.

'I suggest we waste no time in testing the prototypes. They're keen to get initial results both visually and via written reports.' Drew caught a stray piece of foil as it aimlessly drifted towards the air-filtration duct. He placed it in the trash compactor.

'You mean they're going to watch us?' Nadia kept her eyes on the food, incredulous that not only would she have to entangle herself with a stranger but also that any number of people on Earth would be watching.

'Of course, but you must understand that we're simply checking the viability of certain methods.' Drew turned away before half coughing, half speaking, 'Testing positions.'

'We must make this over with as soon as possible.' Nadia fastened the food containers to trays with Velcro strips and issued their rations.

'*Get* this over with,' Drew corrected but Nadia pretended not to hear.

Commander Brigson was attending to routine maintenance and knew Nadia well enough to allow her privacy while in the laboratory. As Drew grappled and unwrapped various contraptions, Nadia reluctantly set up the communication cameras from five different locations in preparation for the broadcast to Earth. Quick-fire Russian pounded through her head, trying to convince herself that, by performing the sensitive experiments, she would not compromise her professionalism.

'Christ, what are they thinking we should do with this?' Drew laughed and waved it around. The web of grey nylon strapping broke free from his grip and somersaulted through the laboratory. Nadia arrested it and studied it disdainfully.

'It looks like a complicated chastity belt, not something that would make you want to . . .' Nadia found herself unable to finish.

'You can say "have sex" or "fuck", you know. I won't be shocked and it won't make me think any less of you.'

Nadia's cheeks coloured and, to her horror, she realised

the blush was not completely derived from Drew's comment. She turned as quickly as microgravity would allow and zipped up her crew jacket. She wanted to make sure that there was as little of her flesh showing as possible and also the greatest thickness of fabric between them.

'Right, let's get cracking, then.' Drew then made their intentions clear to Mission Control and Nadia made a point of completely ignoring the cameras. She didn't want anyone to see the fear in her eyes.

'Slip your legs in here.' Drew assisted Nadia as she threaded her long, slim legs through what she discovered was an elastic contraption designed to pin the two participants together face to face.

'Of course, this works the other way around, too.' Drew winked at Nadia as he inserted his legs through the holes and pulled the straps tight, locking their groins together in an uncomfortable clinch.

'Ouch!' Nadia pushed on Drew's shoulders. It was bad enough having their legs entangled but for their faces to be at such an intimate distance was intolerable. 'What do you mean, the other way around?' They floated helplessly around the laboratory. All protruding instruments and dangerous objects had been stowed at Drew's request and Nadia had scowled when he implied things could get pretty wild.

'I can take you from behind if I strap myself to your back, if that's what madam would prefer.' Drew grinned but then recoiled in slow motion as Nadia's hand buffeted the side of his head.

'That would have been a sharp slap on Earth. Just get on and do what you have to and then let's get out of this stupid thing.' She turned her face sideways and screwed up her eyes, refusing to wrap her arms around Drew's back as he was doing to her. She couldn't help but notice the citrus tang of real shampoo and the laundry freshness of his clothing, leftovers from regular Earth life and likely to haunt her understimulated nose for days to come.

'What on Earth are you doing?' Nadia felt her body being bumped as they tumbled around the lab.

Drew laughed, risking another slap. 'On Earth, Miss Kasparova, we call this making love.' He thrust his strapped-up hips even faster, grinding against Nadia's sweatpants, feeling the V-shape and gentle mound at the top of her legs. 'What do you call it?'

Nadia tried to shut down all of her senses, but the breathy words that left Drew's mouth in time to the pulsing delivered by his hips refused to allow such an escape. 'I don't call being strapped to a stranger against my will making love, Captain Masters, on Earth or anywhere else.'

At that moment, Nadia was ashamed of her body. Not for the toned lines and feminine shape it presented to her pseudo-mate but for the way that it responded to the situation. Nadia could barely accept the internal system error that she was diagnosing and was grateful at least that her mind prevented reciprocal thrusts that the surge of warmth in her belly was urging her to try.

Communication from Florida slowed Drew's thrusting hips. Instinctively, he rotated his pelvis in an experienced way – the way a man would hold himself on the brink of orgasm while nursing his lover's nipples or reaching down to trace a figure of eight at the top of her sex.

'How does that feel?' The chief's voice quivered through the miles, distorted by distance and interference.

'Somewhat awkward, and I suspect in practice this traditional position would be completely impossible,' Drew replied. 'With each forward movement I make to simulate copulation, Nadia's pelvis is shunted away with such a force that even the harness isn't enough to hold her steady. I would float right out of her.'

'Do you feel you are being ... er ... pushed beyond the limits of realistic sexual activity, Miss Kasparova?'

Silence and several beeps as Nadia floated through the laboratory with Drew Masters attached to her groin. She was quite unable to speak.

'I'll take that as an affirmative, Miss Kasparova. Perhaps you could try the harness in reverse. The experts say that a better purchase on the pelvic region can be obtained by securing the female around the upper body with the arms.'

'Copy, chief. Give us a few minutes.' Drew unhitched the harness and Nadia floated away, although she was soon retrieved by a firm grip around her wrist. 'We have work to do. Put this on again but backwards.' Drew leaned in and whispered through Nadia's neat blonde hair. 'Then I have to grip your tits.' He grinned as she recoiled but, unable to escape the impending connection, Nadia sighed and allowed the fullness of her bottom cheeks to be bound against Drew's groin.

'Where's the fifth camera?'

'Below the work station,' Nadia snapped. Her words were followed by a sharp gasp as foreign sensations wound around her body. It took several seconds to realise that Drew's hands were cupping her weightless breasts, his fingers teasing her forgotten nipples into gravity-defying peaks even through the thickness of her jacket. It took several more seconds to realise that Drew had positioned them where his advances would go unnoticed by the cameras.

Nadia mentally kicked herself for the moan that escaped her throat as Drew continued to tease her breasts. If she told him to get off, then Mission Control would know that something was going on and, if she tried to ignore him, well, she wasn't sure how long she could hold back the second gasp that was begging to leave her chest.

'Do you have to do that?' She twisted her head around so she could speak in a whisper, but her mouth was met by Drew's open lips. It was as close to a kiss as Nadia had come in several years.

'Just trying to make the simulation realistic.' Drew grinned and wrapped his legs firmly around the outside of Nadia's thighs so that his now virtually erect cock was nestled in the groove between her fleshy cheeks. Embarrassed by his sudden reaction to Nadia's proximity, he was hoping to conceal his hardness.

'It feels *too* realistic for my liking.' Nadia wriggled away from the bulge pressed into her bottom but it followed her, growing firmer and more invasive through the soft fabric of her jogging bottoms. 'Can't we try something else? I'm beginning to sweat with this much exertion.'

'You're just not used to it.' Drew growled the words in her ear before pushing his cock into her buttocks as far as he could while tweaking both nipples.

'Exactly what do you mean by that, Captain Masters?' Nadia almost squealed his name as she felt her wretched and faithless body responding.

'That you haven't had it for years, have you, Miss Kasparaova?'

'Get off my back. Now!' Nadia struggled and kicked, and finally Drew unhitched them and they drifted apart. Nadia lifted the hem of her T-shirt, exposing her flat stomach, and wiped her face before the perspiration had a chance to bead and float off her skin. She hated the buzzing inside her jogging bottoms and, so foreign was the sensation, she wondered if a bee had stowed away and found its way into her knickers. She wanted to press her fingers down there to arrest the tingling, but touching herself in front of Drew would be tantamount to admitting she had enjoyed their simulated sex. Nadia forced her mind to overcome her body. These feelings – this *arousal* – simply would not do.

'*Ventura* to Mission Control,' Drew called out. 'Harness proved more promising from rear docking position but unwilling subject made simulation difficult.' Drew grinned at Nadia.

'I am not a piece of space junk. Do you think you can dock me?' She flushed and wiped her face on her T-shirt again, allowing Drew a delicious view of the lower portion of her breasts. He didn't realise that military-issue bras could be so alluring.

'What do you propose is the answer, Captain? The research department are keen for solutions.' The chief's voice rattled through the static.

'Personally, I'd suggest dinner, wine, soft lighting, more wine, a bit of dirty talk, even more wine and then tying her up and giving her one. But, like I said, subject unwilling, so results are unreliable.' Drew laughed and began to pack away the harness. 'Allow me to lavish some of my charm on the subject and we'll see what we can do later. There's still the inflatable tube to try. *Ventura* out.'

Nadia watched as Drew left the laboratory. Was that it? she wondered. She felt empty, somehow cheated. He hadn't even offered a parting kiss. And she was so consumed with thoughts of Drew's body shunting them around the lab that she completely forgot to shut down the audio and visual connection with Mission Control. It wouldn't be until later that she realised her mistake.

Nadia usually worked right through her daily rest periods. Breaking the flow of concentration, she believed, was detrimental to her productivity. She only allowed herself to eat, wash and sleep outside of the laboratory.

But today, after the unusual encounter with Drew Masters, Nadia retired to her cabin during the next break. She slowly stripped off her clothing as if it were contaminated, knowing that she would have to put it back on at some point because garments had to last several days at least. She allowed her long fingers to brush over her skin, thankful that her body was free from the ridiculous strapping and the incorrigible Masters.

'How do I get out of this mess?' she considered, while floating freely around the small space in just her white bra and knickers. She hugged her body, concerned that these extraordinary circumstances would challenge the strict control she self-inflicted. She stroked her shoulders and, to her utter shock, she allowed her fingers to slip inside the cotton of her bra and cup the fullness of her breasts. Is this how it felt for Drew? she wondered. Intrigued, Nadia trailed a hand down her lower back and nestled it in the fleshy groove between her buttocks. She smiled. It had been a long time.

'I am not completely without feeling,' she whispered in Russian, trying to ignore that her fingers were nuzzling beneath the elastic of her panties in search of the renewed tingle. Nadia bit her bottom lip as she made contact with the awakening bud nestled between the soft folds, following the channel further until she was able to tentatively slip a finger inside her surprisingly moist sex. 'Not at all without feeling,' she told herself, wondering how she would justify this indulgence over tending to fragile seedlings.

'Nadia, you in there?' Drew's voice drove through the bulkhead, causing her to withdraw her hand. Unaccustomed to spending any length of time semi-naked, Nadia forgot her state of undress and concentrated on steering herself to the cabin entrance. Drew's face acted like a mirror as she slid the door open, his shocked but then approving expression reminding Nadia that she was wearing only a bra and knickers.

'Oh! I was just changing. You caught me –'

'No need. You look fine as you are. How about another romp around the lab? We can practise our moves and then show the chief how it's really done. What d'you say?'

Common sense had been shed with her clothing and Nadia wasn't sure if it was the slow, dragging gaze that Drew applied to her naked flesh or the newly discovered sensations that caused her to float out of her cabin and follow him to the lab.

'Brig's sleeping, so there's no one to bother us.' The

laboratory door closed automatically behind the pair as they entered.

'What's that?' She batted away what looked like an inflatable kid's toy bobbing about on a pool.

'That,' said Drew proudly, 'is our reproductive tunnel of love, as supplied by the kind folks in research. Wanna try it out?' His smooth American accent contrasted against Nadia's like custard drooling over gravel.

'Do I have any choice?' The thought of climbing inside the thing with Drew pressed against her bare flesh sparked the tingle again and, when he wasn't looking, Nadia gave herself a little stroke between the legs for reassurance. Being reckless once couldn't hurt, surely?

Drew needed no further encouragement. While Nadia's back was turned, he removed his T-shirt and pants but decided that he would never get the woman into the tunnel if he removed his shorts too. That, he hoped, would come later.

'It'll be easier getting into the inflatable with skin on skin. Less friction.'

Nadia's shock, when she saw his naked torso, was allayed by this justification at least until he gripped her around the waist and posted her legs through the tube. It was like trying to get into a sleeping bag underwater, especially as Nadia wasn't concentrating properly. Her attention was focused on the expanding package buried within Drew's shorts.

'To hell with this tube,' she said swatting it away. 'My face will not remain straight if we use it.'

'You mean, you won't keep a straight –' Drew stopped himself. Nadia was actually grinning and he didn't want to kill the moment. Truth be known, her silly expressions turned him on. 'What do you suggest, then?'

'Come here and I'll show you.'

To Drew's complete surprise, Nadia offered a slow wink and beckoned him to her. As he approached the

Russian woman's long, lean body – the stripes of a very fit woman visible in the form of streaks of muscle stretched across her tight stomach – he became aware of the enormous erection that now strained in his shorts. How he wanted Nadia to wrap her slender fingers around his shaft and mutter something dirty in her native Russian. How he adored the power she had over him – and she didn't even know it.

'I think the researchers have been approaching this completely the wrong way,' Nadia said. 'What they don't realise, when they invent their clever contraptions, is that, when you've been in orbit for nearly ten months, you don't care how you do it. You just know you'll do it.' She pulled Drew towards her and clamped his body against the length of hers, their groins meeting again but this time with sheer lust holding them in place.

'Who needs elastic strapping and blow-up tubes?' Nadia giggled. 'Now, pretend to fuck me.'

'Affirmative, Miss Kasparova. But are you sure you just want me to pretend?' Drew began to rock his hips but, on the second shunt, Nadia floated away from him as if she were in an orbit of her own.

'That worked well,' he muttered, following her trajectory. 'We need to approach this differently. This position is obviously impossible. One of us must be stationary.'

'Fine,' Nadia said. 'Tie me up to the support brackets.' She took a moment to retrieve four cords from a locker and Drew fumbled and rushed to get her bound to the wall. 'Now I can't float away and you can grip the handles above so that you can push into me. Theoretically, of course.' She winked again.

Nadia's legs were spread wide enough for Drew to work the bulge in his shorts into the tempting mound behind the white panties. As instructed, he seized the support handles and slowly began to press his concealed cock against Nadia's knickers. When she let out a long moan, not even attempting to stifle it as she had before, and began to pulse against his movements, Drew took this as a signal that she wanted more.

'Let's make this simulation as realistic as we can.' He slipped off his shorts and began to peel Nadia's panties down her legs. The angle of her tied legs prevented them going further than her knees, but Drew didn't care. Her desperate, love-starved pussy was only inches from his face and he took the opportunity to swivel around, so that he was inverted in relation to Nadia, and plunged his face into the depths of her sex.

Nadia yelped, partly in protestation and partly from delight as Drew's strong tongue pushed inside her. It took her a moment to realise but, in his new position, he was offering up a feast of his own. Nadia couldn't catch the buoyant erection with her tied hands so she had to seek it out with her lips and, when she did, she was rewarded with a slow and deep lick from front to back.

'Time to attempt a docking procedure, Miss Kasparova.' Drew flipped around again and pressed against Nadia's suspended body.

'Permission granted, Captain Masters.' Nadia giggled, wondering how she had survived this long without sex. Her thoughts were smothered as Drew dipped his mouth on to hers and delivered a deep kiss. She felt the tip of his cock probe the entrance to her sex and suddenly she felt like a virgin all over again.

'I shouldn't be doing this.' She pulled away, overcome by a moment of guilt as she sensed her mind and body letting go.

'Nonsense. It's for the future of mankind. One small step and all that.' Drew buried his face in Nadia's neck and began to ease himself between the folds of her sex. Strapping her to the wall was the perfect solution. Indeed, she could be tied to the ceiling, the floor, a chair – it didn't matter as long as she was a fixed target. He planned to try each position in turn and present his findings to Mission Control. Finally, he was fully engulfed by the warmth and wetness of Nadia's pussy and as he settled into a rhythm, he wondered how he would last more than a dozen strokes.

Nadia was helpless. She had never felt so out of control – both in body and mind – and loved her newfound freedom. As she felt her orgasm approach, she rocked her hips as much as she was able and delivered squeal after squeal as pleasure ripped through her body. Unable to contain himself as he was milked by Nadia's detonation, Drew jettisoned deep inside her.

'I am sorry for yelling so much.' Nadia gasped and laughed and writhed within her straps as she caught her breath.

'We're in space,' Drew said with a smirk. He held himself close to Nadia, unwilling to separate from her smooth skin. 'No one can hear you.'

Static and several beeps suddenly filled the laboratory and the chief controller's voice came through loud and clear. 'That's not entirely true, Captain Masters. Mission Control here.'

The shocked pair frantically looked around the lab at the five cameras and, to their horror, each had a red light above the lens, indicating that they were live. Nadia began to laugh.

'Didn't you cut communications earlier?' Drew whispered.

'I must have forgotten.' Nadia was wide-eyed and a mischievous glint sparkled in the cool blue as the sun rose once again. 'But at least they've got the results they need for EROSS.'

Nadia then addressed the nearest camera and, still completely naked and tied spread-eagled to the bulkhead, she spoke to Mission Control. 'You have caught us with our pants down, sir, and my back is against the wall –' Nadia winked at Drew '– but it is all in the name of science. I am pleased to report that this particular reproductive position has been a success and we will be experimenting further over the coming days. My full report will follow but for now, suffice it to say that the world was out of this.'

With that, Drew flicked off all the cameras and turned his attentions to Nadia again. 'That'd be "out of this world",' he corrected and pulled himself level with her exposed pussy. 'Better clean up the mess before it escapes.' And he set to work.

Pumps Monica Belle

I have a confession to make. There's a naughty habit I picked up in college, or maybe I should say a nasty habit. Yes, a nasty habit, as the Americans put it, because it's something that respectable women very definitely do not do – but it is delightfully sexy.

The first time was at the beginning of my second year. I'd bought an ancient Metro, my first ever car, to get my stuff up to college. It was nearly two hundred miles, so I decided to fill my tank right up and make sure I didn't run out of petrol. After buying the car I had to watch every penny, so I went to the supermarket pumps the night before I left. It was two in the morning and nobody was about except for a bored attendant reading a magazine in his booth. I'd parked a bit too close to the pumps, and when I put the nozzle in the hose pressed to my leg, just a couple of inches from the V of my jeans, so that when I squeezed the trigger ...

I had never realised a petrol pump vibrated like that, so fast, and so powerful, the thick green hose sending shivers right through me, and right where it matters. Of course I snatched it away immediately, sure I'd been seen, but there was nobody there to see me, and that single jolt of pleasure had been far too good to ignore. My car was between me and the booth, and it was more than I could resist not to push the hose against me again, this time right between my thighs, with the trigger squeezed full on.

It made me feel guilty, and slightly silly, but it made me feel daring too, while those vibrations were far, far too good to let me stop. I had to close my eyes, the feeling was so strong, jolting me into a sudden arousal far more quickly than anything I'd known before, and made stronger still by my sense of being naughty and my fear of getting caught. All anybody needed to do was drive up behind me and they'd see, see what I was doing with the thick green hose between my legs, see how improper I was being, masturbating in public, how naughty, how dirty.

I squeezed my thighs tighter, biting my lip in a vain effort to stop the pleasure showing on my face as it rose higher and higher still. A little more and I was going to come, right there on the garage forecourt, to come in public. How bad could I get? I was masturbating in public. I was going to come in public. I was ...

... not going to do anything of the sort, because the tank was full and the automatic cut-off had worked perfectly for once, leaving the hose still thick and firm between my thighs, but not vibrating. I had never, ever felt so frustrated, and, short of rubbing myself on the hose, which was far too blatant, there was nothing I could do. My hands were shaking, and the sense of urgency between my thighs was every bit as high as it had ever been before, even during those exquisite moments an instant before penetration, when you know your lover's cock is going to go in at the next instant.

I was so aroused I even considered propositioning the attendant, something completely outside my experience. He wasn't very attractive, or maybe I would have done, although I doubt it. I'd have lost my nerve, anyway, back then, after just three lovers and all of them very conventional – rather like me really, until then.

There was nothing conventional about what I did when I got home. I desperately needed to recreate my experience as soon as possible. Everyone else was asleep, my room quiet and almost dark, with just the dull orange glow of the street light outside to illuminate me as I stood by my bed, stroking myself through my jeans and struggling to focus my mind on what I'd done.

It wasn't easy. I needed to be clothed and I needed to be standing, but I also needed something thick and rubbery between my thighs, something that vibrated. There wasn't anything. Even if I'd had a boyfriend to hand he'd have needed at least three feet of impressively thick, vibrating cock, and they just don't make men like that. I was going to do it, though, one way or another, and in the end I nipped downstairs to fetch a bottle of salad dressing from the fridge.

I held it between my thighs as I rubbed myself on it, thinking of how rude it had felt to secretly masturbate in public. It did feel good, and naughty, and it got me there in the end, but the thrill was very pale indeed compared with the real thing. Even as I came down from the peak of my excitement I knew I'd be doing it again.

The trouble was, that no matter what, the petrol tank of my Metro was simply not big enough to take me all the way. I tried again and again, all that year and always to much the same routine. Half my money went on petrol, and I was the most popular girl in my hall because I was always willing to give lifts, help people move their things and generally put my car to use whenever I possibly could.

As soon as my tank was empty I'd stay up late, then drive out to one of the big, anonymous petrol stations on the ring road. Sometimes I'd be unlucky and there would be too many people about, but more often than not it would be OK and I would get my moment of mounting ecstasy before driving home to bring myself to climax under sticky fingers.

I soon became something of an expert. For instance, it's always best to go to the right-hand pump, because then there's the best chance of being shielded from the prying eyes of both the attendant and fellow motorists. Unless, of course, your petrol tank is on the left, in which case the reverse is true. Always wear dark clothes, because believe me, walking into a student accommodation block in white jeans with the outline of your sex lips set off with oily black lowlights takes quite a bit of explaining.

Otherwise jeans are good, because nobody comments if you wear them tight, but if I get too excited I make a damp patch, which can be awkward. Slacks are more embarrassing still, because the damp patch shows more easily, but they let the vibrations right through, especially with no knickers on underneath. Skirts are awkward, unless you dare to lift them up, but I'm getting ahead of myself.

All that year it was the same, and most of the next. I did feel guilty about it, sometimes, and that it somehow made me abnormal, but then I'd tell myself it was just harmless fun. Twice I gave it up, once during a brief fling with a fellow student, a law graduate who'd already been through Yale. He was nice, and maybe I even loved him a little, but I knew I could never share my nasty little secret with him and stopped it until we split up. The day after I'd dumped him I was back at the pumps.

The second time was during finals, when I swore I'd stop because it was spoiling my concentration on my work. I succeeded too, although as the days ticked by I could feel my need rising, and while all my fellow students were getting outrageously drunk at our party after the final exam I was on orange juice, the designated driver, which allowed me to visit my favourite service station at four o'clock in the morning.

I graduated with a 2:1 and took up a PhD grant even further from home than before. Most of my friends were going into work, which meant salaries, and it took me quite a bit of willpower not to do the same. Not because I wanted to join the ranks of the wage slaves, you understand, but because it would have meant I could afford a bigger car. A bigger car meant more petrol. More petrol meant more time to fill up. More time to fill up might just mean that I could bring my nasty little habit to the climax that had eluded me for so long.

Being a good girl at heart, I resisted, but it was only when I'd settled down in the north of England to work on my thesis that I discovered the joys of demonstrating. I'd been vaguely aware that graduates could add to their pay by taking practicals, but I'd never realised how well it paid, or how much was available. To the delight of my tutors I took on work in every subject I could handle, and quite a few I wasn't at all sure about.

For the first time in my life I was earning money, and I knew exactly what I wanted to buy. Well, not exactly, because it took me a while to work out which of the models I could afford would take the longest to fill up. I shall skip over the details, save to say that the most fanatic anorak would have been amazed at me as I sat up over my calculations, surrounded by car catalogues new and old, drinking coffee after coffee until I was satisfied.

At last I made my selection, a big old Ford with a fifteen-gallon tank, twice as big as the one in my Metro. I know it sounds silly, and the sort of thing only men are supposed to do, but as I drove away from the dealer's forecourt I felt as if I were going on a first date, and felt bad about 'dumping' my Metro. As usual, feeling a bit silly didn't stop me, and, as there was almost nothing in the tank, I knew it wouldn't be long.

I drove myself home and forced myself to take my time over dinner, then sit down and watch TV for a bit, although my hands kept straying either to my car keys or to the V between my thighs. Only at midnight did I allow myself to go into my bedroom, take off the skirt and knickers I'd worn during the day and slip into tight, slimline black slacks with nothing underneath. One glance in the mirror was enough to be sure it showed, with my bottom cheeks bare and round underneath the thin cotton, and the shape of my sex embarrassingly obvious at the front.

Anyone who saw me would know I had no panties, which made me hesitate, but after half an hour of indecision I told myself to be bold, and out I went. It was still a little early, but I drove out of town, to a big service station beside the road leading up over the Pennines. I knew it was never very busy in the evening, and sure enough, as I pulled in, only one other car was there, a souped-up cabriolet driven by overexcited teenagers.

They seemed to take forever, laughing among themselves and going back and forth from the booth to fetch cigarettes and chocolates, until I was cursing them under my breath. All the while I'd been pretending to have trouble with my petrol cap, and praying nobody would offer to help me. They didn't, and as soon as the other car had roared off I twisted it open, only to discover that the attendant was looking right at me.

I knew why, or I thought I did. The teenagers had been in my favourite spot and he could see me, with the light full on me from behind. His eyes were right on me, and, although I dared not turn around, I could just imagine them lingering on the contours of my bottom, so obviously bare beneath my slacks. I didn't know what to do, too embarrassed to simply drive away, while indulging my nasty habit with him watching was absolutely out of the question.

In the end I put in a miserable two pounds' worth of petrol and endured both the funny look he gave me when I paid and the feel of his eyes on my bottom as I walked back to my car. I was blushing as I drove away, with my hands shaking on the wheel, but I was determined not to give in. There was another service station a couple of miles south on the main trunk road, bigger and busier, but maybe I'd be lucky.

I was. A large van had pulled into the second pump from the right, allowing me to take the perfect place and shielding me from the attendant. My heart was racing as I slipped the nozzle from its holster and into the mouth of my petrol tank, and faster still as I surreptitiously closed my thighs around the thick, rubbery hose. Ready, I made myself wait, just a second, and squeezed.

As the vibrations hit me I felt my mouth become wide in pleasure, and shut it just in time to prevent myself getting caught as the van driver appeared around the front of his vehicle. That gave me a start, but he took no notice of me whatsoever, and as he pulled out my pleasure was already rising towards ecstasy. I was going to do it, I really was, to make myself come with a petrol hose, after so long. That was enough, no fantasy needed, just the way I was, knickerless under my slacks, the hose pumping between my tightly clenched thighs, the vibrations running through my sex, masturbating in public, as usual, but this time to orgasm, my pleasure rising, my muscles beginning to tighten, my bottom squeezing, my eyes closed in bliss, delicious little shocks starting in my pussy . . .

. . . and nothing, as the pump cut out, just seconds before ecstasy overwhelmed me. My eyes came open and I looked down, the thick green hose between my thighs blurred, my legs weak with the approach of orgasm, my hands shaking so hard I could barely put the pump back and twist the petrol cap into place. I paid. I drove away. I stopped, in a lay-by just a few hundred yards down the road, because I quite simply was not fit to drive.

I'd been so close, right on the edge of orgasm, yet I had been denied that final push to take me over the brink. Maybe, just maybe, I'd have made it if the van driver hadn't appeared. Maybe, just maybe, I'd have made it if I hadn't put two pounds' worth in already. It would work, another time, that I knew, but it was no help. I couldn't wait, my frustration too strong to be denied.

Still trembling badly, I wound my seat back a little. Just yards outside my window cars were belting past, and yet I couldn't stop myself. My legs became wide, my hand pressed to the V of my crotch, and I was masturbating, not even subtly, but sighing as I rubbed myself through my slacks, alternately squeezing and spreading my thighs, my eyes shut, one hand to my breasts to tease and stroke my nipples, my mouth wide in pleasure, and then in ecstasy as I brought myself to a shuddering, wriggling climax that left me with spots dancing in front of my eyes and my head spinning and dizzy.

That was the first time I had ever come outdoors, at least alone, which is very different from being in the arms of a lover. Afterwards I was telling myself that it had been a stupid thing to do, especially right beside the main road, and that I would never do it again. You see, the great thing about the petrol pump was that it looked quite innocent, except only that last crucial moment, and I'd spent ages teaching myself to look as unflustered as possible as I came. In the lay-by I'd looked anything but innocent, with my legs wide open and playing with my breasts as I rubbed myself. If a patrol car had happened to pull in at the wrong moment to see what the matter was I'd have been in serious trouble. Or it might have been a lorry driver, or a group of teenage tearaways out for fun, like the ones I'd seen earlier.

I knew I'd be back, but I promised myself I'd be more careful. I was, and I wasn't. The next occasion came quite unexpectedly, when I was asked to drive the departmental minibus to take some students down to York. I agreed to do it, and was telling myself I would be good as I drew in to the very same service station at which I'd come so close before. It was impossible to be good. Just taking the pump in my hand sent a shiver the length of my spine, and watching the way the hose moved had me squeezing my thighs together.

None of the students were looking as I stood behind the van, blocked from sight. It was too much for me. Full of apprehension and guilty excitement, I moved a little closer, allowing the thickness of the hose to press into my sex as I squeezed the trigger home. I was in heaven immediately, but, with the need to keep a straight face and my concern for the students and others using the garage, I knew I would never reach that magic moment. Sure enough, I didn't, but I rode my ecstasy for the full time it took me to fill up that big, big tank, which left me dizzy with pleasure and need.

Naturally, I couldn't do what I wanted to in front of my students, so I was left smouldering gently for the rest of the day. Only that evening did I manage to come, and, as I lay in the warm stillness of my bedroom afterwards, my head was full of plans for that ultimate moment of satisfaction. With my car I might make it, but with the minibus I would *definitely* make it, while it also provided so much more shelter. All I needed to do was find some excuse to book it out for the day, on a trip long enough to make sure I came back late at night and so could replace the petrol I'd used in my own special way.

Which I did. My trip took me up into the Highlands, a beautiful drive, with my sense of anticipation rising all day, until, by the time I was ready to start back, I could barely contain myself. I'd planned which petrol station to use, but I never made it that far. With the tank just on the red I came across an empty station on an empty road, and I took my opportunity.

It was perfect. The attendant was dozing in his booth and there was nobody else around. Now I was going to do it, and just that knowledge was enough to have me shaking as I unlocked the petrol cap, full of guilt and arousal, knowing that this time there was no stopping, no going back. I slid out the pump from its holster and pushed the nozzle deep. I pressed close to the hose, pushing the thick, hard rubber tight against the crotch of my favourite black slacks, beneath which I had no knickers. I squeezed the trigger and closed my eyes, knowing exactly what was going to happen.

The moment the vibrations started to run through my sex I knew I was there. I felt such a bad girl, so deliciously rude. Everyone at the university thought I was such a good girl, ever so diligent, always ready to help, working hard, far too shy and far too serious to even think about men. The last bit was true, anyway. Who needs men? I didn't, not with a two-inch-thick rubber hose pumping petrol between my thighs.

It was going to happen, my excitement rising, my thighs tight around the hose, my head full of naughty thoughts, and I was there, biting my lip to stop myself crying out as wave after wonderful wave of pure bliss swept over me, on and on until my knees gave way and I was forced to stop. I sank down, leaning against the side of the minibus, my head spinning with reaction to what I'd done, my hand still grasping the trigger, pumping petrol.

I became an addict. There's no other word for it. Again and again I would go out, with my car, with the minibus, even with friends' cars once or twice, to run through that same delightful routine: a quiet service station, the hose between my thighs, the trigger squeezed, and taken to heaven by the vibrations.

I was always very careful to keep my nasty little habit a secret, but the more I did it the more I needed it, and the more I did it the less exciting it became each time. I understood full well the path I was on, and I did my best to restrict myself to doing it once a week and to resist the urges of my imagination, which was demanding that I try new and more exciting routines, more exciting, and more daring. I tried to resist, but I failed.

The first temptation I gave in to was to do it with the hose pressed to the front of my knickers, a small thing maybe, but not when it means standing on the forecourt of a petrol station with my skirt bunched up at the front so that I could press the hose to myself. I'd been thinking about it for a while, and how easy it would be in a knee-length skirt. And it was. It was also delightful, with the feel of my bare thighs and the knowledge of how unmistakably rude I would look restoring all the pleasure I'd lost through overfamiliarity. That was one cool summer dawn beside a road in Wales, and it was the first of many times.

The second temptation I gave in to was the urge to feel the touch of the hose on my bare flesh. That was at a petrol station outside Rugby, the first time, when the thrill of pressing the hose to the front of my knickers had begun to fade. I reasoned that, if I dared to push up the front of my skirt to get at my knickers, then why not do it with no knickers underneath? After all, I wouldn't be showing anything else. But I was, flashing my bare sex for just an instant as I adjusted myself, and that made it better still, giving me one of the best orgasms I'd ever had. Once I'd done it bare, there was no going back.

The third temptation I gave in to was to let somebody else see. I'd fought it hard, for two long years, scared by the power of my own needs as much as by the possible consequences of my action. By then I'd taken to doing bare every time, and as often as not after a little routine. I would choose my time and choose my place, then drive out late at night as always. I would be dressed in a sensible, knee-length skirt, stay-up stockings and no knickers. Just being bare was wonderful, and sometimes I would even stop just to take my knickers off under my skirt, even when it wasn't a petrol day.

That was what I did on the day it happened. I was travelling from London to Carlisle in my shiny new BMW, a treat I'd bought myself on getting my new job as a senior researcher with my company. For some reason I was feeling aroused anyway, and as I watched the petrol gauge drop slowly down I decided to tease myself. After pulling off at the next services, I parked in the far corner and slipped off my knickers under my skirt. I had lunch there, enjoying the naughty feeling of having my bare bottom sitting on the chair and knowing that I was bare.

By the time I left the services I was ready, and I stayed ready as I drove north, all the time imagining the pleasure of the climax I was going to give myself that evening when I filled up the car. Had I stayed on the motorway I'd have been in Carlisle far too early, so I turned off beyond Lancaster and threaded my way north through the Lake District. For dinner, I ate at country pub, again with my bottom bare on the seat beneath me, and, not long after I left, the warning for low fuel came on.

For me, that was like a switch. With some women it might be the sight of their favourite film star, for others a pair of muscular buttocks packed into tight jeans. For me, it is the moment that little yellow light comes on and I know that it is time to masturbate. Now was no exception, even though it was a little early. I pulled off the road just a few miles later, at a tiny station high on a hillside. It looked as if it hadn't changed since the 70s, just two pumps, side by side, with no canopy, and a wooden stack in which the attendant was seated, resting the plaster cast that encased a broken leg on a chair. The thought came to me immediately. He could see me. He could hardly fail to see me, but I was quite safe. After all, what was he going to do?

What he was going to do was enjoy the view. I knew he was right immediately I went to the booth to buy a packet of mints. He was young, handsome, friendly in an easygoing way, and yet as I walked back to the car his eyes were on my bottom, watching the way my bare cheeks moved under my skirt. He knew I was bare, I was sure of it, and that alone was a delicious thrill.

Turning to find him smiling at me was more delicious still, and, with my heart in my throat, I decided to do it. I waved, making it quite clear I knew he was watching. I opened my petrol cap and took the pump from the holster, as I had done so often before, but now knowing a man was watching, and my sense of rising anticipation was stronger even than it had been those first few times.

Had I not been so turned on I could never have done it, but I was, and I did. I made sure he was watching. I took hold of the front of my dress. I lifted it, deliberately showing my legs, my stocking tops, my bare thighs and my bare sex, naked and pink in the fluorescent light, bare to his pop-eyed gaze.

That alone was enough to leave me determined to make myself come. I was shaking terribly, but I took the pump and eased it between my legs, showing off with a little wriggle as I made myself comfortable with the hose pressed deep into the groove of my sex. I kept my skirt up, too, so that he could see, every rude detail as I began to do it, squeezing the trigger and rubbing myself on the hose as that wonderful, throbbing vibration began.

Now he was really staring, with his mouth open wide, and that only encouraged me. I began to let my feelings show on my face, maybe even putting it on a little as I wriggled and squirmed against the hose. There was nothing fake about my pleasure, though, my orgasm already rising in my head as I thought of what I was doing: not just masturbating in public, but doing it bare, and in front of a man.

I came, screaming out my pleasure as it hit me, with the hose pumping hard between my thighs, my whole body tight with ecstasy, my sex on fire. He was staring as hard as ever, and, as that glorious orgasm tore through, I locked eyes with him, watching him as he watched me come, holding his gaze until at last I could take it no more and slumped down, spent.

Only then did I realise that I hadn't really thought it through, letting myself get carried away in my excitement. What I'd meant to do was come, then cover myself up, perhaps give him a final teasing wave, and leave. Unfortunately it was out of the question.

I'd come in front of him, and my tank was full of petrol, petrol I hadn't paid for. Forty-two pounds and thirty-eight pence the pump showed, forty-two pounds and thirty-eight pence I was going to have to pay him. That meant walking across the forecourt, handing my debit card to the man I had just masturbated in front of, waiting for him to put it through his machine, signing for the payment and walking back to the car.

Never, ever have I been so embarrassed, my face burning with blushes as I walked, acutely aware not only of what I'd done, but of how I was, and how he knew I was, bare under my skirt. I wondered if he'd say something, maybe call me a slut or a tease, maybe demand that I lift my skirt again and show off for him. He just smiled, which is why he is now my husband, and tonight he is taking me out, to this little petrol station I know just a few miles up the A32.

Are We There Yet?
Portia Da Costa

'Where are we going?'

'It's a surprise.'

'Oh, go on. Tell me.'

'Don't be so impatient, wench.'

Wench? What is this? A sexy pirate fantasy? It's Stone's clapped-out Toyota we're about to board, not the fucking *Golden Hind*.

At least I *think* it's the Toyota. He doesn't usually use the Merc for jaunts like this. But I can't be sure because he's got me in a blindfold.

Yeah, I'm wrapped around in a world of pitch-blackness, strung-out nerves and one man's perverse peccadillos. It's so exciting that I think I might faint.

'Oof!'

I stumble on the gravel, and obscene messages streak along those tight-strung nerves. For one churning second, I have a horrific feeling that something totally disgusting is going to happen. But luckily it subsides just as quickly and I'm back to being weak and girly and clutching at his solid muscular arm as he helps me with all courtesy into the car.

'Are you all right, Miss Lewis?'

His voice is soft and genial as he settles me into my seat and fastens the belt across my chest. He has to do this because he's got me in handcuffs, too, as well as the blindfold. I'm totally vulnerable, but I can't deny that I like it.

'Yes, thank you, Mr Stone,' I answer, keeping it bright

and pert and slightly insolent because that's the game we're playing tonight.

He murmurs, 'Hmm...' as if he suspects my motives, then softly slams the door and makes his way round to the driver's seat.

I know the blindfold is part of the game, but suddenly I wish with all my heart that I could see him as he settles in beside me and starts the engine. I want to see that dear profile of his. The solid, stubbly jaw. Those unexpectedly lush and overtly sexy lips. Long, long eyelashes that make me jealous as hell that it takes three coats of Maybelline to get the same effect. Taken overall, he's not exactly an oil painting but to me he's just sex on two long legs.

He revs the car and the vibrations of the engine play havoc with my insides because of the thing he inserted into me earlier. I hardly dare put a name to it, because it's not exactly the most refined and sophisticated of sex toys. But Mr Stone likes it – so that makes it fine by me.

OK, it's a butt plug, right?

And it provokes the rudest, most insidious of sensations. It feels like ... It feels like ... God, I just can't bring myself to say what it feels like. But at the same time, oh boy, it gets me going!

And Mr Stone knows that. Which is why he put it in me before we set out.

My mind flicks back to the bathroom and I start to sweat as if it were happening all over again. I'm naked, bending over, one foot on the edge of the bath. I'm totally exposed in the lewdest of ways and he's just looking, looking ...

And then there's that sensation. Intrusion. Pushing. Pressure, pressure, pressure, then the give as it goes in. Oh, God! Then I'm exhibiting myself to my lover, slick and dripping, with that stark black rubber base protruding from my fundament.

It just boggles the mind what a girl will do for love.

As I zone back into the world of here and now, I wonder if he's deliberately searching out bumps and potholes. The old car trundles along, bouncing me around in a way that makes me gasp and gulp. The suspension leaves a lot to be desired, and so does my self-control tonight. But Mr Stone loves pushing my buttons and testing my limits.

One particularly juddering lurch has me biting my lip, and, though I can't see him, I know Mr Stone has noticed.

'Are we there yet?' I ask by way of a distraction. And he laughs.

'Impatient, Miss Lewis?'

'No.'

'Liar.'

'I just want to know when we're going to get there.'

'You might not be so keen if I told you.'

My heart kicks, and so does my sex.

Are we going dogging? We've done it before. And done it enough times for me to know that I'm just as much of an exhibitionist as he is.

I remember the first time, travelling there in this car, and it makes me sort of breathless.

I could see, that time, and Mr Stone gave me plenty to look at. And more. He asked me to take his dick out of his jeans and touch him.

Oh, my God, he might even have his dick out now for all I know!

I edge sideways, and begin to lean towards him. I may be handcuffed, but I can still reach over in search of our pride and joy. It's certainly big enough to find in the dark.

'What are you doing, Miss Lewis?'

'Um ... nothing. Really...' I lie. 'Just trying to get comfortable.'

He says nothing, but I can sense that he's smiling. It's a slow, sly, sideways grin. I know it well and it slays me every time I see it. Even after all our months together.

Time seems to dilate and warp. I've no idea how long

we've been travelling. I can measure it only in terms of what my body's telling me. The growing pressure in my belly. The growing wetness in my knickers. The way my clit aches and throbs and throbs and throbs. I want to ask if we're there yet again, but there's a pressure on my tongue too. The awareness of what might happen if I speak.

You might be wondering why I call him 'Mr Stone' when we live together.

Well, I don't a lot of the time. Mostly, he's just 'Stone', or maybe 'Robert'. And sometimes he's 'Bobby' when things are close and sweet and tender. But when we go all formal on each other it's a signal. Let the games commence. I only have to hear him say the words 'Miss Lewis' and I want to come.

'So, are we comfortable yet?'

His words make me jump and that plays havoc with my innards. I have to gasp for breath and gather myself before I can answer.

'Well, I don't know about you, but I'm just fine. Thank you.'

'Really? Is that a fact? I was just thinking that by now you might want to touch yourself.'

I've been wanting to touch myself since the bathroom, but I'm not going to tell him that. Instead I sneakily clench my thighs in an attempt to get some stimulation. It's a huge mistake though, and only makes things worse.

'Why on earth would you think that?' I pause, then add sassily, '*Mr Stone*.'

'Have a care, young lady,' he shoots back. More quickly, I suspect, than he intended. He puts on this act of total self-control. Impassive lack of interest in the sexual tension growing between us. But I know I'd be on a winner if I put good money on the fact that he's rampantly erect.

I get that yearning, burning urge to touch him again, and confirm my suspicions. I fancy that I could come from the simple act of touching his thigh. Which is bullshit, really, and I know it. This isn't some flowery, unrealistic romance here. Like any woman, I need my fair share of purposeful, inter-thigh fumbling to get me off. Fingering. Tonguing. What have you. Or maybe a good hard shag? A bit of old-fashioned, tried and true, pneumatic grinding between the sheets with Mr Stone on top, his big size-eleven feet braced against the footboard so he can really put it to me.

Yum!

'What are you thinking about?'

Oh, shit! I realise that not only have I been quiet for several minutes, I've been jiggling about, trying to get some action by knocking that accursed butt plug against the root of my clit somehow.

'Nothing, Mr Stone. Still wondering where we're going and if we're anywhere near there yet.'

'Bullshit,' he observes roundly. 'You're thinking naughty thoughts, aren't you, Miss Lewis? If you aren't, I'll be surprised—' he pauses for a beat '—and disappointed.'

Oh, no!

'All right, all right, I was thinking about coming. And how much I want to do it. And all the ways I could do it.'

'That's more like it.' He starts to change gear and misses the one he wants. And I laugh out loud.

Touché, Clever Bobby, you're as horny as I am!

He treats me to one of the foulest, most disgusting oaths I've ever heard – all delivered in his most cultured and pleasantly conversational tone. Then, a moment later, he brings the Toyota to a halt.

Before I can ask if we actually are there yet, he's out of the car, round my side, and gently but determinedly hauling me out of my seat. He leads me a few steps away from the car, and simply says, 'Come, then.'

'H-here?' I stammer.

But where is 'here'?

I can hear the roar of traffic in the distance, so we

must be near the motorway, but, other than that, we could be anywhere.

With anybody watching.

Not that that would bother me too much. It wouldn't be the first time I've put on a show. But still, not actually *knowing* whether there's an audience is unsettling.

I reach out my hands blindly in the dark, but I can find neither anything to sit on nor anything to lean against. And, goddamn him, he offers no assistance.

With a resigned sigh – and a great deal of difficulty, due to being cuffed – I yank up the hem of my skirt and fish about in my knickers.

'Tuck it up,' he instructs, 'and then pull down your pants to your knees.'

I feel faint again, and it's not from disorientation. My head goes light and I feel as if I'm floating on a cloud. Scrabbling and tumbling, and trying not to dislocate my shackled wrists in the process, I obey him. And display my crotch to the chilly night and its thousand eyes.

Remembering certain preferences of his, I spread my legs as much as I can with my knickers at half-mast. I know Mr Stone likes it when I lose my elegance. He likes it a lot. His dark side gets off on seeing me graceless.

I half crouch, half squat, and reach for my sex. It's like a swamp down there, and I'm so sensitised that I moan aloud. The erotic tension, the plug, the darkness. It's all brought me to fever pitch far too quickly. I touch my clit and feel a deep throb that seems to grab at the thing inside my bottom. The temptation to go for orgasm immediately is breathtaking, but I know that Mr Stone wants a performance. So I withdraw from the most critical area and start to wiggle.

I must look a bit of a sight. Half crouched and waving my bum about. I drift into a strangely detached state, while inwardly watching both myself and the man who's watching me.

I suspect that he'll be masturbating too. That is if we're

not in a public car park or a lay-by or somewhere with dozens of folk around us. Maybe even if we are? I imagine those big hands on that big dick and I wish I knew exactly where he is in relation to my position. The ground beneath my shoes is soft, and, as Mr Stone is light on his feet, it's impossible to hear his tread. He hasn't spoken for a few minutes either.

But I *should* be able to locate him. After all, he's six foot four and broad with it, and he displaces a lot of air. Yet I've no idea whether he's close by, or many yards away. If it weren't for the fact that I would've heard the engine start, he could have got back in the car and driven away.

And then I nearly faint when I feel his warm breath on the back of my neck.

'You're not trying very hard, are you, Miss Lewis?' he murmurs, so close he could be touching me. And in fact, a second later, he *is* touching me.

I feel his towering form against my back, his erection rampant as his arms come around me. One huge paw cups my breast, and the other swoops low to direct my masturbation.

His middle finger presses mine against my clit and I come like a runaway train!

My mind goes blank for a bit, but as I get myself together again, and realise I'm sagging against a still very insistent prick, I struggle with my cuffs and try to twist around to fondle him.

'Tut, tut! That's enough of that,' he says sternly, swirling his hips away from me while still holding my body aloft.

Even though my entire pelvis is still softly glowing with satisfaction, I feel disappointed. I so want to touch him. I so want to *see* him. I'd love to snatch off this stupid blindfold, reach for his amazing penis, and watch his broad face contort in pleasure as I caress him.

But it seems I'm not to get my wish, because, almost

immediately, I'm being gently but firmly manhandled towards the Toyota with my skirt up and my knickers still at half-mast. I try to right them, but I get that 'tut, tut' again so shuffle along the best I can.

So, I'm to sit here with my bush hanging out, am I?

It seems that way, as Mr Stone restarts the engine.

How long have we been going now? How long have I been sitting here with my pants down and my skirt up? How many astonished fellow motorists have glanced idly to one side at the traffic lights – and got an eyeful?

It seems like an age, and it's not only my wandering mind that's telling me that, either. The cups of coffee I drank before we left the house are beginning to make their presence felt.

God, I need to pee! I really, really, really need to pee!

And it's all made worse by the nasty pressure of the butt plug. There just isn't room in my innards for a full bladder and a great, honking chunk of black rubber, too.

Around a dozen times, I consider surreptitiously clutching myself in a pathetic attempt to control the ache. But, even though he's driving, I know Mr Stone will be watching my every move. And even if he isn't actually looking he'll be monitoring me with his sixth sense. The one that can reach through the walls and corridors of the rambling, shambling Borough Hall building where we both work and tell at any given time whether I'm thinking or doing something naughty.

'Still comfortable?'

The bastard! He's read my mind – although it doesn't really require telepathic powers to deduce what sort of state I'm in. He was the one who offered me a second Americano.

'Fine. Are we there yet?'

'Not yet. Why, are you thirsty? There's a bottle of water in the glove box. Why not have a drink?'

Screw you!

'Well if you won't, I will. Can you get it for me?' he continues, his voice perfectly normal to the ear, although with *my* sixth sense I can hear him laughing his head off.

I refrain from pointing out that I can neither see nor use my hands all that efficiently, and just fumble around until I find the glove box catch.

The water sloshes as I pull out the plastic bottle and that does terrible things to my beleaguered bladder. This time I can't stop myself from wriggling, and twisting my thighs around, and Mr Stone notes that with a soft, impatient sigh.

I uncap the bottle and hand it to him, then have to sit there in a state of delicious agonising discomfort while he drinks deep, audibly relishing the cool water as it slides down his throat. With a grunt of satisfaction he hands me back the bottle.

'Sure you won't have some?'

'Absolutely.' My teeth are gritted but I get the word out.

We drive in silence a little longer, and again he seems to be navigating with the express purpose of seeking out the most dug-up and roughed-up bits of road. With every jounce and bounce of the car, I'm convinced I'm going to either cry out or wet myself or both, and eventually I just can't take it any more.

'I need to pee. Please stop. We've got to find a toilet.'

'But there isn't one near here,' he observes blithely. 'I'm afraid you'll just have to wait.'

'I can't!'

And really I don't think I can much longer, either. Things are getting very serious down there and sweat is pouring off me as I fight to control my water.

He utters another sigh. A big, fake, pantomime sigh this time.

'Very well, then,' he says, as if I were seriously discommoding him somehow, and it's all very tedious. Which, again, is total bullshit, because he's loving every minute of this. He has a special fascination with pissing games, because he knows I once played them with someone else . . .

We get out of the car – very gingerly and awkwardly in my case – and there's the sound of voices somewhere near. And – oh, God! – running water. We must be somewhere near the river, maybe in the vicinity of a country pub or a beauty spot. It's night but there are strollers out and about. People who might see me with my skirt up and my pants down. People who might see me when he makes me do what I've got to do – out here in the open.

I'll just have to take a chance. Not that I've much option. It's either go where he instructs me to or wet myself anyway. If we were in the middle of the Borough Hall car park in broad daylight now, I'd probably have to go. He leads me a little way along what feels like a rough path. Tall stalks of grass brush my legs, and with my knickers around my knees every shuffling uneven step makes me gasp.

'Here,' he says eventually, then, without warning, he swoops down. I feel him pluck at my pants, and I get the message. Feeling as if my eyes are going to pop out beneath my blindfold, I step out of my underwear, moaning with every move or jolt.

I don't know what he does with my knickers, but I suspect that I'm not going to get them back. And I don't care. All I want now is to squat down and let it all go.

But, of course, once I'm down, legs akimbo, I can't. And the multicoloured frustration is so keen I want to wail. Even with the rushing river so close by, I'm all locked up.

'I can't go,' I snivel.

'Oh, poor baby,' he murmurs. 'Poor Miss Lewis. Do you want me to help you?'

Oh, God, yes!

I sense his great presence beside me and, if it wouldn't

be so appallingly uncomfortable that I'd probably scream, I'd fall down on my knees and press my lips against his shoes.

He crouches at my side, and once more he slips his hand between my thighs.

And when one long, square-tipped finger works its magic, I do scream. But silently, inside, behind my bitten lip as everything cuts loose and I piss and have an orgasm simultaneously.

This time I don't blank, but seem to experience a moment of total clarity. The sounds around me come into sharp focus. The running water. The echo of my own torrent. The bashing and pounding of my heart. The heavy, broken breathing of the man at my side, who's unable to mask his physical excitement in the execution of one of his own particular perversions. He's wanted to do this ever since I described once being brought off this way by a girlfriend in a transport café.

Silently, as I come down, he hands me tissues to clean myself with, then disposes of them I know not where. I don't feel as if I can speak as we track backwards back to the Toyota. I want to touch him again. Or, more properly, touch him for the first time in the course of this escapade. But somehow I know it's not the time yet.

How long is this bloody road trip going to last?

'Are we there yet?'

We seem to have been driving for hours. Certainly long enough for my inner tension, and my libido, to crank right back up to screaming point again. I clench myself hard around the intrusion in my bottom, imagining that it's Mr Stone's magnificent dick.

'I asked you not to ask that again,' he states, mock coolly.

I pout, hoping the mutinous thrust of my lip will goad him. I know I'm acting bratty, but I also know that's what he wants. This magical mystery tour is turning out to be a pick-and-mix of all his favourite kinks, and there's one more I'd like to add to the selection.

I wait two minutes, then I ask again.

'No. But we soon will be. And you'll regret it, young lady.'

Bingo! He's taken the bait.

Or have I taken his?

The car speeds up, and we twist and turn through the unseen roads and streets. There's passing traffic, so we're probably not in the country or by the river, I guess. I can't see him, and he doesn't speak, but there's a quality to the air that seems to press on my skin. He's as impatient as I am, and, even though he's a past master at disguising his emotions, I know him. And I can read him in the silence and the dark.

We stop, he wrenches on the handbrake, and says, 'We're here. Are you satisfied?'

'No,' I say pertly.

'Well, we'll see about that, then, shall we?'

In far less time than it takes me to grapple clumsily with my seatbelt, he's out of the car, round to the passenger side, and hauling me out on to the pavement, or path, or whatever. He's so much less measured now, so much less in control of himself, and that sense of the balance of power tipping makes my innards flutter dangerously. There's just one more component in our three-for-one special, and, in that, the one who seems to have the least say in the matter is always the one who's really in control.

Together we almost run along a hard surface. I hear the rustle of trees, and sense a boundary of some kind on either side of us. It's a narrow alley. There might be hedges or walls flanking us. There's the snick of a gate, and Mr Stone urges me ahead of him through the opening.

I smile. But I don't let him see it.

'You're an impatient travelling companion, Miss Lewis,' he murmurs, bringing us to a halt. A tree, above and to the side, sighs in agreement. 'Not very restful. Not very soothing.' He pauses, grasps my linked hands, and then presses them against the front of his jeans. 'In fact you could say that your presence on this journey has really wound me up.'

I'll say! He's even more gargantuan than usual.

'What do you think we should do about it?' He does his tango hip swivel when I try to get creative and grope him.

'Discipline me?' I suggest, all innocence, while contemplating another lunge for his equipment.

'Really?' He's holding me at arm's length now. Effortlessly. A man of his size has rather long arms. 'And would you like that?'

Trick question.

'Oh, no ... Please, no ...' I try for piteous and just get pitiful. No need to worry about my Oscar acceptance speech just yet.

'Actually, I think "yes".'

And with that he manhandles me into position over the back of what feels like a conveniently placed wooden chair or seat of some kind. How handy that something just like that should be there.

I dangle, face down – head resting against my shackled arms, thighs taut, bum in the air. Perfectly positioned. And, when he carefully adjusts my skirt, a perfect target. The black flange of the butt plug will make it easier to gauge the distance, no doubt ...

I hear a slow, sliding, insidious sound. And then the snick, snick of a heavy leather belt leaving the loops of his jeans.

Uh-oh! He means business.

I almost shoot out of my skin when he trails it lightly over my naked bottom as if he's allowing me to try the leather on for size. I almost wet myself – again – with longing, when he drapes it in the length of my crease, nudging the plug, the smooth leather dangling against the stickiness of my sex.

'Just three, I think,' he purrs, still teasing me with the object of my correction. 'And I think it would be a good idea if you tried not to cry out.'

Fat chance of that, although I know why he suggests it.

With that he whirls away and I hear his firm tread as he moves into position. I like his purposefulness in these matters. He doesn't waste time with unnecessary taunts and overdramatic Grand Guignol threats. He just gets on with it.

The first blow feels as if I'd been whaled on the right bum cheek by a two-by-four, and my attempt not to make a sound comes out like the squeal of the proverbial stuck pig.

The second feels as if the left side of my arse had been struck by lightning and I make a sound that I don't recognise as human.

The third blow is much lighter, but it catches me right in the crease and knocks the evil-demon butt plug right against the nerves that connect to my clitoris.

I climax violently, shout 'Oh, Bobby!' and pee myself a little.

Afterwards, I turn into a sobbing, blubbering, shuddering, glowing, thankful, soppy mess, and he takes me onto his lap – heedless of my soggy state. I come again, lightly, when he whips out the plug and flings it away into the bushes, and, like a little kitten-girl, I try to kiss his beloved hands, and his dear face, while he unclicks the handcuffs and hurls them away too, after the plug.

Which leaves only the blindfold.

'Are we there yet?' I whisper, managing to get my lips against his as he reaches for the ribbon that holds the mask in place.

'I think so, baby,' he whispers, returning my kiss as he gives me my sight back.

My lips cling to his for a moment, then I ease away, almost blinded by the nearness of his broad, beloved face.

Then I blink like a baby owl and glance around.

At the chestnut tree. The toolshed. The ironic garden gnomes. Then up towards the bedroom window where there's a soft glow from the bedside lamp he turned on before we set out.

We're here. We're back home again, just where we started from. And I'm so happy because this is where the bed is.

And this time, Clever Bobby, *I'll* do the driving!

Life Boat Virginia St George

The ship was an old-fashioned cruiser with a dress code at dinner and seating plans in a glass case in the hall. Breakfast was served on the pool deck under canvas umbrellas. Sunlight glinted off the artificial blue pool and dark-green ocean – light thrown back like shattered glass. The waiters, busboys and bartenders all wore white uniforms complete with gloves. In the lounge, sequined singers still sang the old songs: 'It's a Wonderful World', 'Never on a Sunday'.

For her high school graduation, Lauren's parents had brought her to Greece. Athens. A bus tour of the Peloponnesus. A week-long cruise of the Mediterranean. At night, she stretched across the old springs of her berth. She thought about sex, love and the future. She imagined her future, herself at twenty-five, an ad exec or lawyer in expensive high-heeled shoes and tight leather pants, a woman who would fuck men and be gone in the morning. She felt so naïve still, on her first trip to Europe, so soft and girlish despite her best efforts to become world-weary and wise. She longed to be a heartbreaker.

The third evening of the cruise, at the dinner table with her parents, Lauren found herself next to an English doctor and his pretty wife, both dressed in white linen. Also at the table were American siblings, in their third month of a year of travelling, they said. 'We're from Utah.' The sister was rosy and dark-haired.

'Are you Mormons?' Lauren raised an eyebrow.

'Oh, no, we despise Mormons. I hope there aren't any on this ship.' The sister looked over her shoulder and giggled, displaying a small gap between her front teeth. The waiters appeared and with a flourish removed the shiny metal covers from their platters in unison.

Lauren studied the brother. He was wearing a sand-coloured corduroy coat with leather elbow patches, unseasonably warm attire. His face was freckled, even his eyelids, and his hair was sandy like his coat; he didn't look at all like his sister. There was a tattoo on the inside of his wrist that peaked out from under his cuff as he struggled with his cutlery: 'INCONCESSUS AMOR' in cursive script.

'What does your tattoo mean?'

'It's a secret.'

The dining room was grand, chandeliered. At the other tables silver-haired gentlemen poured wine for their smiling, round wives. Retirees. Older professionals on summer holiday. The sounds of clinking china and silver was a polite cacophony.

'We're the youngest people here,' Lauren said.

The brother raised his eyes from his swordfish and brushed his hair from his eyes. He smiled. 'I'm Ben. She's Casey. Call her Cass.'

Cass's eyes glittered. 'Have you noticed the waiters? They're young. All male too.'

Lauren blushed and glanced nervously at her mother.

Cass shrugged. 'Don't pretend you didn't notice.'

Lying in her berth listening to the heartbeat thrum of the engines felt like sleeping inside a body, warm and close. Lauren felt the slow rocking of the sea, nestled in the ship's dark depths, cradled in its womb. Before she slipped into sleep, Lauren touched her clit softly, stroking it while thinking of Ben and her ship full of young men.

When Lauren woke late in the morning, her parents had already gone above deck. She put on her bathing suit and a sundress, then, glancing in the mirror, raked her fingers through her hair. Good enough.

The elevator up to the pool deck was empty save the elevator operator.

'Up to breakfast?' His face was tanned and freckled with sun. His dark eyes stood out against his white uniform. He glanced at her, just for a moment.

'Yes.' Lauren stood behind him as he pressed the button with his gloved finger. The doors closed. The young man's hands rose again and he pressed another button. The elevator stopped suddenly. He turned to her, and put his wet mouth over hers. His face was pressed so close to hers, all she could see were his dark eyelashes over his closed eyes. She could have counted them if she'd wanted to. The soft fabric of his gloves grazed her thighs. He tasted like coffee, his tongue bitter and forceful inside her mouth.

She gasped for breath. I could fuck this guy, this nameless guy, she thought. He wants me. He could give me pleasure. For a few moments, I could be the centre of his universe.

The elevator attendant pulled his hands free of his gloves and grabbed her ass as he pushed her up against the wall of the elevator, grinding his body into hers. He fingered the elastic edges of her bathing suit. Lauren could feel herself getting wet, responding to him. He groaned as he pushed his hand into her bathing suit and found her asshole. Lauren cried out as he pushed a finger inside her. It felt lovely, but dirty. It made her hot, but it felt wrong.

'I have to go, my parents are waiting for me.' She pulled herself away from him.

'Please.' He was panting and his eyes were pleading. 'Please?'

'No, I've got to go.' Lauren pulled down the hem of her sundress.

He grabbed her wrists and pushed them around her back. He kissed her again, forcing his tongue deep inside her. Her heart raced with fear and arousal.

He pulled away from her fast as the coppery taste of blood filled her mouth. 'Fuck! You bit me.' Lauren smiled at him, his blood on her teeth.

'Crazy bitch.' He pressed a button and the elevator began to move.

At breakfast, Lauren drank coffee and the cup shook in her hands.

Around noon, Lauren found Cass sunbathing topless on a deckchair next to the pool. Her breasts were milky compared with her round, tanned shoulders and arms. Cass had a fashion magazine covering her face. Lauren thought she was beautiful like this, exposed, embracing her own exhibitionism.

Without removing the magazine, Cass said, 'I'm driving the wait staff completely wild with desire.' Cass's skin glistened with tanning oil and the smell of coconut mingled with sweat wafted off her. She peeked out from under the magazine pages. 'Do you want to join me?' Cass tugged at one of the ties hanging off Lauren's swimsuit. 'Did I mention that I'm doing a tour of the men of Europe? I've yet to land myself a Greek. On this ship I've already had a Hungarian. Did you see him? Tall man, salt-and-pepper hair? Wears the red Speedo bathing suit for his swim each morning? His body is hard as rock.'

Lauren smiled and shrugged.

'Oh, don't be coy. Everyone notices The Hungarian.'

'I haven't.'

'Oh, well. I have a plan, if you'd like to be in on it. To land myself a Greek. A busboy would be good. They look like they would be so appreciative, don't you think? You can have one too. We'll meet here after dinner. Wear something that shows some skin.'

In her cotton tank top and skirt Lauren felt rather unglamorous beside Cass's low-cut red dress. 'I always wear red when I want to just ooze sex.'

'You look nice.'

'You do too. In a sweet, wholesome way.' Cass's eyes moved away from Lauren's body to a young man crossing the deck with a tray of empty glasses.

'Hey, you there. Busboy?' The young man turned and looked questioningly at Cass.

'Come over here for a second. I'm looking for a bottle of ouzo and I don't want to order ouzo drinks all night. I want a full bottle. Do you know where I might be able to purchase such a thing?' The busboy had to struggle not to look down Cass's cleavage as she bent towards him. 'Do you have a bottle? Or a friend who has one? Could I meet you later to buy it from you?'

The busboy looked wide-eyed and overwhelmed for a moment, then shook his head yes. 'Ten minutes, yes? Cabin two-six-five? Both of you come?' Cass smiled, her teeth white against her scarlet lipstick. The busboy turned on his heel and jogged away with his tray of glasses tipping perilously.

'Well, he's cute and he understands English pretty well. I reserve the right to choose him until after we've seen what his friend looks like. It was my plan, so I get first pick.'

'Why would he bring a friend?' Lauren liked the idea of an adventure, but buying a bottle of ouzo seemed unlikely to yield a thrill, let alone score a busboy.

'You'll see. Now that we have ten minutes to kill, let's see if we can't do something about your outfit, OK?' Cass led Lauren towards the elevator.

Cass's cabin was a mess of clothes hanging off the edges of the berths, the chair, the bathroom door. Giant bottles of duty-free perfume cluttered the small vanity. Cass pulled a sequined dress off the chair and offered Lauren the seat.

'You share this room with your brother?'

'Unfortunately. But he knows enough to keep all his things in his suitcase. I travel in style as you can see. I get it from my mother – she was an actress. I think Ben must have gotten his neatness from his dad. He was an accountant.' Cass wrinkled her nose playfully. 'Mother's fourth husband. She really does have a voracious appetite for men. Now she's on to husband number six.'

Cass opened a drawer, which overflowed with make-up, cigarette packages and small bottles of booze like the ones served on aeroplanes. 'I'm thinking black eyeliner for you. Maybe a spritz of Opium. And this.' Cass pulled a backless chiffon blouse out of a lower drawer. Lauren peeled off her tank top and felt Cass's eyes on her body, her gaze sliding languidly over Lauren's shoulders, breasts and stomach.

As Lauren slipped on the blouse, it felt light and luxurious against her skin. 'Now you feel as sexy as you are.' Cass ran her finger slowly down Lauren's neck, from her chin to her collarbone. 'Do you feel sexy?'

Lauren and Cass found the busboy, a friend and an open bottle of ouzo waiting for them in cabin 265. The curtains were drawn over the portal. The room was immaculate, obviously uninhabited. The two boys wore matching uniforms, and even their well-shined black shoes were the same. The friend had eyes that slanted up at the outside corners and showed sharp white teeth when he smiled. I want that one, Lauren thought.

'Good evening, boys.' Cass danced into the room, spreading the scent of her perfume as she moved. 'What do we have here? A little private party?' Cass grabbed the bottle of ouzo, walked into the bathroom and collected four Dixie cups and began to pour. 'Classy.'

'Hello.' The friend made room for Lauren beside him on the berth. Cass looked him over slowly as Lauren sat beside him.

'So, boys, what signs are you? Let me guess. I'm good at this.' Cass handed out the cups. 'You look like a Scorpio. Am I right? And you – a Leo?'

The busboy smiled awkwardly and shook his head.

'I'm wrong? You're not a Leo?'

'Myself, I am a . . . a crab?'

'Ah, Cancer.'

'And was I right about you?' The slant-eyed man shrugged, looked helplessly at his friend and said something in Greek. 'Oh, well. I guess he's yours. No English.' Cass smiled, showing her teeth, then picked up her drink and proceeded to sit in the busboy's lap.

'What's your name?' Lauren blushed as she looked at her companion for the evening.

'Christopher.' He moved towards her and brushed her lips with the tips of his fingers. 'Beautiful, yes?' He held her cheek in the palm of his hand, rough and warm against her. 'Kiss?' Lauren closed her eyes. As he moved closer, she could smell the scent of him, the slight smell of bleach from his uniform, sweat from a long day's work. She couldn't help wishing she could breathe his air, suck in his breath, sweet and wet against her mouth.

She gently bit his lip, plump and full like a ripe plum. He put his hand on her breast, then slipped it into the open back of the shirt, around to the front, and pinched her nipple. Lauren gasped as pleasure pulsed through her body. She could feel herself getting wet, just from a kiss and playful touch.

She put her hand on to his cock, feeling its stiffness through his pants. He wanted her. She could feel it in the electricity off his skin, the way he held his breath when she touched him.

'Listen, boys. This is all well and good, but I've got to tell you. My friend here, she isn't just my friend. She's my lover and watching you touch her makes me jealous.' Cass was standing in the middle of the cabin, towering in her high-heeled shoes. The busboy started talking rapidly in Greek to his friend. Lauren looked up at Cass with a question mark in her face. 'I want you to take your hands off my girl.' Cass pulled Lauren up by the hand.

'Two girls? Lovers?' The busboy's forehead was wrinkled with confusion.

'You do have lesbians in Greece, don't you?' Cass pulled Lauren to her and kissed her on the mouth, then moved her mouth towards her ear and licked her earlobe. The kiss was wet and sensuous and Lauren wanted more of it. Cass whispered into Lauren's ear, 'Not fair for you to have the hot one. I want them both.' Lauren stepped back and looked at Cass: there was a mocking mirth hiding around her eyes. Cass drew back and slapped Lauren across the face. It stung only slightly, but Lauren was shocked by its suddenness, its utter unexpectedness.

'Whore! You're making me jealous on purpose! Why would you do that to me? I want you out of here. I don't want to have to look at your face.' Cass was a queen of melodrama, her voice singsong, her movements exaggerated, her emotion filling the room. She pushed Lauren towards the door and out into the hallway and then promptly slammed the door.

'Cass, I...' A question hung on the end of Lauren's tongue as she heard Cass lock the door from the inside. Lauren's body was buzzing. She felt strangely hollow and confused. She'd only sipped the ouzo. Lauren could hear Cass's giggle through the cabin door. Greedy, insatiable Cass. In that kiss, Lauren felt as if she had been given a clue, a way to possess the woman she wanted to become.

Lauren felt the sting of cool night air as she came up on deck. The expanse of stars and water – the vastness of it – made her feel as if she might explode out of her skin, like an astronaut outside of her spacesuit. Ben's dark shape reclined on a deckchair, eyes glittering, the cherry of a cigarette orange between his fingers.

'You seen Cass?' Ben ashed over the ledge of the deck, into the sea.

'No.'

Lauren settled on the edge of a chair and reached for the lit cigarette. She put it to her lips and took a drag, letting the smoke sting the back of her throat. Ben was Cass's brother, but Lauren could make him her own in a way that Cass never could.

'You don't smoke. I can tell by the way you hold it.'

'So?'

'So, it's a nasty habit.' Ben took a pack out of his shirt pocket and shook a cigarette from it. 'And, if you are going to do it, you may as well do it elegantly.' He put the cigarette in his mouth, lit it and then let the smoke stream effortlessly from his mouth into his nose. 'Let me teach you to French-inhale.'

Lauren sucked smoke into her mouth, then opened it slightly and breathed in through her nose. Smoke rose around her head like a halo. 'Like that?'

'Don't open your mouth so much.'

Lauren tried again.

'Better. But remember it is supposed to be sensual.'

'So I should half close my eyes and try to look like Marlene Dietrich?'

'If it helps.'

Lauren glanced up at his face. Amusement bent the edges of his lips. She leaned towards him and put her lips against his mocking mouth. She would not be coy. Not any more. What was the use of it? It was better to take the man you wanted. It was better to want than to be wanted. He tasted like salt and smoke, but his mouth was soft and warm against hers. She put her hands on his chest and felt the heat of him through his shirt, the hard muscles of his chest, the buried beating of his heart.

'What are you doing?' He moved his face away from hers.

'I'm kissing you.'

She kissed him again, pushing his lips apart and finding the wet centre of him. She ran her hand down his chest, across his stomach and down to his hips. Her fingers lingered on the sliver of bare skin just above his belt buckle. A silky patch of hair ran between his navel and his buckle and, as Lauren stroked it, she could hear Ben's breath falter.

'We can't do this here.'

'We'll find a place. We'll both look around and meet back here in ten minutes.'

This is it, she thought to herself, this is finally it. I will vanquish him and leave him in the morning. Anticipation prickled against her clit, like the throbbing engines far beneath her. Weak, silly boys never had a chance – they were just the fodder for her lust. She watched his ass as he walked towards the front of the ship.

When he returned, Ben was flushed with running. 'I've looked everywhere. Up there is an empty space where there are just ropes and stuff on the deck, but it's open to the sky. I don't know if there is a place.' Ben leaned on the railing, giving up. 'If you don't really .–'

'I thought of a place.' Lauren pointed.

'Overboard?'

'No, look behind you and down.'

Ben looked over the edge of the railing, and then looked up at Lauren. He smiled, and his teeth shone white like a Cheshire cat's.

It was a calculated leap between the rail of the upper deck and the roof of the lifeboat. Lauren scrambled down on to the narrow deck and tried the hatch. It was open. Inside, the air was warm and heavy against her skin, moist and fragrant with diesel, dust and salt. The space was lined with padded benches and the small windows let in only a dim light that made the interior black and white. A hidden space.

Lauren clutched Ben's shirt by the collar as he followed

her into the cabin. She pulled him close and kissed his lips as hard as she could. She would have liked to taste him, if she could have, taken a bite of him. She crushed his body against her own. She needed to get closer. She fumbled with the buttons of his shirt.

'Wait, a sec, I –'

'Quiet.'

Lauren unbuttoned his shirt and slipped it off him. She got down on her knees to unbuckle his belt. The buttons of his fly were difficult and she had to slide her hand under the waist of his jeans. She pulled the denim down from the knees and let the pants settle around Ben's ankles. He stepped out of the pile of fabric, leaving his flip-flops behind too. Ben's boxer shorts were a light, clinging fabric that almost stuck to Lauren's fingers as she pulled them down. In the dim light, his skin looked silvery and his pubic hair was a dark patch of shadow. His body was sinewy and long, and she could see his tattoos in their entirety, a phoenix that stretched across his upper back and sent plumage down one arm. She traced its contours with her fingertips and he shivered under her touch. Ben moved his head to kiss her.

'Wait. I just need to do something.' Lauren ran her hands down his back, feeling the fine hair beneath her fingers. She caressed his muscular legs, his knees. She felt the generous proportions of his buttocks. She smelled the back of his neck, the nape of his hair. He smelled faintly like heat, the memory of sun. She licked his earlobe, it tasted like sweat.

'OK, now kiss me.'

He grabbed her, hungry, and clutched fistfuls of her hair as he kissed her. He pushed her down on to the bench and peeled off the chiffon top and cotton skirt. He smiled at her when he found that was all she had on. Lauren looked down at her naked body, appraising it as she thought he might. Narrow hips, small breasts, but strong and taut. His mouth found her nipple and she gasped. It almost tickled.

His fingers left a trail of fire down her belly to her cunt. They felt big and rough as they moved against her clit. Unfamiliar. Unpredictable. She moved against him. She closed her eyes. Her entire consciousness moved down into her pelvis, the slippery movement of his fingers, the wetness of her cunt, the longing to be filled up with him.

She found his cock with her hands, judged its hardness, its girth, with her touch. Very hard. Shaped like a stick of dynamite and at its tip there was a piece of metal. Lauren opened her eyes. The tip of his cock was pierced with a ring with a barbell on it. Lauren tugged at it gently. Ben sighed.

'Ben, I want to fuck you.'

Ben pushed her knees apart with his legs. He kissed her as he guided his cock into her cunt. She moaned as the tip entered her. Ben pushed his hips into her and his cock slid deep inside her. Pain and ecstasy. Friction and heat. Lauren moved against Ben, rubbing her clit against his pelvic bone. She was getting sweaty and her slick belly slipped against his. The pain made her catch her breath.

'Does it hurt?'

'Yes.'

Ben whimpered in ecstasy, his breath fragmented, broken up with pleasure. Lauren could feel the tension growing in her cunt, coils of energy pulling tight against the walls of her vagina. She sank her nails into Ben's shoulder. She moved against him, faster, harder. She could feel her juices dripping down between the cheeks of her ass. She could feel his breath, staccato, against her neck. She could feel his cock deep inside her, filling her up. And then, for a moment, her mind went blank. There was a small explosion inside her. A flash of white light on the backs of her eyelids. I am the whore of Babylon, she thought. The fucking whore of Babylon.

'Oh, my God. Oh, my God.' Ben was moving inside her. In and out. Faster and faster. She felt a burst of warmth inside her and he collapsed on to her, sweaty and drunk with pleasure. He pulled his cock out of her and his come ran down between her legs on to the bench. Lauren reached down and touched it with her finger, so slippery. She brought her finger to her mouth and tasted it. Like the sea. He lay beside her, cupping her breast in his hand, face tucked into the crook of her neck.

'I know what your tattoo means. The one on your wrist. I asked my mom – she studied Latin. It made me think you might be a romantic. A Romeo. Are you?'

'I have my romantic delusions, I guess.'

'Have you ever been in love?' Lauren asked.

'Yes.'

'What's it like?'

'This isn't it.'

'Good.'

There was a silence.

Lauren slept and dreamed of home. Of the greenness of home, the boys who smelled like their mothers' clean laundry, the girls fated to marry. She dreamed of her high school sweetheart and his tenderness in the back seat of his car.

When she woke, it was light and Ben was gone. She could hear laughter and conversation on deck. The clinking of glasses. Shit. She slipped into her clothes, opened the hatch, and peered up at the deck. She clambered on to the roof of the lifeboat and pulled herself up over the railing. Breakfasters turned and stared, teacups held halfway to their lips, forks frozen in the air. She knew how she looked, dishevelled, sleepy-eyed, a stowaway. A matronly woman with tight white curls pursed her lips in disapproval. A red-faced man laughed for a moment.

'Your young gentleman made his escape almost an

hour ago. Didn't expect that he'd had a companion.' The man's eyes crinkled into tiny slits with depraved delight. You're all voyeurs, Lauren thought. Perverts. She curtsied exaggeratedly, before turning towards the elevator to the lower decks.

Lauren stopped in front of Ben and Cass's door, beige with gold numbers, identical to all the other cabin doors on the whole ship. She knocked. How could Ben have left her alone in the lifeboat? *She* was supposed to leave *him*, lonely in the morning light. She knocked again. Jerk. She tried the doorknob and, when it turned in her hand, she pushed into the room.

On the bed, Cass's enormous naked breasts jiggled as she writhed against the white sheets. Sweat stood out on her collarbone, her hairline, her upper lip. Between her legs, Ben lapped at her clit, one hand reaching up to Cass's mouth, where she sucked on his fingers, the other holding her ass. The embrace wasn't familial. Cass's pinkly round and supple body was passionately enmeshed with Ben's long and sinewy paleness.

Lauren stood stock still, waiting for the image to make sense. For a moment, she wanted to join the wicked, moaning, quivering union and be one with the sweat and the bliss. Lauren looked at Ben's naked back, his phoenix, which only hours ago had belonged to her. Traitor. Ben looked up at her, his mouth shiny with Cass's juices.

'Where are you from, Lauren?' Ben didn't bother wiping his mouth.

'Toronto.'

'We'll check that off our list, then.'

Cass giggled as she pushed Ben's head back down into her cunt. Only then did Lauren notice the words 'INCON-CESSUS AMOR' tattooed on Cass's hip. Forbidden Love.

Silent as the Grave Fiona Locke

A raw October wind swept across the harbour, shrieking through the high, ruined arches of the abbey. Windblown and chilled, Aspen watched the red and gold leaves dancing past her feet. They scurried into the shadows carved on the grass as the setting sun pierced the lancet windows, dividing darkness from light.

She pulled the blue velvet cloak tighter around her shoulders. Her legs, practically bare in torn fishnets, felt encased in ice. And the black tulle skirt barely covered her bottom. But one had to suffer for fashion.

The man in the Barbour coat had circled the abbey more than once, clearly eyeing her up. Aspen pretended not to notice. She was used to being stared at and she welcomed the attention.

'A bit early for the festival, love,' quipped an elderly tourist as he passed her. He gave her a lecherous wink and headed for the visitor centre in what remained of the old Cholmley family mansion.

Aspen smiled and shook her head after him. She wasn't just a twice-a-year goth girl. This was how she always dressed.

Twice a year the goth community descended on the little fishing port. The narrow cobblestone streets were filled with men in opera capes and top hats, women in bustle dresses and bonnets. Brooding teenage vampires in velvet and lace. Fetishists in latex and PVC. And tourists, of course. The goth weekend was the ultimate people-watching venue.

The non-goths gawked at the dark procession. But they entered into the macabre spirit of it, tucking into red fondant-filled chocolate coffins from Justin's Sweet Shop. They feasted on the famous Whitby scampi and the best fish and chips in the country. They bought ammonites and jet. And they undertook the climb to the abbey like a pilgrimage – 199 steep and winding steps up to St Mary's churchyard. Aspen often heard them counting as they climbed, as though expecting a 200th to have sprung up just for them.

From the corner of her eye she saw the Barbour man surreptitiously aiming his camera at her and decided to play along. Enjoying the objectification, she obliged him by braving the cold and removing her cloak. Her wasp waist was exquisitely showcased in a tight-laced black satin corset. Her long scarlet hair streamed out behind her in dramatic contrast to her tragically pale skin. She lifted her chin as her ballet teacher had taught her, showing off the lace choker at her throat.

With an appreciative grin, the photographer snapped away, inching closer to capture the poses she adopted for the camera. Her vanity indulged, Aspen placed her hands against the ragged stone wall of the north transept, arching her back and thrusting her bottom out.

A small knot of tourists were watching the display. They probably assumed she was a model. But Aspen was just an exhibitionist. And, if the photographer had the courage to ask her to strip off completely, she'd squirm with delight and make a few half-hearted protests before complying. She wasn't easily abashed.

She thought of the beautiful boy at the cemetery. The one who drove the hearse. He always stood by the car while the funeral party was at the graveside, watching solemnly. Waiting. And as the mourners filed away, he would slip into the long black car and drive away. Aspen would watch as it snaked its way along the curving lane out of the cemetery. Out of sight.

If he was curious about why she went to so many funerals he never showed it. But she could hardly keep her eyes off him. She would lower her head and pretend to stare into the grave, furtively raising her eyes enough to see him. And he was always watching her.

She imagined him watching her now, wantonly disporting herself for a stranger. Would he be shocked? Jealous? She had no idea. He was a complete mystery. But he'd made her blush with a single look.

Aspen had always felt at home in churchyards, among the canted tombstones. The fancy carved calligraphy and loftily worded epitaphs took her back in time. She was fascinated by the tiny ancient markers at the outer edges of the burial ground, worn so smooth nothing could be read. As a child she'd done grave rubbings. As a teenager she'd taken pretentious black-and-white photographs. Eventually she'd gone simply for the atmosphere.

One day she had chanced on a funeral. Dressed in black, she joined the mourners inconspicuously at the graveside, unnoticed except by the young driver.

He was striking. Gorgeous pale skin and sharp, gaunt features. Long dark hair pulled back from his face, emphasising the high cheekbones. There was something of Christopher Lee's Dracula about him – an extraordinary stillness that belied intense passion within. He watched her, but never approached. Aspen was sure the etiquette books would disapprove of flirting at funerals, let alone crashing them.

The second time she saw him she flashed him a mischievous smile, confident that her audacity would entice him into sticking around. He met her eyes impassively, but didn't react. She took his severe expression as a rebuke. Aspen wasn't used to being refused. His black look made her feel deliciously guilty, as though she'd flirted with a priest and he'd reached through the confessional grille to smack her hand. Her sex pulsed hungrily, making her feel even naughtier, and she blushed, biting her lip through the rest of the service.

She stalked him. She got the name of the undertaker

and noted the list of forthcoming interments. Each time she saw the driver she tried a different tack. She'd coloured her hair the last time – Red Death. A shameless bid for attention. He noticed, but still he kept silent and aloof. The dance was tantalising, but it would become a stalemate if one of them didn't act soon. If only he were watching her now, as she posed for the photographer.

Crossing her wrists, Aspen raised her arms high above her head, as though suspended by invisible bonds. She stood on tiptoe in her Victorian riding boots, leaning back against the worked stone and wincing at the chill. The ice turned to fire in her mind as she displayed her back again, imagining the punishing strokes of a whip along her spine. A wanton flogged at the stake, a spectacle for the villagers who secretly lusted after her.

At last the photographer was done. He hesitated a moment before turning to leave, glancing back over his shoulder one last time. But all he offered her was a conspiratorial little grin and a chaste wave of thanks.

Married, thought Aspen with a smug grin.

Shivering, she retrieved her cloak and gazed up at the crumbling pinnacles of the abbey, starkly outlined against the deepening sky. The darkness fell early and the nights grew intolerably long and bitter as winter took hold.

It wasn't long before the last visitors left and Aspen had the grounds to herself. She admired the rich tracery of the rose window in silhouette against the unearthly glow of the moon. This was how it must have looked to Dracula when he arrived in Whitby.

As the moon climbed higher the wind began to intensify. Over its howling she felt rather than heard footsteps. She stared intently into the gloom of the choir end of the abbey, half expecting to see a shadow detach itself from one of the gaunt sandstone pillars and drift towards her, the ghost of some murdered monk.

Just the wind, Aspen told herself. But wasn't that what

they always said in horror movies? She wondered whether Bram Stoker had been this easily spooked. No, there was nothing there. Nothing but her own overactive imagination.

She followed the path around the abbey pond, watching the flickering reflection of the ruins in the choppy water. From there she could see the dim glow of headlights in the car park. So she wasn't alone after all. Perhaps it was her photographer, waiting to see if she'd flaunt even more skin for him away from the tourists.

The lights made her slightly nervous, but she pressed on. She wasn't going to be intimidated. Not by a vampire or a ghost. Not even by a shambling zombie risen from the Saxon churchyard of St Mary's.

Cresting the hill she could just make out the vague elongated shape of a car. There was something oddly familiar about it. As she drew nearer it came into focus and her breath caught in her throat. It was a hearse.

The boy got out and stood beside the car. Just a silhouette, but she knew his movement signature. The beautiful boy. A flush spread over her face and throat, warming her from within. How long had he been watching her, following her?

Aspen couldn't have stopped if she'd wanted to. She felt compelled by some magnetic power as her feet carried her towards the car. It was a gleaming, vintage Daimler. The high-roofed casket compartment sported large oblong windows on both sides, draped with red velvet curtains. On the roof, the chrome wreath rail shone like a silver serpent in the moonlight.

The boy wasn't in his usual black suit. Instead he wore a dark Victorian frock coat with white lace pouring from his cuffs and throat. The sight of him plunged her back a hundred years and the tight-lacing suddenly felt too constricting.

She tried to think of words, but none would come. None were needed. The driver walked round to the rear of the hearse and opened the back door. A little throb of fear ran through her. But there was no silk-lined casket waiting for her. The hearse was empty. There was only a cushioned floor where the bier and coffin runners should have been.

Her escort didn't say a word. She met his eyes. They were Scandinavian blue and piercing, accentuated by the dark hair that hung loose around his shoulders. His gaze exuded competence, authority. But still he said nothing. Her legs felt weak.

He gestured formally and she climbed inside, mesmerised. But, instead of joining her, he closed the door. She expected to hear a resonant boom, sealing her fate. Instead it barely made a sound. Somehow that unnerved her even more.

Aspen had seen plenty of hearses, but she'd never been inside one. She had supposed it would be chilly. Instead, the padded interior was warm and comfortable. She surveyed her surroundings as the driver took his seat behind the wheel.

Two ledges ran along the curtained windows on the sides of the car. She guessed they were where the bier had rested. There was a row of red candles in brass holders spaced along one of the ledges. Lighted, they would create the perfect ambience.

A flutter of red velvet covered the rear window. She drew it aside and caught the pearly eye of the moon as the car bore her away. She had no idea where he was taking her. But it wasn't for her to know; she wasn't the one in charge.

She took off her cloak and folded it beside her, watching the abbey shrink into the distance as the hearse crept along the winding road out of Whitby.

'Who are you?' Aspen whispered, unable to take the silence any longer. He probably wasn't used to being addressed from back here. Unless he did this sort of thing often.

He didn't answer, but she thought she could see the corners of his mouth turn up slightly in the rear-view mirror. She thought of Poe's raven, uttering only the single cryptic word, 'Nevermore.' He would reveal what he wanted her to know when he wanted her to know it.

Morbidly unable to resist, Aspen lay on the cushioned floor and crossed her arms over her chest. The compartment was almost five feet high and long enough for her to stretch out fully. Of course. She closed her eyes and listened to the tyres singing on the road as the driver increased his speed.

So he was a goth boy after all. She couldn't believe she'd never seen him at the festival. Why had he been so distant all this time? All those funerals! He could have given her some sign of encouragement. But, then, that wouldn't have been half as much fun. Clearly he loved a good mystery as much as she did.

It wasn't long before the car began to slow. She felt the soft rolling bump of the tyres over grass and she sat up and looked out of the back window. The moonlight cast a numinous pall over the desolate landscape of the North York Moors. In the distance she could just make out the bleak outline of the abbey perched on the windswept headland. A dramatic testament to the durability of stone over flesh.

At last the engine stopped and the driver stepped out. Her heart began to pound as she watched his form slip past the curtained window. The back door swung open on its hinge and Aspen's breathing quickened. Without a word he climbed inside and closed the door, settling on the ledge beside the candles. The car's dome light dimmed and she was alone with him in the dark. Outside the banshee wind continued to wail, rocking the car gently.

Her first question had gone unanswered, so Aspen wasn't keen to ask another. She decided to follow his lead. To wait for instructions.

A match flared and his features came into view again. He held the match to each candle in turn and the flickering flames made the shadows dance inside the hearse.

In the candlelight he was a vision from another era. He removed his frock coat, folding it carefully and laying it aside. The billowy white shirt beneath it became a canvas for the wandering shadows as he sat back and considered her.

Aspen was used to being the one in control and his silence threw her off balance. She didn't know what to do. Unsettled, she stared at the candles. They gave off a rich, cinnamonny aroma. As she watched, a creeping droplet of wax slithered down the length of one of them, pooling at its base. She noticed that the ledge was crusted over with dried wax. Nervously, she passed her finger back and forth through the tall, licking flame. The feeling of subordination was unfamiliar, but also exciting. There was something about her companion that she dared not challenge.

He looked her up and down, as though appraising a slave girl on an auction block. Slowly, he stirred his finger in the air, directing her to turn around. There was no question that she would obey. She turned on her knees, facing away from him.

He patted the ledge in front of her and she placed her hands on it. His shadow loomed before her on the curtains, vampire-like.

She gasped at his touch. Just a finger, stroking sinuously along the lacing of her corset, down to the starchy layers of tulle below it. Her tutu-style skirt left little to the imagination. He had an unobstructed view of her bottom, clad in black-lace French knickers and framed perfectly by her fishnet holdups.

Aspen looked around to see what he was doing. But he stopped her, winding a hand in her hair and firmly guiding her head back so that she was facing forward again. She weakened at his show of authority and began to tremble. He smoothed her hair down, sweeping it across her right shoulder to expose her back.

There was a creak as he shifted his position. A scrape. Something uncoiling. It was all she could do not to peek. Suddenly, there was a flash of sensation across her bare upper back, accompanied by a leathery smack. Disorientated, she was uncertain whether it had hurt or not. Slowly the feeling built and began to burn. With a moan she arched her back, inviting another stroke.

This one was harder and her yelp was of genuine pain. She gritted her teeth and prepared herself for the next. She saw the shadow raise the whip with both hands. One hand held the tails in place while the other prepared to strike. He released the tails at the last second and the well-aimed stroke fell across her shoulder blades with another sharp crack.

Aspen sensed he had been sizing her up at the funerals. Testing her resolve with his detachment and his unspoken rebuke. She also sensed that he expected silence from her as well, a sign of her surrender.

Again the whip fell and she writhed as it stung her chilled flesh. When seconds passed with no more, she sighed with relief and disappointment.

She flinched in surprise when she felt his fingers at the lacing of her corset. A quick tug and the knot was undone. The boned panels parted and she relaxed gratefully as he released her waist. He slipped his finger under the laces and loosened them until there was enough slack to unfasten the front. Reaching his hands around her, he unhooked the metal studs and grommets with practised ease. His familiarity heightened her submission and she closed her eyes as he freed her small breasts from their confinement.

Then he pulled her skirt down to her knees. He lifted her right foot and slid it down her leg. She whimpered as he repeated the action with her left foot, undressing her like a child.

Still in her panties, stockings and boots, Aspen felt more naked than if he had stripped her bare. It was different when she was the one exhibiting herself. She never felt vulnerable then. This was different. This was scary.

And when he slipped his fingers inside the waistband of her panties she resisted.

'No,' she moaned softly, reaching back to stop him.

The silence deepened unbearably.

She felt his disapproval like a blow. Slowly, deliberately, he replaced her errant hand on the ledge. Aspen bowed her head, a wordless apology.

When he touched her again it was with the same uncanny stillness that had captivated her since she first saw him. She knew he was going to punish her. Her skin prickled with fear and need as her panties came down. He eased her out of them as he had her skirt. She knew the gusset would be soaked and she surrendered to the delicious misery of embarrassment.

One at a time he positioned her hands on the padded floor of the hearse, guiding her head down until her forehead touched the floor as well. The position raised her bottom, a perfect target, and she moaned with shame.

He made her wait. The seconds seemed like hours. She dreaded and yet craved the whipping to come. Outside, it had begun to rain. The water drummed violently on the roof of the Daimler like a tribal beat. Primitive and lust-driven.

She heard the soft creak of leather and held her breath, anticipating the sting of the whip. It struck her bottom sharply, harder than it had her back. Aspen yelped, pressing her hands into the floor to avoid breaking position. Each time the lash found her tender flesh she cried out, sinking deeper and deeper into submission.

He whipped her soundly, awakening unfamiliar feelings. She wanted to please him, to make him proud. More than once, the tails crept in between her legs, their tips biting into her sex. Whether deliberate or not, the searing pain got her attention. She genuinely regretted her disobedience and she resolved to do whatever was necessary to earn his rewards.

She was breathing hard when he stopped and she knew her bottom was well striped.

With a gentle tap he urged her up and around. Every movement made the candles flicker in response, as though reflecting her arousal. She knelt before him, her heels pressing into the punished skin of her bottom.

Again he gathered her hair, this time sweeping it behind her to uncover her breasts. He positioned her hands on top of her head, giving her wrists a firm squeeze before releasing them. A command. A warning. Aspen squirmed at the exposure. But she'd learned her lesson; she didn't protest again.

She pressed her thighs together, flushing deeply at the warm pulse between them. There was a strange security in punishment. It absolved her of all responsibility. There were no decisions to make. All she had to do was obey. The discovery made her feel feverish.

He smiled with his eyes, but his lips didn't move. He'd known how she would respond.

Breathless with anticipation, Aspen watched as he prised a candle loose from its holder. At last he smiled, showing his teeth. A sly, wolfish grin. He held his hand up in front of Aspen, palm down. He raised the candle above his hand and allowed a single drop of wax to fall on it. Transfixed, she watched as the wax spread itself into a thin film before it began to harden. The red faded to a cloudy white bloom before her eyes.

Trembling, Aspen held her breath.

The candle paused a foot above her right nipple. She stared wide-eyed at the liquid pooling around the wick, shimmering just at the edge. The candle tilted just enough to release a few drops of wax. They landed precisely where they were aimed and Aspen cried out as the fiery droplets clung to her tender skin like molten lava and began to harden and cool.

More drops of wax found her other nipple, making her gasp in astonishment at the pain. The initial sting was overwhelming, but soon it faded to a pleasant warmth, leaving the punished skin throbbing.

The space between them was charged with electricity and she stared at him, bewildered. This didn't happen to her. Such vulnerability was completely unfamiliar. *She* was the one who prowled, stalked and conquered. She lured boys to her like a siren. She used them and then released them, dazed and drained, back into the wild.

She looked down at herself as another sprinkling of droplets fell across the swell of her upthrust breasts. Hissing through her teeth, Aspen twisted from side to side as the burn peaked and dwindled.

He tilted her head to look into her eyes, as though assessing her endurance. He arranged her arms so that they rested on the floor behind her. With a gentle tap he directed her to arch her back. She obeyed, exposing the soft and pale expanse of her belly.

The candle tipped again, and this time the wax trickled down to form a tiny pool in her navel. She gritted her teeth, groaning deep in her throat as she writhed help-lessly in her invisible bonds.

Over and over, the cruel candle dripped wax on to her sore breasts and belly. The torture was symmetrical, moving from one breast to the other and then to her abdomen.

The pain dominated her landscape of sensation, excluding everything else: the rain, the wind, the spicy perfume of the candles. Nothing existed but the pain and its agent.

The candle moved to her thighs, sprinkling wax along

her flesh in an upward motion, moving closer and closer to her sex. The fishnet stockings afforded no protection. She gasped at every kiss of the burning liquid, shivering and sighing as it hardened and dried. She could just imagine how she must look – like a victim spattered with the inauthentically red blood from a Hammer horror film.

When she thought she couldn't possibly take any more, he held the candle up in front of her face. She stared fearfully at the flame, wondering what he intended to do next. To her relief, he blew the candle out, and she was fascinated by the frantic guttering of the flame before it died. As though the wax still yearned to torture her smooth, delicate skin.

With one finger he pushed her down on her back. She didn't resist. Well trained now, she lay submissively on the cushioned floor and waited. Outside, the merciless gale battered the car, causing the remaining candles to throw dramatic shadows across the interior.

He opened a small compartment beside her and took out four lengths of rope, doubling them carefully. Her stomach plunged as though she'd dived off a cliff. He wrapped the ropes around her wrists and ankles, securing them one by one to the large chrome rings at the four corners of the compartment. She hadn't noticed those before.

Her limbs spread wide, she shuddered in anticipation. He watched her for several seconds before cupping his hands around her vulnerable breasts and squeezing. The wax crumbled beneath his fingers, a strangely pleasant sensation.

He drew his fingers along her bound and waxed body before unlacing his shirt. He peeled it off, revealing a lean, wiry frame. Strong, but not overly muscled.

The ropes weren't necessary. Even if she'd wanted to resist, she was completely under his spell. He had stripped her of her power as easily as he had stripped her of her clothes. But the physical experience of being bound and helpless was exhilarating. She was at the mercy of a stranger and she could indulge the fantasy of being taken by force. Kidnapped and driven out to the lonely, barren moors. Punished and ravished. He would have his way with her and then take her back to his lair. Keep her prisoner and use her for his pleasure.

Delirious in her hunger, she squirmed impatiently as he skinned down his trousers and knelt above her. She felt the tip of his cock at the opening of her sex and she strained towards him, urging him to take her. He smiled cruelly and didn't oblige.

Frustrated, she yanked at the ropes, resisting the urge to demand with her voice. She knew he would punish her if she spoke unbidden again. Not that the idea was entirely unappealing. He was master of many more sexual torments, she was sure.

At last he pushed inside her. Barely an inch, but enough to make her gasp. His restraint was incredible. He stayed just inside for what seemed an eternity.

Aspen bit her lip to keep from begging. She'd never been so desperate in her life. She pleaded with her eyes and bucked her hips against him in frustration.

Without warning he plunged himself inside her, up to the hilt.

Aspen cried out in pain and surprise, then surrendered gratefully to his rough penetration. The friction was even more painful for the burn of the hot wax. And every thrust pushed her bottom against the padded floor, reawakening the sting of the lash. The pleasure and pain melted into one and she abandoned herself to the fusion.

Her cries were lost in the driving rain and the shrieking wind. She yanked at the ropes so violently she half expected to snap them. But, oh, the freedom to be so wild and primitive! He could do anything to her and she would take it. She would love it. And as she felt the rising tide of his climax she caught a glimpse of the ruins through the window, over his shoulder. She felt just as ravaged.

She thrashed in her bonds as her own orgasm began its exquisite crescendo. She'd never come before without elaborate and careful manipulation, but the hearse driver had taken her to a strange new world. He had transformed her. She was his slave. Out of control for the first time in her life, Aspen wept as the climax racked her body.

Wrapped in her velvet cloak, Aspen looked up into his eyes. He smiled at her, gently massaging her wrists. She sighed as the blood flow returned. The ropes had left deep, telltale imprints whose passing she would mourn.

Utterly drained, she curled into a ball, laying her head in his lap. As he stroked her hair she murmured, 'I don't even know your name.'

By the time he told her, she was lost to the world of dreams.

The Brinks Job Sophie Mouette

My palms were sweating, my hands slick on the steering wheel. I glanced in my rear-view mirror. The dark sedan had been following me for several miles, even when I'd turned on Slater and looped around across the park at Kingston to try to shake him.

Nope, he was definitely following me, despite my defensive driving training. Nobody came through this industrial area after hours unless they lived in the development on the other side.

Or they were looking for an illegal rave on a Saturday night.

Or they were planning to hold up a Brinks van, like the one I was driving.

The fact that I knew about the hold-up, knew even the identity of the person in the dark sedan and had planned the heist with him, didn't matter. He gunned the accelerator. Spraying gravel pinged against my window as he tore out in front of me and wrenched the wheel sideways, effectively cutting me off.

I slammed on the brakes, adrenaline making my ears ring and my vision sharp. I had been trained for this, and my hand automatically went to my gun before I remembered I'd wisely removed all the bullets.

It wasn't just adrenaline coursing through my system, either. My nipples had beaded the moment I'd stepped up into the truck half an hour ago, and I'd been squirming in my seat as I drove, my clit throbbing gently in time with the engine.

My pursuer was at my door, face ominously covered by a black ski mask, gun shoved in the space where I'd cracked the window for air. Unsure what to do, I put my hands on the steering wheel, in plain sight. 'Get out of the van, Kay.'

Hearing my name almost broke me out of the fantasy. But he'd pitched his voice low, gravelly, unfamiliar. I heard the threat, and shivered at the implied danger. If I didn't do what he said ...

Reluctantly, I put my hand on the door handle. If I rammed the door open, his gun might go off, and, unloaded or not, it was close enough to my head that I didn't want to take the chance. I pulled the lever. It clunked loudly, a sudden counterpoint to my harsh breathing and the drum of blood in my ears.

Donny – I didn't know how else to think of him; my assailant? – took a smooth step back, just far enough so I could open the door.

The gun never wavered. I was impressed, actually.

I eased the door open.

We were both so intent on the moment that neither of us heard the crunch of gravel or the sound of a motor as a second car crept up behind the van.

Police lights flashed, piercing the darkness, half-blinding me. I bit back a scream. Donny threw up an arm to shield his eyes, and I took the advantage. I could have shoved the door open and nailed him with it – but I didn't want to hurt him. Instead, I jumped down from my high perch and grabbed Donny from behind, my arm around his neck and his arm behind his back before he could fight back.

'Freeze!' the cop shouted. 'Put your hands in the air!'

'Well, which is it?' Donny asked. 'Do I freeze, or put my hands in the air?'

Dammit. I couldn't stifle a snicker. It didn't help that Marc had his big ol' mirrored cop glasses on in the middle of the night.

'Don't give me any lip, boy,' Marc snarled. Metal clinked as he deftly unhooked his handcuffs from his belt.

The cuffs glinted in the strobing light. Despite myself, I shivered, right down to my damp panties.

Let the games begin.

'Nice work, ma'am,' Marc said. He was staying in character well. Except for the obvious bulge in the crotch of his polyester cop pants. He took Donny from me and slapped one end of the cuffs around Donny's left wrist.

As planned, I ran to the back of my van and unlocked the door. The back was empty, of course. I didn't get to carry money around when I was off duty.

Empty except for a queen-sized mattress and an array of pillows, which in fact made it pretty full. The mattress filled the back from wall to wall and was bent up a bit on one side where a rack attached to the wall interfered with its lying flat. If there had been racks on both walls, we'd have been in trouble.

Marc secured the other cuff to the rack. I knelt on the mattress next to Donny and whispered, 'You're doing great, honey. Do you remember your safeword?'

He licked his lips. 'Daffodil.' His voice was hoarse.

I kissed him, a deep kiss with an interplay of tongue that made me tremble. We'd been together for three years now, and his kisses still held so much promise of things to come. Oh, yeah, we were going to have fun tonight. I put my hand on his thigh, slid it slowly up in search of his ...

'I'll take it from here, ma'am,' Marc said, returning from turning off his car lights. I noticed that he'd also retrieved a small duffel bag. 'It's my job to interrogate the criminals.'

I squeezed Donny's hand reassuringly, and retreated to the other side of the van. I loosened my jeans and stretched out comfortably at the other end of the mattress, leaning back against the metal wall. I'd let Marc call the shots now, as we'd planned earlier.

My boyfriend had admitted from the start that he was bi-curious, but had never found the right way to explore his interest. Marc, on the other hand, was unabashedly bi, something I'd learned when I dated him, very briefly, when we were both at the police academy. We later determined that we were far better as friends. We'd stayed close even after I left the force to do private security work, and then he and Donny had become friends as well. The three of us frequently hung out together.

Naturally, our conversation had turned to sex. You might have expected the three of us just to tumble into bed for a sweaty, extended romp punctuated only by ordering pizza, but we all have a flair for the dramatic. Plus, Donny needed an added incentive to push his curiosity into reality. He wasn't submissive per se, but he wanted to let someone else take control, to allow him to feel less responsible for what was happening to him.

What started as a drunken chat after Sunday football and beer had turned into an elaborate scheme involving a local map, schedule co-ordination and detailed shopping lists. I swear we synchronised our watches.

It was all turning out wonderfully so far.

The light in the back of the van cast a wavery, anaemic glow on both guys. It washed out colours and blurred some details, but I knew them well enough that I could fill in Marc's warm, swarthy complexion and dark eyes, Donny's fairer skin, which would be flushed now with excitement, his sandy hair, now tousled by the ski mask.

When Marc knelt down beside Donny, grabbed handfuls of that sandy hair and pulled him into a brutal kiss, everything snapped into focus for me, despite the poor light.

Donny was on his knees, unable to struggle much even if he'd wanted to due to the way he was cuffed. (Real police cuffs hurt if you struggle. Donny had been coached to stay fairly still until we could get something on him designed for restraining lovers rather than suspects, but we couldn't resist giving him that initial shock of cold metal.) For a second, Donny froze, unsure what to do. His free arm stayed at his side, but I saw it twitching as if he wanted to put it around Marc and pull him even closer.

His body, though – his body knew how to react. He knelt up, rising to give himself more to the kiss. His hips strained forward, pressing against Marc.

I imagined their cocks touching through fabric. It was easy to imagine Donny getting harder, pushing at the fabric of his sweatpants, easy to imagine the heat rising in him. I'd seen it often enough. I'd caused it often enough. But it would be different now, feeling himself brushing against the length and hardness of another man for the first time. While Marc and I hadn't been ideal romantic partners, I certainly had fond memories of his body. I felt a stab of heat imagining how it must seem to Donny. Bigger than it really was, probably, magnified by imagination, lust and a bit of fear. He'd be thinking about what might happen next, where that cock might end up.

And, God knows, I was thinking about that too, and the thought was making me frantic. I slid one hand inside my jeans and stroked gently at my eager clit.

Donny had told me his fantasies, whispered at night in the dark. I'd encouraged him, telling him stories Marc had told me about two men together. Donny had liked some of those an awful lot. After he fell asleep, I scribbled down everything I remembered, and that's what I'd passed on to Marc.

But tonight wasn't only about fulfilling Donny's fantasies. Long before I'd met Marc, I'd masturbated to the idea of being with two hot men. I'm greedy, and more cock to enjoy (not to mention two pairs of arms to wrap around me, two sets of nipples to tease ...) sounded like a great plan. Once Marc told me some of his adventures, the fantasies expanded. I wanted to see men together, men kissing, men sucking and fucking, beautiful male bodies doing wonderful, nasty things to each other as well as to me.

And now I was getting my chance.

Donny's arm jerked again, then went around Marc's back, sliding down to his bum. I knew exactly what cop uniform pants felt like, imagined the unappealing texture and under it the far more appealing curve of a fine male ass.

The kissing continued for a long time, enough time for me to decide the jeans and shirt were in my way and scramble out of them. My panties had soaked through already.

It was tempting to make myself come now, but I decided that, if I enjoyed the show while teasing myself at a leisurely pace, it would be that much stronger in the end.

Marc broke away from the kiss first and said something I couldn't quite hear, prompting me to crawl closer.

Donny's eyes were wide.

'I said, did you like that?'

Donny didn't answer. I wasn't sure if that was part of the game or if something in his brain had short-circuited.

'Take off your clothes,' Marc said, his voice husky and commanding.

'I can't.' Donny sounded shaky. I'd almost felt sorry for him, except I knew how lust could break up his voice. He took a breath and composed himself. 'I really can't. Not handcuffed like this.'

'Let it be noted that the prisoner refused to co-operate, so we had to step up the interrogation efforts.' Marc's smile was deliciously evil. I'd been on the receiving end of that smile before. Usually what happened next made me come a lot. He wasn't hardcore kinky, but he was a master of the fun head-fuck.

As he proved when he reached down to his belt, pulled off a butterfly knife and opened it with a practised flick.

I'd thought Donny's eyes were wide before.

Marc started at the bottom of the worn black T-shirt and cut up, not a grand slash, but a careful, controlled gesture.

Donny held his breath. I think I did, too, because in the silence I could hear the tiny noise of fabric parting.

Marc paused, stretched out the neck opening as wide as it would go, cut at the fabric.

The shirt fell entirely open and Donny let out an *ooof* of held breath. Another snick cut the drawstring on Donny's sweats, which tried to fall around his knees but hung up on his erection.

Donny moved his free hand to wriggle the pants free, but Marc beat him to it, brushing along his cock lightly as he got the pants out of the way. Oh, yeah, my guy was enjoying this.

Putting the knife away, Marc rose, one hand following the line of Donny's torso as he did. 'Could you give me a hand here, ma'am?' he said, a gleefully ironic tone on the 'ma'am'. 'Cuff the prisoner's hands in front of him. I have another set of cuffs in the bag.'

He tossed me the key for the police cuffs, but, before I unlocked those, I rummaged through the duffel. Nestled between a box of condoms and a coil of rope was what I was looking for.

Marc might not be hardcore kinky, but he was kinky enough to invest in some sweet toys. The cuffs were thick, cushy, cobalt-blue leather, lined with sheepskin for comfort. The straps that actually held them shut were black for contrast. They fastened together with a metal clip.

I fastened one around Donny's free wrist, then reached behind him to unlock the metal cuff that held him to the van wall. He leaned back into me, his body hot against mine.

'Doing all right, love?' I asked. I ran my hands over his hips to cradle his balls as I asked. Parts of him were doing just fine, but I wanted to make sure his brain was as well.

'God, yes.' He craned his neck, clearly wanting a kiss, and I was glad to give it to him.

I imagined I could taste Marc on his breath, and that made me want to devour him. The position was awkward, though, so I reluctantly let him go and finished releasing him from the wall.

Finishing the job of recuffing him took longer than Marc probably expected, but not because Donny was struggling. Once I moved in front of him, I had to kiss him again, feeling his arms around me, his warm strength, the urgency of his erection straining to rub against my slickness if he couldn't enter me. Partly it was pure pleasure, both sexual and emotional. Partly, I was feeling a little competitive after watching Donny respond so eagerly to Marc's world-class kissing effort. I was glad to find that he seemed equally eager with me.

Then, once I did get him cuffed, I had to take advantage of his relative helplessness to suckle on his nipples, which always makes him squirm. Finally, though, I turned him back to Marc and sat back down. The metal wall felt cold against my bare skin, but I figured the action would soon be hot enough to distract me.

Marc had taken advantage of the interruption to undress.

Nice view. Definitely a nice view. I hadn't seen Marc naked in more than six years, but he hadn't let himself go after getting out of the academy, as a lot of cops do. His abs and pecs and thighs were as muscular as they'd been when we were doing intense workouts every morning. 'Buff' was the word. Buff and strikingly hairless in certain areas. That was new, but I could see why he did it. His cock, which I remembered as being good-sized, but not gigantic, looked immense and inviting springing straight from his body without a thicket of fur.

I tore my gaze from that pretty sight long enough to

glance at Donny. He wasn't quite drooling, but it was close. Something else seemed to be mixed in with the excitement. Probably nerves. I reached out and put my hand on his arm to reassure him, but he hardly seemed to notice, so taken with the gorgeous hunk of man in front of him.

(This was almost funny, because I knew he'd seen Marc naked a lot more recently than I had, in a gym locker room sort of way. But I suppose with the entire recreational basketball league in there too, he hadn't ventured to take a good long look.)

Time seemed to stop in the back of the van. None of us moved. I don't think we even breathed. In the distance, the sound of a siren cut through even the armoured walls of the van. I went even more still, thinking some good citizen taking a shortcut might have phoned in what looked like a Brinks van in trouble, before I correctly identified the sound.

'Ambulance, not police.' Marc breathed what I'd just processed.

Having to speak broke the spell. Marc stepped forward, gave Donny a gentle shove that didn't so much push him backward as signal him to lie down. Without being directed, he put his bound hands above his head, giving Marc free access to his body.

I hadn't been sure what would actually happen once the guys got naked together. Given the scenario, I'd imagined a little rough stuff, Marc using a bit of force to pretend-take what Donny wanted to give anyway. That was one of his fantasies, but it was one of many.

Instead, Marc lay down on top of him and started another of those incredible kisses.

There's only so much a girl can take. I lay down with them at a skewed angle so I could, with a little effort, see both faces and Marc's glorious butt. Then I began to kiss and stroke wherever I could reach on either of them. Even through the muffling kiss, Donny was making low, animal noises. The van was starting to smell like male musk, accented by my own arousal.

Marc raised his head and began kissing his way down Donny's body. He lingered at one nipple, the one further from me.

Again, what's a girl to do? If one mouth on one nipple would make Donny ecstatic, two ought to do better.

Apparently it did, if the indrawn breath and the squirming were to be believed.

When Donny was bucking and wriggling, Marc shifted again and continued kissing his way down my boy's torso. I kept working on the nipples and enjoying the view.

Marc licked and kissed down, breathed on the rampant dick without actually touching it and kissed his way to the hipbone, where he rested his cheek.

I knew that move: letting the anticipation build for both of you, drinking in the intimate, animal scent of your lover's balls. I don't think I've ever been able to keep it up for long, though. Marc couldn't either.

I held my breath as his hand closed around the base of Donny's cock.

Donny groaned, struggled against the cuffs.

Marc's mouth opened. Before he filled it, though, he looked at me. 'Get on his face or something, Kay. Not much point in having a threesome if everyone's not getting some.'

The sound coming out of Donny was inarticulate enough that he had to repeat it before we understood. 'Daffodil.'

We froze. 'You all right? Do you need to stop?' Marc asked, moving his hand.

'Please. Don't stop. Don't move ... your hand away. It's wonderful.' The words sounded like words again, but he was pausing between them like a graduate of the William Shatner School of Acting. 'But the cuffs. I want ... if Kay ... I want to ... touch you both.'

Marc grinned. 'Kay, honey, I think our criminal's done his time. Let him loose and see if he attacks us.'

'We can only hope!'

After I unfastened Donny's wrists, I considered straddling his face, then reconsidered. This was his first time ever with a man. He should get to enjoy all the aspects, including visual. Instead, I cuddled up next to him, took his hand and put it where I needed it, right on my throbbing clit.

As Marc's mouth closed on his cock, Donny rolled over and bit my shoulder. So much for my generosity in letting him see.

'Is it good?' I asked – a silly question under the circumstances, but dirty talk is dirty talk, and Donny liked it. 'Does it feel different, knowing you're being sucked by a man? How do you like Marc's mouth on you?' I wasn't expecting a sensible answer, which was good because I didn't get one.

'Your cock looks so beautiful going in and out of his mouth.' That got him to look again, and to nod tightly in agreement. 'He looks like he's really good at sucking cock. I guess he should be; I know he loves doing it.' I couldn't be sure, but I thought I saw Marc flush.

Marc did look like he was good at it, taking Donny in avidly, with a combination of tenderness and speed that was eliciting some pretty extraordinary noises. Despite the distraction, Donny was doing a fine job on me, his fingers circling my clit for a sweet, slow build that gathered in my pelvis waiting for release. But watching the guys was at least as exciting as those sensations. I could never see Donny's face well when I was blowing him; it was quite a study. Did he make those hot, half-pained faces when I was doing it?

And what exactly *was* Marc doing, anyway? I felt as though I should be taking notes. Surely I could learn something about sucking cock from someone who had a cock of his own.

He interrupted himself, keeping one hand on Donny's cock but reaching around to fumble in the duffel bag.

He came out with lube, poured some of the thick substance on to his hand and stroked it rather showily down his fingers until they glistened.

'Open up for me,' Marc breathed, and moved the lubed hand out of sight. I didn't need X-ray vision to imagine what he was doing, gently but inexorably pushing one finger – maybe the first of several – into my boyfriend's body.

Donny's body tensed.

'Relax,' I whispered. 'You've done this before. More than this.' We'd played with butt plugs sometimes. I hadn't been crazy about the sensation, but Donny had been. 'You'll love it. You know you will.'

I kissed him and could almost feel the tension draining from him. Then Marc must have found the sweet spot.

Donny's face flushed clear down to his nipples. His body strained.

'Oh, no, not yet.' Marc took his mouth away, but left his hands where they were, one working the cock, the other hidden, but obviously playing with Donny's ass. 'One more finger at least. And maybe later my cock, unless you suck me off instead.' His tone was calm, conversational, but his face wasn't. The noises Donny was making were barely human.

And, when Marc took him in his mouth again, they ceased to be human at all.

I thought that, lost in his own pleasure, Donny had forgotten about me. (I didn't blame him. With all that happening to *me*, I know I'd lose co-ordination.) I was just about to take matters into my own hands, relieve the pent-up pressure, when he managed to choke out, 'Let me lick you.' I climbed on to his face in record time.

He was moving under me as well as licking, writhing from Marc's attentions and channelling what might have been screams, otherwise, into me. Already on edge from all the voyeuristic fun, I teetered there for a little while, loving his hot mouth, loving the waves of sensation, loving the glorious sight of a handsome naked man pleasuring the man who was pleasuring me. Donny was shaking. I could see his abs ripple.

And then he bucked his hips. I couldn't see his orgasm, but I could feel it coursing through him, and I could see Marc's eyes light up as Donny's come flooded his mouth.

Those things, more than anything Donny was capable of doing at that moment, pushed me over the edge I'd been teetering on.

It's a good thing Brinks trucks are armoured, or they'd have heard me at the housing development five blocks away.

We collapsed in a spent heap on the mattress. A corner of the duffel dug into my hip, but at first I didn't have the energy to reach down to move it. I rested my head on Donny's chest and felt his heartbeat pound against my cheek and listened to the sound of the three of us panting.

Finally I roused myself, threw on my shirt (just long enough to skim the tops of my thighs), and eased out of the back of the truck to retrieve bottles of water out of the cooler in the front seat.

The night air was soft and refreshing, and a few dim lights glowed at the corners of warehouses, not strong enough to dim the sharp glitter of stars above. I paused just long enough to smile up at them, tossing out a silent thanks to anyone who might be listening for the fact that everything was going so well.

When I returned, the tiny space was filled with the hot heady scent of sex and sweat, so strong it made me flutter, deep inside. Donny lay with his head in Marc's lap, eyes half lidded, stroking Marc's hard cock with languid movements.

Such a sweet picture – except it reminded me that Marc hadn't come yet.

I tossed each of them a water bottle and was rewarded with promises of undying affection. I had to admit it tasted like nectar to me, too. I'd gotten pretty sweaty and dry-mouthed from howling in pleasure.

'What about you, sweetheart?' I asked Marc, joining Donny's hand in its slow caress along the length of Marc's penis. The taut skin was hot, sticky with pre-come. I ran my thumb along the head. Marc's response degenerated into a moan.

Donny took a deep breath. I recognised his expression: he was steeling himself to say something. Was everything OK?

Then he said, 'I want ... Marc ... to fuck me up the ass.'

The last words came out in a rush. Oh, my sweet boy! Marc's cock twitched under our hands.

It took only a moment to change positions on the mattress: Donny on his hands and knees, with Marc crouched behind him. As Marc lubed up his fingers again to prepare Donny's ass for something larger and longer, I scooted beneath Donny and reached for his penis, already half hard again. I could taste Marc on him, and Donny's own come, as he grew in my mouth. It didn't take long for him to get fully erect, what with Marc's ministrations, or for Marc to get Donny opened up and relaxed.

Another shift, and I was kneeling in front of Donny. He slid in, and I groaned at the feel of him filling me. Oral sex is all well and good and fun, but there was something about a steely cock buried in me that made my toes curl.

But I had to wait for the actual fucking part, as Marc slowly pressed himself into Donny's virgin ass. I could feel them gently rocking back and forth as Donny opened up enough to let the tip pop in. They both froze for a moment, revelling in the sensation.

Then Marc slowly, relentlessly, slid full length into

Donny. I know because it made Donny press deeper into me.

It was awkward at first, setting up a rhythm that we all moved to. It wasn't perfect – we had moments of rueful laughter as things went awry at times – but it was *right*. Donny whimpered my name, then Marc's. I could only guess what he was feeling. I just knew it had to be exquisite.

Knowing what they were doing set off a chain of hot images in my head, pushing me on. I imagined I could feel Marc's cock inside Donny's, both of them stretching me, filling me, fucking me.

Donny reached around me, cupping my breast, pinching my nipple. Then I felt another hand rub my ass – the same side – and realised Marc was reaching around to touch me, too. We didn't exactly form a circle, but at the same time it was much more than a simple line. We were all touching each other, all connected by energy and arousal – and love.

That last bit didn't penetrate my lust-fogged brain clearly. It was just part of all of the images and sensations and intensity. I felt it more than I thought it.

It was a combination of everything that sent me over the edge: the emotions, and the feeling of a hard cock in me, and the vision of how Donny and Marc looked together on repeated loop in my mind's eye. I was screaming again, and the boys were joining me. I felt Donny's cock swell inside me just before he shot his load, and his frantic pumping was matched by Marc's. Yes, oh, yes, oh . . .

We collapsed in a heap again, somehow ending up with me in the centre, cuddled close by both boys, who clasped hands together across my stomach.

We couldn't stay this way for long. I had to have the truck back well before dawn, before anyone noticed its absence, and we'd have to clean out the back thoroughly before that. (Marc had used his own car, with the detachable police light on the dash.) But I wasn't ready to move quite yet. I felt safe. Warm. Loved.

I loved Donny, and he loved me. I hadn't been able to commit to Marc as a solo relationship, but now, now I wondered . . . Could the three of us . . .? It was too soon to say. And, if we just all stayed as good friends, that would be fine, too.

Either way, it had been a hell of a ride.

Beauty and the Bull
Heather Towne

The conductor barged through the connecting door to the passenger car, pressed blue suit and walrus-moustached face looking sternly officious. Sylvia slid out of the comfortable seat, walked towards the rear of the car, as the man started demanding and punching tickets. The shuddering train threw her off balance, and her hips brushed the bloated arm of a businessman in a pinstriped suit.

'Sorry, sir,' she whispered.

He angrily shook out his newspaper, growled around a long, green cigar, 'Watch where you're –' He stopped when he glanced up at Sylvia, greasy black eyes sliding all over her. He pulled his stogie out of his mouth and smacked his thick lips in appreciation.

Sylvia had on a simple yellow sundress, the well-washed material stretched tight over her rounded bottom and mounded breasts. Her slender arms and legs gleamed brown from the sun, her sleek, black hair tied back with a yellow ribbon, high cheekbones framing a pretty, hungry face, eyes blue and burning.

The businessman shifted his bulk around in his seat like an excited child, surveying Sylvia's body as if it were a piece of meat on display at the Kansas City stockyards. Meat wasn't cheap in these days of Depression, except for certain kinds of meat from certain kinds of desperate animals.

He stared at the plump hams that were Sylvia's breasts, said, 'No harm done, honey. I should've watched where you were going.' He coughed out a laugh, an oily grin spreading across his face. Then he plugged his cigar back in and climbed to his feet, gestured with a swollen hand for her to take the seat next to him.

She shook her head, swaying with the train. He puffed like a locomotive and blew smoke in her face, his mass blocking her way. The car shook violently and he was thrown off balance, and Sylvia slid past, murmuring, 'Excuse me, sir.'

He grabbed her wrist and twisted her arm, his hand hot and wet on her cool skin. 'What's your rush, honey? The night is young.'

Sylvia looked away from him, at her reflection in the carriage window, the black nothingness of Missouri racing by alongside unseen. 'I have to go to the bathroom.'

He barked like a seal. 'Full of piss, huh? How 'bout vinegar?'

Sylvia's eyes shifted to him, clouded with revulsion. She tore her arm free and hurried to the end of the car. She didn't hesitate, pulling the door open and stepping out on to the platform, pulling the door closed behind her, the businessman and the conductor watching her every step of the way.

The night exploded with noise: the thunder of the train steaming down the track, the howl of the wind whipping around the open platform. Sylvia was almost blown off her feet, but she gripped the iron railing and held on tight. The cool, rushing air blew away the smoky stench of the stuffy passenger car, the smell of fear.

Lights from a distant farmhouse sailed by, but otherwise all was deafening blackness, an inky emptiness that you could step into at forty miles an hour and be swallowed up for ever. Many a hard-done-by man and woman had done just that, solving all their problems.

Sylvia shivered with cold, but her hands were damp on the railing. She clenched her jaw in resolution; desperate times called for desperate measures. She climbed over the railing, out onto the clanking coupling that joined the last passenger car to the first freight car in line. She easily hopped the blind and climbed the iron ladder on the front of the wooden freight car, crawled out on to its roof.

The wind was even stronger up there, the vibration of the train more violent. Her dress blew up over her head and she went flat on the metal catwalk that ran the length of the car, clinging to its edges. The boxcar bumped and humped, as if it were trying to buck her off. The train was making good time for Kansas City at the end of the line, and nothing was going to hold it back.

Sylvia was just as determined, though, and she crept along the catwalk on her hands and knees, clear to the end. Then she groped for the ladder, shifted her body around, and climbed on down. She jumped the next blind, scaled the next car, crawled halfway down its danger-ously shifting rooftop, before going flat on her belly again. She took a deep breath and crab-crawled to the edge of the clattering freight. Then she curved a hand over the side and felt open air. She swung her body out over the edge.

She hung over the racing, hard-packed gravel grading for a second, the wind catching and blowing her side-ways, her damp hands slipping on the dirty wood, the thunder of the steel wheels blasting her ears. Then she was inside the boxcar, landing catlike on the gritty floor.

She sprang to her feet, brushing her hands off and straightening out her dress, anxiously scanning the black interior of the freight for any sign of humanity. A match hissing alight told her she'd found some.

'Well, lookee here,' a male voice crowed, confirming Sylvia's worst fears.

Another match sparked to life, and another, and in their spitting, yellow glow she made out three men, squatted down against the closed door on the opposite side of the jolting car. Hungry men.

'Consider the wondrous works of God,' one of the men whooped, stretching out his arms and giggling insanely.

Someone tossed their match into a coffee can on the floor and a small fire sprang to life, a Hoover hearth. The orange flames gave Sylvia a clearer picture of the danger she was in, gave the three men a clearer picture of the woman who had dropped so unexpectedly into their ragged lives. A lone female rider was a rare and welcome sight indeed, and the men stared at Sylvia.

'H-hello,' she said, eyes searching the interior of the boxcar. It was stacked to the ceiling with bales and bales of paper-wrapped cotton, the only open space the narrow aisle between the two side doors, the three men at one end, certain oblivion at the other.

One of the men suddenly got to his feet and stepped forward. The two others quickly followed, one of them limping badly. Their clothes were tattered and torn, pants and jackets patched and repatched and still gaping holes. Two of the men were bareheaded, while the third, the tallest of the three, the one who had risen first, wore a battered fedora pulled down low on his forehead. He spoke, 'Welcome aboard, little lady. This here's the gravy train, and we're just about to dine.'

The men all laughed, wiping grimy hands on soiled pants and licking cracked lips. The tall man reached out and touched Sylvia's bare arm. She jumped backwards, too far, teetering on the very edge of the flying boxcar.

She pulled herself back in, holding out her hand to hold back the men. She knew what these men would do if they got their hands on her, so she knew she had to stall for time. 'How would you boys like some ... entertainment before you dine?' she said. Her voice broke only a little.

They looked at each other. 'What you got in mind?' the tall one asked.

'Any of you boys ever seen a burlesque show?'

'I seen one once, sure,' the giggler enthused, clapping his hands together and giggling. 'You gonna do one?'

'Soon as you boys sit back down,' Sylvia replied, gaining confidence as she took control of the situation.

The giggler grabbed his companions and pulled them back against the door. They squatted down as they'd been before, the tall man tearing paper off a bale of cotton and feeding the fire.

Sylvia leaned back against the stacked cotton as the train rattled over a rough patch, stalling for time and strength. She closed her eyes, taking comfort in the warmth and softness of the cotton, her body swaying to the rhythm of the train, forcing her mind to a place far beyond the cold misery of the rumbling boxcar. A vivid imagination had sustained her through many a dark day in the past.

Sylvia had actually never seen a burlesque show herself, but she'd heard stories, heard the music through the doors of a theatre once. So, when one of the men whistled, she stepped out into the middle of the rolling stock, threw her arms up over her head and moved her hips in a gyrating motion. She bumped and ground to a rhythm all could hear, imitating the performances she'd put on in front of her bedroom mirror. The men cheered, the tall one pulling off his hat in a gesture of respect.

Sylvia slowly pulled the yellow ribbon out of her hair, her eyes closed and her body undulating, until her black locks fanned out loose on her back. She shook her hair out so that it spilled over her shoulders, half covered her face, and that drew more cheers from her audience. She smiled to herself, moving her hands to the front of her dress and toying with the buttons there.

The men went silent, breathless, eyes shining and mouths hanging open as Sylvia unfastened a pair of buttons at the top of her dress and let the garment hang open. Cool air washed over her partially bared chest, and she shivered with something other than cold. She wasn't sure what a lady of burlesque actually did to herself on stage, how far she went to please her audience, but she knew what pleased her. She slid a hand into her dress, under the silky material of her slip, closed it around her breast.

Sylvia's body was suffused with a heavy, languid heat, and, when she brushed her fingertips across her stiffened nipple, she tingled all over. She pushed her dress and her slip strap off her shoulder and the worn-thin material dropped down to her elbow, fully exposing her glowing breast. She moved her hand back over her breast, cupping and squeezing it, filling herself with a heated sensuality. She took her nipple between her thumb and forefinger and squeezed, and her body arched with delight.

The temperature in the swaying boxcar skyrocketed thirty degrees – at least to those concerned – the three men panting with excitement and anticipation, Sylvia whimpering with uninhibited passion. She pulled on her swollen nipple, sending sexual electricity shooting throughout her, revelling in the heady mixture of danger and desire, the mounting tension.

She could have been anywhere now – inside a boxcar stuffed full of raw cotton, putting on a dirty show for dirty men; or in a silken boudoir stretched out on the fine-woven cotton sheets of a canopy bed, putting on a very private exhibition for only herself – kindling her passion into a raging inferno, only the thin moonlight and flames to illuminate her lust.

The train slowed down as it pulled into and through a town station, allowing a big man in a blue uniform, holding a lantern, to swing aboard the caboose. But no one in Missouri Pacific boxcar 10445 took the least bit of notice of the speed or the man.

Sylvia pushed her dress and slip away from her right shoulder, fully revealing her rising and falling chest. The men groaned their appreciation, marvelling at her hanging breasts and upturned nipples, the way her tits jounced with the motion of the train. She cupped her breasts and worked them with her hands, rolling engorged nipples between trembling fingers, her dizzy head floating off into the clouds, her mind free and easy and open to anything.

Then, keeping one hand locked on one breast, she plunged her other hand into her panties, on to her soaking pussy. 'Yes,' she moaned, jolted by the impact. 'Ye–'

Something thumped on to the roof of the trundling boxcar. The men sprang to their feet, shunting their dreams aside with a ruthlessness borne of brutality. They scrambled to the open door, pushing Sylvia aside, listening grimly as heavy footsteps trod the top of the car. They knew what that sound was, and what it meant, and without a glance backwards they leapt off the moving train.

The men landed hard on the grading, taking the brunt of the fall on their shoulders, rolling into the ditch alongside the tracks and disappearing into the veil of darkness. It was a survival technique they'd perfected over hundreds of trains and thousands of miles of track.

Sylvia watched them go, startled when a pale face suddenly appeared hanging upside down over the door of the boxcar – a man's face, dark eyes gleaming at Sylvia's half-naked form. The face disappeared, and then a big body swung into the car, landing on the floorboards with a thud. The man rose to his full height, reached up and brought down his lantern from the roof of the car. He held it up, putting Sylvia in the spotlight. 'Paying passengers ride up front,' he growled.

He was clad in a blue cap and blue, brass-buttoned uniform, shiny black leather belt and boots. A short, thick club dangled from his belt. Stitched into the breast of his uniform was the name Cole Jansen. The badge on his cap identified him as a railroad cop, a 'bull', a man whose job it was to keep the trains free of hoboes and tramps, the rod and roof and car riders who didn't pay their freight. And he was allowed to perform that job just about any way he saw fit.

Sylvia studied the man's rugged face, the glittering eyes and thick, slightly savage lips, the strong Roman nose. Her gaze wasn't frightened, though: it was bold and direct, a challenge to the bull in the blue serge. Making no attempt to cover up her breasts, she breathed, 'I'm willing to pay for my ride, Officer Jansen.'

The train was picking up speed again, back in the dark country. Sylvia slid her hands up the sides of her body, along her ribs, underneath her breasts. She pushed her breasts higher, then tilted her head down as she tilted her nipples up, licking at the rigid nipple on her left breast.

A hard swallow was Jansen's response, the raised lantern shaking with more than the motion of the train. Sylvia wagged her tongue back and forth across her nipple, then took it between her lips and sucked on it. 'Yes,' Jansen exhaled.

The boxcar rolled along faster and faster, Sylvia nursing on her nipple, slashing her tongue across the glistening, cherry-red bud. A knowing smile lifted the corners of her mouth as she watched Jansen unbuckle his heavy belt, shove his uniform pants and cotton drawers down. His cock rose up, pointing arrow-straight and accusingly at her.

She obeyed the railroad bull's silent command, releasing her breast and sinking to her knees and crawling across the dirty floor to the man and his cock. The boxcar lurched, and she grabbed on to his cock.

'Yes,' he grunted, bracing himself, Sylvia's soft touch rocking him more than any train could.

She gripped his pulsing length, then slowly began moving her hand back and forth, staring up at him and feeling him grow. She swirled her hand up and down his cock with more and more speed, polishing him to rock-hardness. She stroked him to the very edge of ecstasy, pre-come leaking out of his yawning slit. Then she abruptly stopped, leaving him dangling.

Jansen gritted his teeth, his enraged cock twitching in the warm wash of Sylvia's breath. He pushed forward. Sylvia smiled and cupped his furry balls, encircled his swollen hood with her forefinger and thumb and pressed his cock up against his uniform. She examined his veined shaft for a tense, teasing moment, before pushing the damp tip of her tongue against the base of his cock. His body jerked, jerked again as she dragged her tongue up his shaft in one long, wet stroke.

'God have mercy,' he gasped.

She licked his blood-engorged skin over and over, painting his throbbing shaft with her warm saliva, driving the bull wild. While, way off at the head of the train, the engineer blew his whistle in warning as they roared over an unguarded highway crossing.

Jansen dropped his lantern and sifted his fingers through Sylvia's hair, his body vibrating. Then he pulled her head away before his tongue-lashed cock boiled out of control. 'Suck my balls,' he muttered.

She complied, taking his testicles into her mouth and tugging on them. He staggered forward, cock spanking her upturned face. He regained his footing, Sylvia never letting go of his balls, her dancing tongue and sucking mouth fondling him in the most vulnerable of places.

He could take it only so long. He grabbed her arms and yanked her upright, his sodden sac popping out of her mouth. Then he gripped her dress at the waist, was about to rip it apart with bullheaded desire, when she stopped him. Good dresses were hard to come by, and she couldn't afford to lose one.

She pushed her dress and slip down to her feet, shimmied out of her panties, turning so that he could watch the tight-fitting cotton garment slide smoothly over her rounded bum. She gathered up the precious garments and carefully placed them atop a bale of cotton.

Jansen grabbed her and spun her around. He mashed his mouth against her lips, his passion fierce, crushing her against his chest and savaging her mouth. She returned his fire, flinging her arms around his neck, welcoming his tongue into her mouth with her tongue.

Another one-horse town came and went, the heavy rumble of the train going briefly flat as the steel wheels rolled over a street crossing. The lights of the farming community flashed a fast-moving picture of a man and a woman entwined together in a boxcar, the woman brazenly naked, the man with his pants down around his ankles, their mouths locked together in a fiery embrace.

The beauty and the bull didn't see the lights of the town, feel the change in the rhythm of the train, however: they were utterly lost in the wicked intensity of their need. Their tongues entwined again and again, Jansen squeezing Sylvia's bare buttocks, Sylvia squeezing Jansen's neck, their bodies melded together and their ragged breath coming as one.

Many miles on, Jansen finally pulled back his head. He grinned down at Sylvia. Her eyes were closed and her mouth open, her tongue out and seeking his. 'Don't say I never give a freight rider a fair break,' he said. He dropped to his knees and pushed her legs apart and plunged his tongue into her sex.

'Oh ... God,' Sylvia wailed, jolted by the impact of the man's tongue. She knocked his cap off and clawed at his sandy-blond hair, as he sank his hardened tongue deep into her dripping twat.

He hung on to her clenched cheeks and pumped her with his tongue, moving his head back and forth the best he could with her hands riding him. His pink spear pistoned in and out of her pussy, and Sylvia's legs quivered and her head spun. And, when he fingered her lips apart and touched her puffed-up clit with the tip of his tongue, she almost collapsed under the sheer weight of sexual bliss.

He licked and sucked on her clit, until her body trembled so badly and her breathing got so laboured that he feared she was coming. Then he pulled his face away and licked his lips, climbed back to his feet. He tossed some bales aside, forming a ledge on to which he picked up and placed Sylvia.

She leaned back and spread her legs. He grabbed her legs and roughly brought them up against his chest, shouldering her ankles, spilling her on to her back. Then he gripped his cock and punched its bloated head through her pussy lips. He slammed his hips forward, burying himself to the hairline inside her.

Sylvia revelled in the stuffed-full feeling of Jansen's cock in her pussy, his balls pressing into her ass. She pushed her splayed breasts together and pointed their pink tips at him, hissing, 'Fuck me.'

He teased her, instead, holding on to her thighs and easing his hips back and his cock out. Then he slowly pushed forward again, sliding back inside her. She screamed at him to go faster, but he only grinned and continued to plough her, slow and easy, cock all the way out, then all the way back in again. It was more than Sylvia could take. She reached up and pinched his hairy nipples.

He grunted as if he liked it, but began to build up some steam, moving his hips more quickly, no longer pulling out of her. He churned faster and faster, blunt fingers digging into the soft flesh of her thighs, his big body slapping against her rippling ass. He pounded cock into her, driving her harder and harder, sweat rolling off his twisted face and on to her shuddering tits.

'Punching your ticket now, huh, baby?' the bull gritted. Sylvia moaned her appreciation, and they rocketed down the track, the cool, slumbering countryside a stunning contrast to the scorching action taking place in boxcar 10445.

'I'm gonna come, baby,' Jansen hollered, stoking the fire higher, pumping her in a frenzy.

Sylvia glared up at the thundering man, her buffeted body shimmering with electricity, then overloading. Orgasm detonated in her cock-stroked pussy and shock-waved through her body, her mouth breaking open in a silent scream as she was devastated by ecstasy. And even before her first orgasm had fully dissipated, a second one rocked her, and then a third, sending her flying to the very brink of consciousness.

Jansen frantically thrust into her, then roared with his own release, spraying hot semen deep into her being. He sawed wildly back and forth inside her, his body jerking, her gripping pussy milking him of everything he had to offer.

Still tremoring with the aftershocks of multiple orgasm, Sylvia felt Jansen topple over on top of her, his cock still plugged into her and their shared joy. She had strength enough only to cling to his neck and whisper, 'Thanks for the free ride, lover.'

She stood on the platform of the passenger car, struggling to brush off and smooth down her dress in the vicious breeze. Her face and body cooled rapidly in the cold, rushing night air, and she was racked by an involuntary shiver, the harsh, metallic rumble and rattle of the train frightening her now. She took a deep breath, slid the door open, and stepped inside the car.

The businessman in the pinstriped suit folded his finished newspaper and watched her walk stiffly by in a rustle of silk. He unplugged the green stump of his stogie from his mouth and sniffed the air, smelling a strange mixture of perfume and dried sweat and ... cotton.

She halted when she reached the middle of the car,

then folded down into an empty bench seat, slid over to the window. She was just settled in and thawing out when a short, red-faced man wearing wire-rim spectacles shoved his way through the connecting door at the front of the car and dropped down next to her.

'Did you win this time, honey?' Sylvia asked, covering the man's tiny hand with one of her own, just then noticing the dirt under her fingernails.

'Your hand's cold,' the man grimaced. He jerked his hand away, barely glancing at her. 'Naw. The boys took me again. Might as well just add twenty-five bucks to the price of the ticket every time we go to KC. We'll just have to tighten up back home – to make up for it.' He pulled a train-copy newspaper out of his jacket pocket and rattled it open to the financial page. 'Anyway, it passes the time. What've you been up to?'

'Just waiting for you to come back, honey.'

'Like a good wife, huh?' he muttered, eyes never leaving the stock quotes.

Sylvia's eyes were on the window, gazing at the reflection of the pretty young woman with the satisfied smile on her slightly smeared lips. She was thinking about the return journey through the night-shaded Missouri countryside, about another stolen encounter with her long-time railroad lover, the jostling rhythm of the rumbling train reverberating in her loins.

Après-Ski Candy Wong

'Swiss finishing school, my ass!' snorted Sheryl, taking another drag on her untipped Gauloise. 'A backstreet hooker's got more class than *that*.'

She looked up at me and winked, and I watched as she raised her glass to her lips and the tiny blonde hairs on her toned, tanned arm shimmered in the half-light. We were sitting on the floor of one of the bunkrooms, in a rough circle around an ashtray, a bowl of pretzels and a ceramic jug of mulled wine.

We were five that night; often up to ten of us squeezed into one of the cramped rooms, but a few of the other chalet girls had flown to Paris for the weekend, including Rebecca Jane – the one Sheryl had just been so scathing about.

The windows of the room were flung open to the chilly night, and beyond them the sky was a vast indigo canopy flecked with diamonds. We worked hard, God knows, and earned little, but at moments like this, life was good. Better than good.

I'd packed in my job in London on a whim, tired of the long rush-hour trips by Underground, of the lecherous advances of my boss at the lads' mag where I was a picture researcher, of my long-stale relationship with a drippy guy I'd met at my yoga class. Despairing of ever being able to earn enough money to live somewhere half-decent or to have a good time in such an expensive city, I'd bailed out with barely a second thought.

I didn't regret it, especially on evenings like this, when Sheryl was at her most delightful, her most acerbic. It wasn't that she was a bitch indiscriminately. But she didn't withhold her scorn when it came to people who treated others like something they'd stepped in on the sidewalk, and that was precisely her problem with Rebecca Jane.

Sheryl was the kind of girl I'd have loved as a best friend at school, or back in London. The kind who can lift your spirits in just about any situation. Since I'd been here, I'd seen her buy one of the other girls a drink when her boyfriend back in Manchester dumped her by text message, even though Sheryl was down to her last ten euros. And when I'd thrown up for an entire morning after one of our sessions, it had been Sheryl who'd cleaned up after me and made sure I drank plenty of fluids, despite having had plans that day.

I liked most of the other girls, but Sheryl was by far my favourite, and I sensed that she was especially fond of me too. The only thing that got my goat, in fact, was the attention she received from Serge, one of the ski instructors at our resort. Most girls would have killed to have a guy like Serge so much as cast a glance in their direction. Those sea-green eyes of his, part concealed by a floppy chestnut fringe, had the power to stop people in their tracks. But his avid glances always bounced off Sheryl: she just refused to acknowledge his amorous intentions. And that really riled me.

OK, I was jealous, I admit it. Serge was *gorgeous*. Sheryl was gorgeous, too, but not so much that she had the right to blank him completely. That seemed to point to an arrogance in her that I was loath to acknowledge, to some secret store of snootiness that made her little better than someone like Rebecca Jane.

I often thought to challenge her about it, about how she could remain indifferent in the face of such beauty and ardour, but I always wimped out at the last minute. One look at those ironic pale-blue eyes set in a heart-shaped face both awed and scared me. Despite her readiness to help people out, she had something of the ice maiden about her, and I feared being frozen out.

That night, though, with the *glühwein* firing her, and the candlelight dancing in those eyes, she was the flame to which we were all drawn. Leaning forward, arms folded and balanced on her raised knees, she talked vivaciously about her cheerleader days back in Pennsylvania, her short-lived career as a trolley dolley, and her equally brief affair with a well-known French rock star.

As she talked, her little flared denim skirt had slowly crept up her thighs, granting the barest glimpse of a pair of lacy pink knickers. They looked expensive – Aubade or Lejaby, or somesuch brand. Pulling on my cigarette, I closed my eyes for a moment and imagined the matching bra cupping her perky golden breasts, the flimsy fabric stretching to allow her nipples to show through in places.

I went to bed, as I often did, with my head spinning from the effects of the red wine and the cigarettes, and perhaps more than a little from Sheryl's talk. My roommate, Jenny, climbed into her bunk above me, and for a while her grunts and snuffles as she settled into sleep kept me awake. I thought of Sheryl, and then I thought of Serge, of how he must have women throwing themselves at him all the time. To have someone ignoring him as Sheryl did must come as a bit of a shock. But perhaps I was wrong to feel sorry for him – in all likelihood he was seeking solace at that very moment in the arms of a pretty bargirl or holidaymaker.

Sleep, and alcohol, began to overwhelm me. Sheryl's seashell-pink knickers swam into my consciousness again. She lay on the ground, ash-blonde hair fanned out on the snow glinting silvery around her, swooning as hands tugged at those pants, drawing them down over her hips. And there she was, naked on the slopes, her body lit by a fat metallic moon, pulling Serge down towards her. As she moved inexorably towards her climax, her long manicured fingers pressed into the flesh of his smooth brown shoulders.

Beneath the sheets, I slipped one hand between my legs and masturbated almost convulsively. I came, violently, biting on my other fist to stifle my cries.

It seems a waste now, that I waited so long to take advantage of the free ski lessons that came as part of my contract, but in truth I'd allowed myself to get swept up into the frenetic social life of the resort. When I should have been up at six every day, perfecting my moves on the deserted pistes before starting my duties, I was invariably nursing a hangover of epic proportions.

I came to my senses when I heard that Serge would be leading the lessons for a week. The instructors took it in turns to do this early shift, which wasn't just for the benefit of the chalet girls but for all the resort employees, from management to sous-chefs. Few people seemed to take them up; they probably started out with the best intentions but, like me, found it just too damn warm and toasty under their duvets.

I went to sign up for the classes the following week, feeling a little guilty that I hadn't mentioned it to my fellow chalet girls, especially Sheryl. Not that they'd necessarily be able to summon up the motivation to join in, even when Serge was involved. Still, I didn't want to blow my chances. The only person I did tell was Jenny, since I knew that she'd be suspicious of my leaving the room early in the morning. I even persuaded her to sign up with me, as moral support. It helped, I confess, that she was the dumpiest and plainest of my colleagues.

I was being overly cautious when it came to Sheryl, who almost certainly wouldn't have come. More than any of us, Sheryl lived for the convivial nights in the bars, or, if it was the end of the month and we were waiting for our pay cheques, in our rooms. She was regularly being cautioned for not starting work on time, to no avail.

I'm not even sure that I believed that anything could happen between Serge and me – he seemed way out of my league. But just the thought of being up close to him, of being the focus of those electric-green eyes, of hearing my name uttered by that sexy French drawl, had me growing moist. And, God, but those hands would have to touch me.

It was just my luck that, the Sunday preceding my first class, we'd just been paid and Sheryl was in the mood for a big night out in Joe's Bar. I tried to resist, protesting that I had PMT and fancied an evening in bed with a hot-water bottle and a gossip mag, but she wouldn't hear of it. She came bustling into my room in her low-cut mohair top, clouds of Chanel Cristalle billowing around her, and virtually commanded me to get my party dress on. I looked at her taut, pink, rosebud mouth, her smiling eyes, her cleavage the colour of demerera sugar, shining with body oil, and I opened my wardrobe door. You couldn't say no to Sheryl.

'See you in my room in five minutes,' she said over her shoulder as she walked out. 'I'll mix you a sneaky cocktail before we go out if you're lucky.'

I followed her to the door and watched her retreat down the corridor. Her hips swung softly, nonchalantly, from side to side; her buttocks were sublimely sculpted by her tight black trousers. There was no VPL, so I knew she must either be wearing a thong or going commando-style. No wonder Serge virtually foamed at the mouth every time she walked by – I was a fool to think I had the ghost of a chance with him as long as there was someone like Sheryl around.

I slipped on the floaty mauve dress I saved for special occasions and hurried to her room. After tapping at the door, which she had left ajar, I walked right in without

waiting for a reply. Sheryl was standing in front of the
full-length mirror on the back of her wardrobe door,
stripped down to her underwear. I'd been right – she was
wearing a satin thong with a heart-shaped cut-out just
above the line of her pubic hair. On top she sported a
balcony bra in similar fabric, which pushed her breasts
forward and upward at the same time, like some kind of
offering.

I stood behind her, eyes flickering from her magnificent rear to those dusky globes, the skin of which looked
almost as silken as the material in which they were
encased, and from which they threatened to spill like
apples from an overloaded fruit bowl. I didn't have a bad
figure – it went in and out in all the right places – but I
couldn't hold a candle to this stunner.

'You OK, Sonia?' she said, turning round and flashing
me a big smile. 'You're very quiet. Still feeling a bit
ropey?'

'I was just admiring your underwear,' I laughed
nervously.

'Yeah, pretty swanky, isn't it? That asshole rock star
bought it me in the South of France, just before I found
out he was fucking one of his groupies.' She smirked, and
a dimple punctuated her right cheek. 'I got heaps of great
lingerie out of him, so it wasn't a total waste of time.'
She reached behind her.

'Changed my mind about that outfit,' she continued.

She slithered into a black dress that clung to her like
the skin of a snake. Leaning sideways to take her cigarettes and lighter from the desk, she looked over at me.
'Do me up, honey, will you?'

She turned away from me again and I wound my
fingers between the luxuriant fronds of hair that trailed
down her to find the zip fastener nestled in the small of
her back. Yanking it up towards the nape of her neck, I
felt my knuckles trace the supple line of her spine. I
closed my eyes and inhaled her scent again – her perfume

mingled with some kind of coconut shampoo, and underlying it all something indefinable, indescribable, something sweet and musky and compelling.

'Thanks, sweetie.' From the desktop she handed me a tall glass filled with a pink liquid. 'Don't ask,' she said at my raised eyebrows. 'My own concoction. Cheers.'

We clinked glasses and emptied them, feeling the night reach out its tendrils, pulling us into it, as the alcohol flooded our bloodstreams. Exhaling a plume of smoke, Sheryl slipped on a pair of high-heeled black shoes. They could have been tarty on the wrong person, or combined with the wrong outfit. On Sheryl, with that simple, understated dress, they were chic.

As if echoing my thoughts, she looked me up and down and let out a soft whistle. 'Hey, now,' she said. 'Don't you look just great? That dress really suits you. The colour sets off those beautiful eyes of yours. Don't take this the wrong way, but you should think about investing in some really good lingerie. You'd be amazed how much difference it makes to the hang of a dress, to the look of an outfit. How say next time you have a little spare cash we pop into Geneva and try a few things on?'

I giggled shyly. The thought of huddling into a changing room with Sheryl and trying on expensive underwear was both absurd and irresistible.

'In fact, here, try these,' she said, turning away to forage in a drawer. 'They won't be quite right, but we're more or less the same size.' She held up a pair of spanking white pants and a bra with a subtle foliage motif.

'I kept these from a shoot,' she explained. 'Did I ever tell you I did a bit of modelling, mainly swimwear but a bit of lingerie too? I got bored of it quite quickly, but I did get to keep a lot of the gear. In fact, if it fits, keep it. I've got more than I know what to do with.'

I took the garments from her and rubbed the soft fabric between my fingertips. 'Thanks so much,' I said, a little embarrassed. 'I'll just put them in my room.'

'OK, honey. See you downstairs in a couple of minutes.'

My alarm went off at 5.45, and to my alcohol-pickled brain cells sounded like the splintering of metal beneath some kind of terrifying machine. Moaning, swearing, I hauled myself up in bed in time to see Jenny's hairy calves swing down from the bunk above me.

'Holy shit!' I heard her mutter. 'My head's killing me. I can't believe you're dragging me into this. You really owe me one.'

Jenny shared my aesthetic appreciation of Serge, but I suppose she reasoned that, if I was out of his league, she was off the radar. In any case, she had already found her beau in the form of Raphael, a mustachioed little waiter at one of the resort restaurants.

I massaged my aching temples. 'Why do we always overdo it?' I said, as much to myself as to her. 'Why can't we just go out for a sociable drink or two?'

'It's that Sheryl,' said Jenny. 'She's an evil temptress.'

'You're telling me,' I replied.

'She's cast a spell on us all,' she continued. 'It's like we all lose our marbles when she's around. It's weird.'

We dressed in the dawn light that filtered through the half-open curtains. Jenny had a point, I thought blearily – until now, I'd loved how Sheryl had taken charge and organised us into a partygoing little gang, but now I wondered if it was a little unhealthy, the way she encouraged us to spend all our money on drink, to spend all our evenings together.

'I'm ready,' said Jenny, interrupting my train of thought, and together we headed downstairs and out of our accommodation block towards the resort hotel, in the lobby of which Serge – my heart began to flutter a little at the prospect – would be waiting for us.

I was wearing a powder-blue ski suit hired at a discount from the resort outfitter; it fitted me so snugly it was as if it were made to measure. In the morning light, it had an attractive platinum sheen to it; I hoped that would detract Serge's attention from my washed-out complexion and bloodshot eyes. I hadn't even had time to remedy matters with a touch of foundation and mascara. The suit made me feel slinky, though, and I remembered with pleasure Sheryl's compliments about my figure the previous evening.

Serge was standing by the reception desk, as heartstoppingly handsome as ever in his navy ski suit. Beside him was another man I recognised as the hotel's restaurant manager, and I felt a little relieved that it wouldn't be just Jenny and me taking the lesson, given our current state. Seeing us enter by the revolving door, Serge nodded curtly, ground out his cigarette in a nearby ashtray, and took hold of two pairs of skis propped beside him.

'*On y va,*' he said, striding towards us. I swallowed painfully, choking back my disappointment. He was so uninterested in us, he hadn't even greeted us by our names. I might as well be back in bed, sleeping off my hangover. Having handed us our skis, he ushered us back out and into the harsh light.

As we walked towards the chairlift, I sensed Jenny's eyes on me, and I turned to meet her glare.

'Tomorrow you're on your own,' she hissed before I had a chance to speak.

I would have been in half a mind to drop out myself, only I'd just caught sight of Serge's arse all trussed up in his ski suit, and my pulse had quickened. Nothing was to come of it, clearly, but to be able to admire such a splendid physique from close quarters for a few days – for that I would put up with every kind of offhand treatment.

Once he'd questioned us and established that we all had a reasonable level of competence, Serge was happy to take us up to some of the higher pistes without preamble, and we ascended by chairlift, two by two. From

behind, I watched Serge's shiny chestnut locks shake as
he turned to talk to the other man, then looked back at
the scenery around us, and I told myself that someone so
arrogant deserved no sympathy for being snubbed by
Sheryl.

But, Jeez, I still fancied him. Up on the slopes, with
the snow glittering in the sunlight and the valley spread
out below us like a fairytale landscape, I gave myself
over to his able tuition. I admit I probably played up the
gaps in my knowledge and technique, exaggerated my
shortcomings, just to feel his large, strong hands on my
shoulders, at my elbow, on – oh, God – my haunches,
guiding me, steering me, supporting me. But who hasn't
cooked up little ruses to get closer to the object of their
desire?

The hour's tuition was over all too soon, and Jenny
and I returned to our block before starting work. For me,
at least, the rest of the day passed in a bit of a haze – the
sleep deprivation, and the lingering hangover, put me in
a spaced-out frame of mind in which all I could think
about was Serge's arse as he bent over to adjust his skis.
From there it was no great leap to my undressing him in
my mind's eye and, stepping up behind him and running
my hands over those honed buttocks before slipping one
between his legs and enfolding his silken scrotum in the
palm of my hand.

The encounter gave me an added impetus to get an
early night, whatever Sheryl might have planned for us
all. I passed her in the hallway before dinner, and she
told me that they were all taking taxis over to a club in a
neighbouring resort.

'I can't make it tonight,' I said, avoiding those intense
blue eyes.

'Why not?' she almost squawked. 'What are you doing
instead?'

'Nothing,' I replied defensively. 'I've just – well, I've
just been overdoing it a bit and I need an early night.'

'Aw, c'mon, Sonia, that's pretty lame. You only live once, after –'

'And other clichés,' I interrupted. For the first time, probably because of what Jenny had said, I felt a little tetchy towards Sheryl. Why couldn't she stand it when I didn't want to go her way? Was she some kind of control freak?

Sheryl was staring at me, evidently stunned by my reaction.

'I'm sorry,' I sighed. 'But I won't be alive at all for much longer unless I slow down a bit.'

'Fine,' she snapped. 'Be a boring old cow, then. We won't miss you. Sleep tight now.'

I watched her disappear into the lift, a frown blighting those lovely features, and felt unendingly sad. Was I really jeopardising this new and exciting friendship for the chance to try to engineer a spot of frottage with a guy whose interest in me was zero? And yet, in the back of my brain, a little voice kept telling me that Sheryl's annoyance was unfounded, out of all proportion to the supposed slight.

Obsessively replaying the conversation in my mind, I slept badly, and it was difficult to get up again the next day. 'I might as well have gone out,' I complained to Jenny as we walked over to the chairlift, after persuading her to give it just one more day. 'Did you have a good night?'

'It was OK,' said Jenny. 'But Sheryl was in an odd mood.'

'What do you mean?'

'Well, she was really quiet to start with, subdued, and she kept looking at the door all the time as if she was expecting someone to come in. It's not like her to be distracted. And then she spent the rest of the night smooching on the dancefloor with one of the ski instructors.'

'Not –'

'Don't panic, it wasn't Serge. In fact that's the strangest thing of all. It was Woody, the ugliest one of all. She can do much better than that. What was she thinking of? I guess she must have been drunker than she seemed.'

We'd reached the chairlift, where Serge was waiting for us with the other man. We followed them up as before and spent an hour practising our techniques with Serge looking on from one side, occasionally turning away to light another cigarette. It must have been this coolness, humiliating and tantalising at the same time, that got me in such a froth, as the tuition had been disappointingly hands-off. All I know is that, by the time we were descending the mountain again, I would have given almost anything in the world to straddle that divine face of his, to smear those perfect features with the juices he was calling forth in me.

'Sonia?'

'Mm?'

'You didn't answer my question.'

'Sorry, Jenny, I was miles away.'

'No shit. I *said*, did you remember it's the launch party tonight?'

'What launch?'

'The Nid d'Aigle.'

'Shit, yeah, I *had* forgotten.' The previous month, it had been announced that a local millionaire was setting up a new restaurant in a former monastery further up the mountain. To our surprise, we'd all been invited along to the opening party. Perhaps, we'd decided, they'd been short of eligible females.

I was through with Serge, I decided. Not, as I've said, that I was ever really deluded enough to think I stood a chance. But suddenly, the knowledge that I was getting all of a lather about some conceited prick who couldn't even bring himself to remember our names made me feel cheap and nasty. And, more to the point, I had fallen out with Sheryl because of this guy. I resolved to set things right with her as soon as I got back to the block.

She was on her bed, wearing the little teddy in which she must have slept, in eggshell-blue jersey. With one hand she was painting her toenails a subtle 'nearly nude' shade; with the other she was holding a cigarette.

'Hi,' I said, after drinking in the sight for a moment in the open doorway.

She looked up, and I saw a smile play around her features for the briefest of instants before her brow creased.

'Where have you been?' she said, gesturing at my ski suit.

I blanched. I'd been in such a hurry to make amends, I'd forgotten what I'd been doing.

'I've been out for a lesson,' I admitted.

She gazed at me through narrowed eyes. 'Why so keen all of a sudden?' she asked, and I heard that brittle edge to her voice I so feared.

'Just – you know – I felt stupid not taking advantage –'

'Taking advantage, my ass!' she spluttered, her laughter a glacier-bright peal. 'It's that dick Serge, right? Woody told me it was him taking the lessons this week. Oh, God, Sonia, you've not fallen for that jerk?'

I looked away from her. 'I know, I know,' I said finally. 'I've got no chance –'.

'I wouldn't be so sure.'

'Oh, come on, Shez, he's only got eyes for you. What have you got against him, anyway?'

She harrumphed, fed the little lacquer brush back into the narrow neck of the bottle and twisted it. 'Nothing,' she said at last. 'He's not worth wasting our breath on. I'm just upset you stood us up in favour of him.'

'So am I,' I said. 'And I'm sorry I bit your head off last night. I'm finished with those lessons.'

She smiled. 'Then you're coming to the party tonight?'

'Wild horses wouldn't keep me away.'

Dressing in front of the mirror that night, holding my outfits up in front of me in turn, I wondered if I dared ask Sheryl whether I might borrow something of hers: as she'd pointed out, we were similar in build. I'd already used up my favourite dress the last time we went out, and the rest all seemed lacklustre given the glamour of the event.

After throwing my second-best option, a cerise wraparound, on to the bed in disgust, I put my hands on my hips and tried to imagine how I would look in those clingy black trousers and that scooped-neck angora top of hers. Pushing my breasts up, I drew the pads of my thumbs lightly over the creamy beige flesh of my nipples and watched as they sprang into life beneath my touch. It was then that I remembered that I did have some clothes of Sheryl's. How could I have forgotten?

I pulled open my underwear drawer and fumbled about for the lacy, virgin-white confection that she'd lent me, excitement fizzing in my groin. Looping the bra straps over my shoulders, I leaned forwards slightly and lowered myself into the cups. A frisson ran up through me as my areolae grazed the delicate fabric. Having adjusted my breasts a little, I fastened the clasps at the back and lay down on the bed to put the knickers on.

It was too much I hadn't even got them over my ankles when a thrill rippled through me like an electric current. My cunt was on fire, almost throbbing with the need to be touched. I brought my hand to it and marvelled at the sheer wetness of it, at how, almost independently of me, it was making its demands known. My fingers slid in all too easily, four of them, as if drawn in by some incontrovertible force. With my thumb, I massaged the hard little bead of my clitoris, applying a little pressure now and then but releasing when the pleasure became almost too intense and I feared losing control.

I glanced down at my breasts and saw how they jiggled like jellies as my hand worked its magic. I wondered if Sheryl had ever worn the bra and supposed she must have, if only once or twice. Slipping my free hand inside one of the cups, I tweaked at the erect nub of nipple. I felt wide open now, my cunt deliquescent, gaping, on the cusp of the contractions that would bear down on me like waves.

I couldn't help myself – I wrenched the knickers off my ankles with a cry, brought them up towards me and buried my face in them, inhaling their sweet aroma – was it lavender water or Sheryl's pussy juices? – as my climax ripped through me, leaving me limp as a ragdoll.

I was late down to the reception, and the other girls had all set off without me. All except Sheryl, who – bless her – had been worried when I hadn't shown up and had been just about to come and check my room.

'Jenny said you were showering when she left,' she said. 'I thought maybe you'd fallen asleep or something.'

I smiled uneasily. I was flattered she'd thought about me, and cared enough to hang back, but what would she think of me if she knew I'd been masturbating myself to a frenzy in her underwear? A few minutes more and she might even have walked in on me. Even now, ten minutes later, my muff felt engorged, still damp, against the gusset of her knickers.

We walked away from the hotel, snow crunching under our feet. Sheryl had forgotten her gloves and was blowing into her hands. In the moonlight her eyes glinted mischievously. She was in her element, on the way to a big night out.

''Who knows?' she mused. 'Maybe we'll meet the millionaire of our dreams tonight. Someone who can take us away from all this.'

My belly flipped.

'I know,' she whispered, seeing my look of anguish. 'It's hard to think it could ever end, this life. But it will – you know it has to.'

She glanced down, rifled through her clutch bag for her party invitation, then looked back up at me. Her amethyst eyes were wide, childlike.

'We'll stay in touch,' she said, smiling. 'You and me.'

Inside me, something unlocked. I stepped forward, tended my palm towards her cheek.

'*Salut!*' came a voice behind us, and we both started. Serge emerged out of the darkness, looking for all the world like George Lazenby in an immaculate smoking jacket, a cigarette burning away in the corner of his mouth. He was staring at Sheryl, an oddly amused expression on his face. *Aha, I got you now*, it seemed to say.

Sheryl, for her part, was making a show of looking away from him, but I could tell from the tense way she held her neck and shoulders that she was fighting the urge to say something to him.

The doorman who had been posted at the bottom of the new cablecar built to ferry guests up to the Nid d'Aigle stepped up to us. 'You must be the last three,' he said, running his finger down a list of names on his clipboard. 'May I see your invitations?'

We each handed one over and he inspected them briefly before opening the door to one of the cars and gesturing us to board. As we climbed in, he handed us three flutes of champagne. '*Bon voyage*,' he shouted, as he slammed the door.

Once inside, we sat on the cream leather banquettes and looked up expectantly. In the distance, a faint rash of lights gave us an idea of where we were headed.

'This is going to be some party,' said Serge.

Part of me was loath to reply, given his indifference to me during the ski lessons, but Sheryl clearly wasn't going to acknowledge him, and I didn't think I could bear the frosty atmosphere all the way up the mountain.

'Apparently he's a Swiss newspaper tycoon,' I said. 'The owner.'

Serge nodded, still gazing out of the window. 'A multimillionaire, I heard. He's brought over chefs from New York.'

The car had begun to mount now, slowly, smoothly, revealing the valley twinkling below us like a basket of jewels. Serge and I both stood up to gain a better view, pointing out landmarks as we identified them. Then Serge sat down and began patting at his pockets for his cigarettes and lighter.

I glanced at Sheryl, discomfited by her silence. She was gazing at Serge, one hand running – unconsciously, I guessed – up and down her thigh.

I smiled bitterly. So she *did* like him. It had all been a sham, probably to get him even more interested. And now she had decided to make her move. I only hoped she could wait until we got to the party. I didn't have the stomach to play gooseberry if they actually did get it together.

Sheryl looked at me now, forehead lightly filmed with sweat, and her face dissolved into a curious, indecipherable smile. Her hand slipped between her legs. I shot a glance at Serge. The phrase 'rabbit caught in headlights' could have been invented for him at that moment. His eyes were disbelieving, his mouth open like a fish's. He looked – well, he looked ridiculous.

Sheryl was staring back at him, another strange smile flitting around her lips. She took hold of the bottom of her dress and pulled it up and over her head in one deft movement, flinging it to the ground in front of her like a matador swirling his cloak in front of a bull. My breath caught in my throat, both at the sight of Sheryl's body and at the anticipation of what it would unleash in Serge.

There was a long moment of silence, and then she held her hand out. Serge stepped towards her. In the silence of the mountains, he sounded as if he was panting, his breath was so laboured.

'No,' said Sheryl. 'Not you. *Her*.'

Serge jolted backward, as if electrocuted.

'But –'

'But nothing,' said Sheryl, standing up and taking my hands in hers. Her nipples, high and proud on those firm breasts, swung alluringly in front of me.

'C'mon, Sonia,' she said, teasing at the lace-up detail on my shirt. 'God knows, this loser doesn't deserve it, but he's gonna get the floorshow of his life.'

The passion between us, pent up all this time, released itself in a kind of fury. After undressing me rapidly, Sheryl pushed me on to one of the leather banquettes, tore her white knickers off me and began lapping at my pussy with her mouth and tongue. Every few minutes, she would let out a long, low moan and, as if urged by some inner compulsion, move her hand down between her legs and rub madly at herself. Then she would focus on me again for a while, tonguing my lips and clitoris and sphincter in turn, exploring them with her hands before moving them up to my breasts, where her digits flitted like butterflies.

Then, sated of me for a moment, she sat up, legs spread, knees bent, one foot on the bench on each side of her, and offered me her own cunt, waxed Brazilian-style, glistening in the light from a moon that hung heavy and full beyond the cablecar window.

I was too much in the moment to even look at Serge, although now, thinking back to the incident, I would give anything to know what he was doing all that time we were screwing each other's brains out. Maybe he was wanking himself senseless, inflamed by the sight of two bodies in such perfect synch, able to elicit such pleasure in each other. More likely, knowing Serge, he was just sitting smoking a cigarette, an incredulous look on his face.

But right there, right then, in that cablecar on the way up to the stars, Sheryl and I were lost to everyone but ourselves.

The Wildest Thing
Teresa Noelle Roberts

The wildest thing I ever did? That would have to be the night ferry from Nice to Corsica, back in college.

I know, that was closer to twenty years ago than I like to admit. Without hearing the story, I must sound like one of those pathetic losers who settle down after graduation as muck settles to the bottom of a pond and have had no fun since. But you both know that's not true. Joan in particular, even if it was just that once when we were both between lovers. Oh, Joan's blushing – how cute!

It's just that in terms of sheer 'I can't believe I did that but I have no regrets', nothing beats the ferry. Refill your drinks and sit back, girls – it's story time!

I was nineteen and studying in Paris for a year. Well, studying is what I called it to placate my parents, but school had very little to do with what I was learning. It was all about experiencing as much as I could, seeing anything I could, travelling wherever I could. But not sleeping with whomever I could, at least not as much as you might think. The French guys I met were determined to believe that American girls were easy and I didn't want to give them the satisfaction of knowing that, in my case at least, they were right. So you have to understand I was a little jumpy by the time that Nancy and I decided we needed to blow off classes for a few days and go to Corsica.

Nancy was a friend I'd made through the exchange programme, a long, tall drink of blonde Texan who liked to play with her stereotype and tromped around Paris in a Stetson and scuffed cowboy boots, talking with an exaggerated drawl. She was the daughter of a small-town librarian and a pharmacist, but that was back when *Dallas* was popular – Fiona, don't try to pretend you're too young to remember it! – and our French friends just assumed she was either from some wealthy, dysfunctional family or lived on a vast ranch. But that's neither here nor there.

Nancy and I looked good together. I was also heavily invested in playing with my stereotype: art student with wild vintage clothes and hair a different colour every week. We made a nice contrast. I looked curvier and funkier next to her; she looked leggier and racier next to me.

I can't remember now what prompted Corsica: something we'd read, something we'd dreamed, someone we'd met. Maybe it was just that none of the other Americans we knew had gone there. We got up one morning at the crack of dawn and hopped a train to Nice, where we wandered around lugging our big backpacks, staring at the well-dressed, fabulous people, splurging on dinner in a waterfront café. Then, in the evening, we got our third-class tickets and boarded a night ferry to Ajaccio, Corsica.

These days, I understand that the ferries are pretty nice, and much faster than they were back in the 80s. Even then there were cabins on the night ferries, and a little restaurant, and all the other creature comforts a traveller might wish.

Not for people travelling in third class, though. We got bright orange airport-lounge chairs in a big, bare cabin, not hideously uncomfortable but not the best for spending the night. We got diesel fumes and a stuffy below-decks ride that was guaranteed to bring on seasickness if you were prone to it; fortunately I'm not. We got all the food you could carry on board, which in our case was bread, cheese, some peaches and a jug of the cheap red wine we called 'Château Clochard' (*clochard* means bum),

which cost about as much for a two-litre bottle as a loaf
of bread did at home. We thought, for a few minutes,
that we'd get a crying baby and a whining toddler, along
with Mother, Father and Granny, but Granny took a look
around at the other people in the third-class cabin and
marched everyone out, presumably to get a ticket
upgrade.

At first, I figured I was the cause of her disgust. I can't
remember what I was actually wearing that night, but
my fashion statement at that age was designed to make
old ladies twitch. Probably purple hair and black lipstick,
or maybe the other way around, and definitely ripped
fishnets. But then I realised it wasn't me.

It was the ten young French soldiers who made Grand-
mère nervous. The cabin was a sea of olive drab, punctuated by fresh, grinning male faces and smelling of harsh
French cigarettes, garlicky food and brandy just as cheap
as our wine. Every single one was staring at Nancy and
me like a dog staring at a steak.

'Maybe Granny had the right idea,' Nancy whispered.
'What do you think?'

I thought two things. One was that, if I upgraded to a
second-class ticket, I'd have damn little money for Corsica. Dinner in Nice had set me back more than I'd
planned for.

The other was the one I actually voiced. 'I think some
of those guys are cute. That's what I think. And, if we
pool our food and booze with theirs, we'll have a good
party.'

Nancy looked the group over and drawled, 'I do believe
you're right, Allison.'

And then we all froze. Two American girls stared at
ten French soldiers and the soldiers stared back. If it had
been a porn movie, someone would have done something
raunchy immediately to get the ball rolling, but, since it
was real life, it took a while for anyone to even speak.
'Hello, I'm Allison and my friend's Nancy,' I finally said

(in French, of course. Don't ask me to repeat the whole conversation in French now. It's been a million years). 'Do any of you boys have a cigarette?'

I did smoke back then, mostly cloves, but I said it because it was the first thing that came to mind. You have not seen funny until you've seen ten French boys fighting to be the first one to whip out the ciggies when a semi-pretty girl asks for one.

The first one to get to me with a cigarette was a dark, trim kid with brown eyes that seemed to see through me and see I didn't really want a cigarette at all. He was short, but nicely built, not gorgeous, but full of this great energy and intelligence that was very sexy.

Once the ice was broken, Gérard introduced us to his friends. Soon we were all passing bottles of cheap booze and a couple of joints that one of the guys had, sharing our bread and cheese and the garlic-laced roast chicken the boys had picked up, and talking like mad. (Even if we did have to get them to slow down and repeat themselves sometimes, what with regional accents and unfamiliar slang that you'd never hear in a classroom at the Sorbonne.) It turned out that short, clever Gérard, like Napoleon, was from Corsica, as were a couple of the other boys. The rest were coming to visit during a short leave, planning to do some hiking and hunting. They weren't career military, just doing their compulsory service, and to a man they hated it.

Jean-Paul was sandy-haired and pretty, with the slight build of a younger boy. For all of that, he drank more than the rest without showing any ill effects. Claudel was a *mec*, a tough guy, scrappy and scarred, with a Provençal accent so strong I could barely understand him. I assumed he was from some slum in Marseilles, but it turned out he was a doctor's kid who'd spent his life getting into trouble and finally flunked out of university. Probably the name. If I were a boy named Claudel, I'd turn into a troublemaker, too. Paul looked almost Germanic, tall and fair. He was from Alsace and when his military service was over he was going back to work in his family's vineyard. He was the only one who turned up his nose at the cheap wine, drinking something out of his own hip flask that I discovered later was an eau-de-vie his grandpa made. The others have kind of blurred together into an amorphous mass of attractive young guys wrapped in olive drab and wearing big trench coats.

Nancy was flirting heavily with Paul. Don't know to this day whether it was his height or the contents of his hip flask that intrigued her, but she was the only one who got to taste the eau-de-vie. Gérard, though, was the first to make an actual move. He'd seemed equally attracted to both of us at first, but, like Napoleon, Gérard employed strategy and pressed his advantage where defences were weaker, i.e. me. After some wine, some brandy and a few months of celibacy, I wasn't bothering with defences at all.

Was he a good kisser? Hell, I don't know. Probably wouldn't impress me that much now, but I was nineteen, tipsy and very, very horny. I tried to maintain a little decorum at first, at least as much decorum as you can get when a cute boy is leaning over you and sticking his tongue into your mouth and you're enjoying it a lot. Then the ferry lurched, pitching him forward into my lap so I could feel his erection pressing against my mound. I went almost instantly from having a nice enough time to being a cat in heat. I needed some of that, and I needed it five minutes ago.

The next thing I knew we'd sprawled on the floor, he'd spread his trench coat over the two of us, we were fumbling with buttons and zippers, his hands were working my skirt up and I was rubbing against his crotch, liking the nice, thick bulge I was feeling. Have you ever noticed that short guys sometimes have surprisingly big ones?

Well, I didn't expect *you* would have, Joan. We all

know cocks aren't exactly your thing unless they come in a little box from Toys in Babeland. Let me get on with the story.

Anyway, just about when I got Gérard's pants unfastened and a fat, uncircumcised cock in my hand, someone tapped him on the shoulder and interrupted us. It was Claudel, who was very drunk, even by comparison with the rest of us. 'Hey, buddy,' he slurred. 'Are you gonna share that?'

I had about two seconds to decide whether to slug him (or encourage Gérard to do it for me) or say 'What the hell!' and go for it. In those two seconds, I glanced towards Nancy.

Nancy had a sweet set-up. Paul was on one side of her and some other guy – I'm not sure I ever did hear his name – on the other, trading kisses back and forth with both of them. She was resting one hand on each boy's thigh, and, if the hands hadn't worked their way into their laps yet, it was clearly just a matter of time. The guys had gotten her shirt partly open, enough that I could see her bra was hot pink and pretty much sheer.

With a view like that to encourage me, 'What the hell!' was the way to go. I asked Gérard if he minded.

He shrugged in a stereotypical Gallic way. 'You know if you start that, our other friends will want to play too,' was basically what he said.

'Is that a problem?'

I'd been having a long dry spell. It had always been a fantasy, being at the centre of a gangbang, men everywhere, one after another using me – or me using them, or us using each other, however you want to look at it – until I was aching all over from orgasms, my jaws hurt from sucking so many cocks, and I was limp as a come-slick ragdoll. But it wasn't like I was about to suggest that fantasy to anyone back in the States. I didn't want to be known as the gangbang bitch, and, even at a school as big as New York University, that's the kind of story

that would get around. This was my chance, with a bunch
of hot guys I'd never see again. Nancy went to college in
Texas, so it wasn't like she could spill the beans to anyone
I knew at home. And everyone knows that what happens
during junior year abroad – and especially what happens
on a road trip during junior year abroad – doesn't count
anyway.

Yeah, I suppose if I'd had a bit of sense, I'd have
thought about awful diseases or at least the possibility of
some child lost on the way to the rest room walking in
on us. But, if you tell me you had that much common
sense at nineteen, I'll tell you you're lying.

Claudel was squatting next to us, stroking his crotch
practically in my face – I told you he was a thug, deliberately crude, but when I'm in a certain mood that can be
hot. Gérard looked confused, but still was fumbling
between my legs and hitting the good bits pretty often
for someone who wasn't paying full attention. Nancy and
her boys were getting hotter and heavier and five out of
six of the other guys were staring hungrily at one or the
other cluster.

(The sixth took advantage of everyone's distraction to
abscond with all the alcohol and the remains of the joint.
I don't know whether he was queer, shy or a voyeur, but
he and the intoxicants stayed in the corner for the rest of
the night and seemed happy that way. No, it wasn't Jean-
Paul, but a square, muscular North African guy who looked
somewhat older than the rest. So much for stereotypes.)

I helped Claudel open his pants. He was hairy, also
uncircumcised – just assume they all are unless I say otherwise, a lot of Frenchmen are – and smelled like Camem-
bert. Stop with the faces, Fiona. I know it doesn't sound
all that appealing now, but think about it. You're in the
bowels of this ferry, rocking back and forth, hearing the
Mediterranean slapping against it as you move through
the night. You're young, on your way to someplace you've
never been, someplace that smacks of bandits and *The*

Count of Monte Cristo. You're about to fulfil one of your top ten masturbatory fantasies, and someone has just succeeded in ripping your tights and is nudging the head of his big cock against you, trying to push his way inside. At a time like that, the hairiness and aroma just seemed French, and thus exciting.

'*Arretez!*' I said – that's one French word I remember even now, not that I said 'Stop' a lot for the rest of that night – and repositioned myself on hands and knees. The guys got the drift immediately.

As if they'd counted to three, Gérard entered me, filling me so sweetly that I felt my whole body ripple with it, and Claudel forced his way into my mouth. Not like he needed to force, but he wanted to, wanted to pound into my mouth like it was a cunt. No finesse, but, then again, I wasn't giving him my best, either. It's hard to concentrate on an artful blow job when someone is fucking you at the same time. And if Claudel lacked technique, unless you consider tonsil-tickling a technique, Gérard had it. He knew how to use his length and thickness to good effect, and, bless him, he remembered that girls have clits and like them touched even while they're enjoying a hard cock stroking against all sorts of wonderfully sensitive places on the interior.

My long-deprived body was relishing all the attention. I was bucking back against Gérard, trying to get even more of him inside me although his balls were slamming against me and it was clearly impossible. I would have been moaning, but my mouth was full. It was a little hard to breathe around Claudel, and drool was running down my chin, and I was glad that his cock wasn't the size of Gérard's, but, for all that it wasn't that comfortable, I liked feeling his excitement as I gobbled him, liked feeling his hands in my hair, liked the way his hips snapped as he moved in and out of my mouth.

He finished first, long before the boy in my pussy did. One second he was fucking my face, the next he was arching back and howling like a wolf in the moonlight and shooting down my throat. He was so deep in my mouth that I felt it, but didn't taste it.

Then he pulled away and another boy joined us. I couldn't tell you his name, but his hair was reddish and he politely asked, 'May I?' before he knelt in front of me.

I expected another cock in my mouth immediately. Instead he kissed me. I really didn't expect that, not with Claudel's spunk still lingering on my breath, but he gave me a sweet kiss and ran his hands over my breasts, playing with my nipples, making me gasp.

Then he pinched, and Gérard did something especially clever with my clit, and between the two of them I caught fire and burned, clamping down on the cock inside me. At that, Gérard lost control and began slamming against me, making me come again, or pushing the same orgasm to a higher level, until he came himself.

The red-haired boy smiled. 'It worked,' he said sweetly. 'Sorry, my friend. I like fucking better and you were taking too long. If the lady will permit me?'

His graciousness should have been funny under the circumstances, but I was still having little aftershocks and I desperately wanted another cock to replace the one that was slipping out of me. I nodded.

The redhead got behind me and another boy claimed my mouth.

In the brief stillness while they were arranging themselves, I heard moans from the other side of the room. 'Do you want to see?' Gérard asked, and, when I nodded, he helped me herd the other boys around so we all had a better angle.

Nancy was sprawled in one of the ugly orange chairs, her long legs open. The Alsatian kid, Paul, was going down on her, a couple of fingers working in and out of her pussy. I'd always vaguely wondered if Nancy was a natural blonde. From the bit I could see, I'd have to say she was. She also was having a very good time, if the moans and groans were any indication. (I think this might have been the moment I decided that I'd have to try playing with a girl myself sometime. I'd never seen another woman getting off before and it was damn hot. Joan's blushing again – but am I right or am I not, Joan? Hot, hot, hot. If you've never tried it, Fiona, you really should.) The other boy was leaning over her, working on her breasts and kissing her, but leaning into Paul as well. Something about the way they were working together said to me this wasn't their first time tag-teaming a girl, and that maybe they'd been naked together without a girl being involved as well. I didn't think anyone else would be breaking into that threesome.

Excellent. More for me.

This time, the boy who wanted my mouth lay down in front of me and the redhead tipped me forward a little, allowing me to use my hands. A little more control let me pull out some technique – teasing his head with the tip of my tongue, playing with his balls, drawing back when it seemed he was getting too hot too soon. This one *was* circumcised, which made him a bit easier to work with, more what I was used to.

Meanwhile, the one fucking me was going great guns. No sophisticated skills, but a lot of energy and enthusiasm made up for a lot. That, and a lovely snap to his hips that hit the top of my cunt just about every time, getting my cervix in on the action. He was leaning forward, kissing my neck and back and sometimes biting down pretty hard, hard enough that if I hadn't been worked up it would have hurt. I could tell where his hands were, so I was a little confused when I felt a gentle touch on my clit.

Then I realised it wasn't a finger. It was a tongue. Better yet.

Jean-Paul, as I've said, was a skinny little thing who hadn't reached a man's height yet. That was an advantage for him under the circumstances: it let him slither under me and get his tongue in there where one of the bulkier guys would have had to stop the action and rearrange everyone to do so.

I had to stop sucking so I could scream.

And then . . .

OK, ladies, you're absolutely right. I don't actually remember all this so clearly. Certain high points, sure. Gérard was one of the better lays I'd had at that age, so he stands out, but even there I'm probably misremembering some of the details. Jean-Paul sneaking in to lick me was impressive, maybe not for the skill, but the sheer surprise of it, and the sensory overload on top of everything else that was going on. I'm pretty sure I did come like a banshee then.

The rest? Some of the story may be real memories, but they're probably in the wrong order. I may even be making up the names, except for Gérard. The rest is pieced together out of blurry impressions of flesh, pleasure, the gently rocking ferry, the smells of diesel and cigarettes and sex filling the stuffy third-class cabin. You asked for the wildest thing I'd ever done, not the best sex I'd ever had. I honestly can't remember if most of the fucking and sucking was good in itself or if the excitement came mostly from knowing I did something so outrageous. I mean, I get all kinds of hot remembering it now, but at the time – sheesh, who knows? How good are a bunch of half-drunk kids likely to be?

You know what else I definitely remember? Sometime just before dawn, when we were all fucked out and the wine was gone, we all bundled back into our clothes and wandered up on to the deck. The air had a nip to it, and the breeze was strong, but it smelled like ocean and, faintly, like herbs. Pale stars still hung in the sky, and, at the eastern horizon, the sky was just starting to turn pink. We didn't snuggle or anything, even though it was cool enough that it would have made sense to huddle together for warmth. We just stood there, holding the rail, letting the sea breeze wash the funk and smoke and stale alcohol off us, not talking, until the sun came up and Corsica came into focus through the fog.

Then what happened? Nothing. The ferry docked and we said goodbye, kind of sheepishly, I guess. The guys went wherever they were going. Nancy and I found a youth hostel in Ajaccio, took a shower, and then slept until they booted us out at lunchtime. We were a little awkward with each other for about a day, like we'd seen too many of each other's secrets. And then we hopped on a bus heading up into the mountains, not sure where it went or particularly caring, to find more adventures. We found them, too: thousand-year-old houses and wild goats and an old woman who told our fortunes and a Danish artist who'd bought a house in the hills and who tried to seduce Nancy. But nothing like the ferry. Probably a good thing, too.

All right, ladies, who's next? What's the wildest thing *you* ever did?

Stretched Severin Rosetti

Claire had phrased the ad so simply and concisely that any man could understand it: 'stretched limo driver' was what it asked for, just the three simple words, but still the applicant *would* insist on reading so much into it, see so many possibilities.

Was it the limo that was stretched, for example, or would it be the driver? The first, quite obviously, though the second would be an amusing alternative, and when he asked for some clarification she gave him a weak smile.

'What a clever question,' she said patiently, her icy stare challenging his smug lop-sided grin. Quite a charming grin, but still a little too smug.

'So? Which is it?' the man pressed, but she simply asked him if he wanted the job.

He said he did, she told him it was his, and so the briefest of interviews was concluded.

'You can start this evening – pick up the limo here,' she instructed him, scribbling down the address on a piece of paper and handing it to him. 'Seven thirty sharp.'

Once he had left, Claire scribbled down some observations for her partner, noting that the successful applicant was young and well presented, pleasant to the eye and affable in manner, that he had the requisite clean licence and some modicum of intelligence. Then she added a postscript, wondering if intelligence might also mean curiosity and cautioning her partner to watch out for any signs of this.

* * *

The drive of the house was long enough to accommodate a small fleet of stretch limousines, though only one was parked there, and broad enough for the vehicle to have easily negotiated a three-point turn in it. The taxi that dropped Lenny off seemed lost in the expanse of carefully raked gravel, a black speck of a beetle against the sleek white limousine with its darkened windows.

'Some place,' said the taxi driver, admiring the sprawling ranch-type house as he took Lenny's money, then frowning at the meagre tip he received, as if he thought the address entitled him to more.

'Hey, mate, I'm just here to work, not take up residence in the fucking place!' Lenny told him, walking from the taxi to the house's imposing façade.

And it *was* an imposing façade, the length of the terrace he had been brought up in, with broad double doors approached by three shallow steps, coach lamps illuminating the porch and so many windows that they made a mosaic of lights. For a moment he wondered whether he would have the courage to actually knock at this house and demand entrance, his step a little hesitant as he approached. Thankfully, though, he was spared this test of his resolve, for, as he approached the doors, they swung open.

'You'll be the driver,' supposed the woman who stepped out, and even as he nodded she was giving him instructions. 'Right, here are your addresses and directions,' she told him, handing him a clipboard. 'Other instructions might be passed over the intercom and there will be no need, absolutely *no* need, for you to get out from behind the wheel. Understood?'

Lenny understood, though in truth little of what the woman said had sunk in, so distracted had he been by her manner and her presence.

In her heels she was his match in height, a fraction of an inch over six foot, wore a dark pinstripe suit, crisply cut jacket and tight skirt just reaching the knee; black hair was drawn severely back from the face, and steel-rimmed spectacles and the leather briefcase she carried gave her the air of a professional woman.

But what manner of profession could have a woman – a young woman, not yet in her thirties – living in such a house and travelling in such a vehicle? He had little time to ponder the question, though, since her brusque manner would permit him no time to dawdle. Realising that she was to be his passenger, seeing her go to the rear of the limousine, he hurried to beat her to the passenger door, but she waved him away.

'That won't be necessary. You drive, you don't open the door,' she told him, ducking into the vehicle, flashing silky slim thighs and elegantly tapered heels as she drew her legs in after her.

Fair enough, thought Lenny, and got behind the wheel, started the engine and slipped the car into gear.

The first address on his schedule was some ten miles away, on the other side of the city, a suburb as prosperous as the one where he had collected the limousine. So who would he be picking up? A boisterous hen party? he wondered. Some rich man's daughter celebrating her eighteenth birthday with the daughters of other rich men?

Apparently not, for as he pulled up outside the mock-Tudor house he saw just one man come hurrying down the drive to the car, and in the wing mirror saw the passenger door swing open to admit him.

To be taken where?

Lenny checked his schedule again and was surprised to see that the man was to be taken nowhere, that the limousine was to remain there, parked outside the man's house for the next sixty minutes.

Shrugging, Lenny sat back in his seat, fingers drumming on the steering wheel as he counted down the minutes on his watch. There was no radio set into the dashboard, though there would no doubt be a sound system and other entertainments in the main body of the vehicle. The glove compartment was empty and so were the side pockets in the doors. Nothing at all to distract him, not even a workshop manual.

He wished he had brought along a newspaper or a book, but all he could do was wait and wonder, imagine what his two passengers might be doing. There were no sounds from beyond the black glass that separated them from him, just the occasional rocking of the car on its suspension, but that was only slight, as if heavy traffic had passed.

But what traffic? The neighbourhood was quiet, the lane deserted. His passengers were shifting in their seats, then, making themselves comfortable; the vehicle was a limousine, after all, and its suspension would be the best, sensitive to any movement.

Making themselves comfortable for what, though? This was Lenny's next thought, his mind mulling over the possibilities, fighting the boredom. He recalled the briefcase the woman had carried. They were discussing business, then? But why not in the man's house rather than the car?

A sudden more vigorous lurch of the car on its springs snapped him out of his reverie and he chuckled softly to himself. Of course! The dirty buggers were having it off back there! His employer had scheduled some sordid assignation before the business of the evening began for real!

Lenny checked his watch. Two minutes to eight. Now he counted down the seconds rather than the minutes, right on schedule heard the passenger door open and shut and turned to see the back of the man returning to his house.

'Right, next stop,' the woman's voice crackled over the intercom, and Lenny moved the vehicle slowly forward.

The next address was in the city. There were some narrow streets and awkward turns to negotiate, but Lenny made the rendezvous more or less on schedule.

This time his passengers were a man and a woman. There was nowhere to park, so he followed the route as described on the clipboard beside him, out of the city and around it, checkpoints listed and carefully timed.

Some job this was! Where were the hen parties he had imagined? The puking teenagers, the pissed-up sluts, the horny old hags celebrating someone's entry into middle age?

After returning the couple to their apartment in the city, he noted that they left the vehicle less quickly than his first passenger, the woman with head bowed as if with guilt, the man looking back with something like reluctance or regret.

And it would go on. In the five hours up to midnight he had carried maybe a dozen people, all in groups of one or two or three, when the vehicle could have accommodated maybe twice that number at any one time.

One or two or three – and his employer.

What *was* the woman up to?

Penny's mobile vibrated, a couple of minutes past the hour, as they travelled from one appointment to the next, and she flipped it open to receive the call.

'Hi, Penny! How goes it?'

'Fine, just fine,' she answered.

'No problems?'

'The new couple were a little nervous, I think the wife was rather less keen than the husband, but apart from that everything's been OK.'

'I was thinking more about the new driver than the clients. No problems with him?'

'The driver?' said Penny, glancing at the dark partition that separated him from her. 'No, no problems there. He seems quite competent, keeping more or less to schedule, and he hasn't hit anything.'

'And he's behaving himself? Doing as he's told? No awkward questions or signs of curiosity?'

'Discreetly dumb so far,' Penny answered. 'And if there *should* be any curiosity, well, you know how we deal with that.'

There was a wicked peal of laughter down the phone before the call finished with, 'Bye then, see you later.'

Evil cow, Penny thought as she smiled to herself. She *wants* the man to be curious.

The last call on Lenny's schedule was at a country club some miles out of the city, a place he knew of but had never been able to afford to frequent. He was to arrive there at midnight, or as close as possible, and remain there until one, after which he was finished.

'Drop me at the door and then park,' he was instructed, the voice over the intercom harsh and grating again; and, as he brought the vehicle to a halt his single passenger stepped out, ran lightly up the steps and into the club.

No briefcase now, Lenny noticed, as he set the limousine in motion once more to turn it in a broad arc, moving it to the furthest corner of the spacious car park, as far as possible from the bright lights of the clubhouse.

He switched off the engine, stretched, but still felt too cramped by the confines of the vehicle. Needing fresh air after five hours behind the wheel, thinking to have a cigarette now that he had made his last call of the night, Lenny got out and lit up, inhaling deeply, then filled his lungs with the crisp evening air.

He walked around the limousine, stroked its smooth flanks and polished sides as he sometimes stroked a woman, then rested against it as he finished his cigarette.

The windows weren't just smoked but as black as tar. Though he bent down and cupped his hands around his eyes it was impossible to see inside.

'Wonder what it's like in there,' he said to himself, dropping his cigarette to the floor and grinding it out with his foot. 'Wonder what the icy bitch carries in that briefcase of hers.'

He yawned and stretched and made another circuit of the vehicle, moving uninterestedly as he glanced across to the clubhouse and saw people leaving – but their cars were parked close to the building and they came nowhere near him.

'Let's have a peep, eh? A taste of stretch-limo luxury?' he said, when the car park was dark and quiet again, and bent to open the passenger door.

The courtesy light was as bright as a beacon in the night, but that was not what startled him, what caused him to catch his breath.

'What the fuck is *that*?' he asked, looking into the limo's interior.

There was a bank of dark leather upholstery at the rear end and similar seating at the near end, next to the black screen of glass that separated this compartment from his. But in between, filling the rest of the interior . . .

A fucking rowing machine? he thought at first, seeing the contraption of steel and leather. Surely something out of a gym.

He saw parts where feet might be placed, parts where hands might grip, a pillow of black leather where a head might rest and enough chains and straps that for all the seeming rigidity of the polished frame it was obviously also a thing that had flexibility.

'A portable gym!' He laughed. 'She's got a portable fucking gym in her limo!'

'No, dimwit! Not a gym but a rack!' he heard, as a foot pressed hard against his arse and sent him tumbling inside. 'I just knew you'd be the curious type who wouldn't be able to resist a peek!'

Lenny tried to rise, roll over, but the foot came down hard in the small of his back, keeping him pinned, and all he could do was twist his head, peer back over his shoulder to see a second woman standing beside the one he had been driving around all evening.

'My colleague and partner, Claire,' he was told. 'Remember? She interviewed you for the job?'

'Pleased to make your acquaintance again, Lenny,' said Claire mockingly as she grinned down at him.

She too was dressed as if for business, as professionally as she had been for his interview, her tailored jacket hugging her waist, white silk blouse open at the neck to show a single strand of pearls, her skirt just short enough to be alluring in a subtle and discreet manner.

The two women looked like company directors. Claire's briefcase was on the ground at her feet.

'So how do we respond to curiosity, Claire?' Penny wondered.

'How about you start by letting me up?' suggested Lenny, and thought they were about to do so, when he felt the foot lift from his back, only to have the breath driven from his lungs by a knee slamming into him.

'Shut up! We decide when or if!' Claire told him, settling her weight on him as she turned to her colleague. 'Perhaps our nosy driver's curiosity should be satisfied.'

'You think?'

'Yes. Let's. It might be fun.'

Lenny felt the car sink on its springs as Penny – having picked up Claire's briefcase from the tarmac outside – climbed in beside him. He saw her skirt riding up black silk thighs as she shuffled forward, and then the two women were manhandling him, flipping him over on to his back, raising his arms above his head and stretching them out.

'Don't struggle, you'll only hurt yourself,' Penny told him, winding leather straps around his wrists and buckling them tight.

'You should be grateful to us,' Claire added, having turned around so that she was sitting on his belly, facing his feet, leaning forward to fasten more straps around his ankles. 'Men pay a lot for this,' she told him, tugging on the straps to satisfy herself that they were secure enough. 'In fact, they've been doing so all night. And their wives, sometimes.'

'Adds a whole new meaning to the idea of a stretch limo, doesn't it?' chuckled Penny, as the two women, satisfied that their victim was securely fastened, sat one to either side of him.

'Comfy, dear?' Claire asked, smiling at first as she stroked his cheek, but then frowning as Lenny did, turning his face from her. 'Well not for long!' she told him, her long nails scratching his skin as she snatched her hand away, letting it fall out of sight, by the side of the contraption on which he lay.

His head lifted a moment, trying to see what she was doing as he felt the straps that gripped his wrists tighten and contract, pulling his arms out further.

'See? It *is* a rack, not a fucking exercise machine!' Claire spat, slowly turning the small chrome wheel, which stretched him. She enjoyed his alarm as her other hand on a second wheel caused his feet to be pulled in the other direction.

A final quarter-turn of each and Lenny was stretched to his limit, the muscles in his arms and thighs straining, his chest filling, his belly tightening.

Penny began to unbutton his shirt, lacquered and manicured nails deftly popping each button free until she had his chest bared. Then she moved to his trousers, unbuckled his belt, tugged down the zip, worked them over his buttocks and down to his bound ankles.

'Toss you for who drives,' said Claire.

'Toss what? A coin, or this?' asked Penny, resting her hand on Lenny's groin, rolling his genitals around inside the cotton of his shorts.

Both broke into delighted peals of laughter, while Lenny tried vainly to squirm his way free of Penny's rough caress.

'Lovely! But that comes later!' said Claire, wiping the tears from her eyes. 'For the moment just call it. Heads or tails?'

'Heads.'

'Tails.'

'Damn!'

'You drive.'

They manoeuvred themselves around inside the car, Claire moving to the front of the vehicle, to the bench seat that backed on to the driver's compartment, Penny opening the passenger door on her side to swing her legs out.

Then she popped her head back inside and said, 'The blindfold, do you think?'

'Good idea. It's so disorientating for them when the car's moving,' Claire agreed, opening her briefcase and rummaging inside.

Seated at Lenny's head, her legs parted, one foot to either side of him, she draped a soft leather blindfold over his eyes, said, 'Head up, darling.'

Instead Lenny tossed his head, trying to shake the blindfold free, so she clenched her fingers in his hair and tugged, lifting his head just high enough to knot the blindfold.

Darkness fell as Lenny heard doors open and close, the ignition turn and the engine fire, and felt the limousine begin to move slowly forward. The vehicle turned in a broad arc, as did his head, as if he needed to follow the movements of the car. A shallow dip down to the main road caused his stomach to lurch; a quick left turn followed by a sharp right made his head spin; and, but for the hiss of the tyres on the tarmac, his world was as silent as it was dark.

'Are you still there?' he asked, and heard a soft chuckle. 'Why are you doing this? Speak to me!'

There were moments more of silence, the nauseating movement of the car, and then Claire finally said, 'Your arms will begin to ache soon, your thighs too. You will get cramp in your calves and beg to be released.'

'Why?' Lenny wanted to know. 'Why?'

'You will ache in other places too,' Claire continued. 'The things we will do to you will cause you so much anguish and so much delight that you will scream and sob and plead.'

'But why? *Why?*'

'Hush! Do you want me to gag you too?' Claire asked, and he felt her fingers lightly brush his lips, not so much a caress as a threat. 'You'll be quiet? Yes? Good!'

And as her fingers continued to stroke his face, as the blind motion of the car made him feel dizzy and disorientated and his immobilised limbs ached as much as she had promised, her voice droned hypnotically on: 'It's not so much sensory deprivation as sensory enhancement, as your movement is restricted and your sight deprived so other sensations are heightened. Touch, for instance.'

When her fingers trailed lightly across his belly it was as if he had been pricked by needles, and Lenny's body lurched, despite the pain caused by his straining against his bonds.

'See? And you are perhaps aware of my perfume now? The warmth of my body?'

Yes, he thought he was. A musky odour pervaded his nostrils and his cheeks burned as if a soft heat were scorching them.

He heard the rasp of a zip, a rustle of fabric, and then that heat increased. He had to gasp for air.

'Of course, such delights that we can bring you have to be earned, which is why I am now lowering my body on to your face,' Claire told him, and, before he could protest, her soft fragrant flesh enveloped his features, muffling his protests.

She had removed her skirt, and knickers if she wore them. Her buttocks moulded themselves about his face, the wet lips of her cunt about his mouth.

'Now lick me,' he heard her say, softly, as if from a great distance. 'Please me if you hope for any pleasure yourself; satisfy me if you want your own curiosity satisfied; serve me if you want any relief from your discomfort.'

Lenny did as he was asked. He had no option. He licked dutifully at the soft vagina that smothered him, and the last words he heard were again as much a threat as they might have been a promise.

'And you know the most wonderful thing of all?' Claire said, her thighs gripping him firmly, her cunt so abrasive against his face. 'Once this is over, once you have the relief of release, once sensation returns to your limbs and the blindfold is removed – then your gratitude will be such that you will surrender yourself to the first person you see. You will be too weak to resist. I will fold your weary body in my arms and you will be helpless, you will be mine.'

'You impatient cow! You couldn't wait?'

The limousine had come to a halt, Penny had returned to find Claire smiling behind closed eyes, her cheeks flushed, her buttocks fat around Lenny's face, her body rocking gently backwards and forwards.

'Sorry, the luck of the toss,' Claire said, as weak mewling sounds escaped from beneath her.

Penny moved deeper into the limousine, reached out, her hand working its way between her friend's thighs.

'You're sopping wet! Absolutely sopping! Get off him before you drown the poor bugger!' she said, pushing Claire back.

Chest heaving, Lenny gasped for air as Claire fell away from him and Penny shuffled to his side.

'His face is positively drenched, and it isn't just sweat!' she said, running her hands over his face, feeling his brow slick, his lips dripping, the leather that covered his eyes sodden. She was about to peel it away when she glanced up at her friend, saw the blank and blissful expression on her face. 'What are you doing? We're supposed to be in this together!' she exclaimed.

'You were driving,' Claire said. 'I need to have a driver.'

'He's ours!' Penny corrected her, leaving the blindfold where it was. '*We* will have a driver!'

Having got his breath back, his body contorting to try to ease his discomfort, Lenny said, 'Please, let me go. I ache.'

'Soon, darling, soon,' Penny said, hunched at his side as she stripped off her jacket, her blouse, struggled out of her skirt.

In just bra and pants, stockings and shoes, she was quickly curled up beside him, her breasts against his cheek, her hand flat on his belly with her fingers pointing towards his groin.

'My slut of a friend has made you hard,' she said, seeing the way the damp cotton of his shorts was now fighting to contain his erection.

Lenny's fingers flexed, as if he were trying to claw his way free, as he said, 'Please ... please ... let me go.'

'But without your comfort? Without your relief?' she purred, her finger tracing the outline of his cock, her nail scratching its tip. 'I know you want it, I know you need it,' she said, slowly, tantalisingly easing his shorts down.

'Oh! Oh, yes!' he agreed, as her fingers closed around his erection, raised it, brought it close to her lips.

Rather than kiss it, though, or fasten her lips on it, she simply blew on it.

Lenny squealed with delight and forgot his discomfort as his buttocks lifted and he strained towards her, and strained again as she drew back from him, and then once more until every joint and muscle protested.

'So yes? You do want your relief?' she said, and, nudging Claire from her blissful reverie, said, 'I'm going to take him, I'm going to have him. Do you want to share?'

'Oh, yes! Yes please!' Claire sighed, turning and curling

into his side, her arms reaching out, one beneath him to embrace him, her other hand slipping down to take his cock from Penny.

She held it upright while her friend positioned herself astride him, then slowly rocked it back and forth against Penny's damp knickers. The lace, though damp, was abrasive against his swollen cock and brought soft squeals of delight from him.

'Yes, slowly, back and forth a little more,' said Penny, now pulling her knickers to one side, 'and now just the head inside me.'

Her body dipped. Claire held Lenny's cock still, and Penny took no more than the tip of it inside her, then a little more, just enough for Claire to be able to release her hold on it and embrace him with both her arms, crushing his face against her breasts.

'Push a little, Lenny,' Penny encouraged. 'I know you must be tired and aching, but, please, just a little effort, eh?'

She smiled down at him, caressed his chest, stroked his nipples and then pinched hard. As he gasped and she flexed her cunt he was drawn suddenly inside her.

'Ah! So nice! Now thrust into me slow and deep and let me feel you grow ever harder inside me.'

Lenny groaned aloud, muffled by Claire's smothering embrace, trying to rise to meet Penny as her friend ground her groin against him, his buttocks lifting weakly.

'Please,' he begged.

'I know, you need to come,' Penny said. 'And I promise, soon. Just move into me a little more quickly now. Make me come and then you can.'

He cried when her fingernails scored his chest, sobbed with the effort as he did his best to slam his cock into her, gasped as she thrust back down on him. As she felt the tension build in him she clenched her cunt around his cock, pulsing rhythmically as her chest heaved, a sensual warmth suffusing her body as her heart raced.

'Any moment now,' she warned. 'I'm coming... Any moment now.'

'Coming so *you* are allowed to come,' said Claire, her own body bucking against Lenny's, her groin driving against his hip, her labia viciously scouring his skin.

'Yes! So you can!' Penny echoed, sobbing with laughter and delight as she fell from his body, leaving his cock spitting wildly, without control, spitting his spunk all over his belly.

She fell into the arms of Claire and the two women kissed as their faces came together, cheek against cheek just inches above him, their eyes devouring him, licking their lips as if already feasting on him. Fingers manipulated his cock, his balls, prolonging his delight; Claire slipped her free hand down by the side of the rack to release the traction that held him while Penny whipped the blindfold away as the last spasms of his ejaculation shook his body.

Lenny's orgasm was so strong, his release so sweet, that he seemed to fold in on himself, as weak as a child, and helpless as, through his tears, he blinked up at the two beautiful women who wrapped him in their arms, hugging him to them and claiming him as theirs.

It was as if the terms of his contract were finally settled, his service secured. He wasn't just employed by them: he belonged to them.

On Tour Andrea Dale

No, I can't tell you his name.

Even though his wife's the really kinky one, he's still a part of the scene, and he's too well known for me to ever be able to say who he is. But you've seen him on MTV. A lot. Honest.

I'm getting ahead of myself, my thoughts tumbling over themselves. That happens when I'm lying here, bound and gagged and blindfolded, knowing only darkness and the swaying of the tour-bus bunk and the low hum of a vibrator stuffed inside me. Not purring hard enough to make me come, but almost. I'm never sure whether that's a good thing or not. I'm not supposed to make any noise. If I do, I'll get punished.

But that's all part of the game.

I'm way ahead of myself again. It's so dark, and I'm so horny that my toes are curling. Gives me time to think about how this all got started.

It all started with a song. OK, a video. MTV was well established by the time I started watching it, and I don't know what it's like not to immediately have a visual image to go with a song. Music and video, intertwined. It created a whole new type of musical artist. Bands had to pay more attention to how they looked. Some even got signed for their looks rather than their talent.

He had both – talent *and* looks. Raspy, sultry voice, kick-ass guitar. How often had I fantasised about his hands? In my masturbatory dreams, I knew the tips of his fingers would be rough with calluses. I imagined he would play me like an instrument, coaxing music out of me until I vibrated like a taut guitar string, wailing and screaming.

Sometimes, when I'm tied up, they put headphones on me, and I have to listen to his songs in the dark, alone. Just as I'd done before, only now my hands are encased in soft mittens, and, even if they weren't shackled to my thighs, I wouldn't be able to dip my fingers between my thighs to stroke my throbbing clit and bring myself the relief I so desperately craved.

Lots of women have fantasies about rock stars, and groupies are a dime a dozen. But every so often you hear the story about one who gets through, one who catches the artist's eye, one who gets plucked out of the crowd like Courteney Cox in that old Bruce Springsteen video.

Like me.

Unlike some of them, I didn't get installed as wife (he already had one) or even mistress. Well, not exactly.

I'm not really making much sense, am I? The gentle rocking of the bus is just making things worse. We don't play this elaborate a game unless it's going to go on for a long time. I have no sense of time, lying here in the dark, on edge. My thighs keep clenching, and I have to force myself to relax them. It's not going to help. She knows just how high to set the vibrator to keep me on this excruciating edge without pitching me over.

For a long, long time.

It's not that hard to get backstage if you're young and pretty and willing to dress the part. I won't bore you with those details. Suffice to say I was on a mission. I wanted more than the brief pleasantries and hastily scrawled autograph during a crowded meet-and-greet.

Platters of cold cuts and cakes, tubs of ice filled with water, soda and beer. The rest of the band and the roadies wandering in and out. Me in a tummy-baring top and tight jeans that show off my ass. A few other select women, all of us eyeing each other warily, knowing there was only so much prey to go around, and some of us would leave hungry.

And then he was there, too, hair damp from his after-concert shower and a wicked glint in his dark eyes.

My heart rate accelerated, and my hips twitched.

And then we were back in his dressing room. I unbuttoned his shirt slowly, one button at a time, revealing the smooth chest I'd longed to lick sweat from since I was old enough to understand what urges like that meant.

No sweat now, but the licking still seemed appropriate. He liked it when I teased his nipples.

Then his hands were on me, pinching my nipples as he gauged my reaction. I'd always liked it rough, and he not only seemed to know that, but was able to take it up a notch, up a level to where it wasn't exactly uncomfortable but certainly was beyond pleasure into some heightened state I'd only played at the edges of before.

To say I liked it ... well, I'd always wondered what it might be like to come this way.

But he didn't let me. Leaving me teetering on the edge, he led me to the sofa. I assumed he'd want a blow job (which, I supposed, might hasten my own orgasm – how long had I been fantasising about *this* cock in my mouth?), but instead he had me straddle him.

I sank down, taking him all the way, enjoying every last inch of him inside me before settling into a rhythm of posting up and down that seemed to please him. It certainly worked for me. I reached up to play with my breasts, but he stopped me. Wrapped long, strong fingers around my wrists and held them firmly at my sides.

He watched me as he did it, his dark, glittering eyes not letting me look away.

My orgasm was a long, slow crescendo, starting quietly but inexorably building to triumphant climax. It roiled through me like the pounding of a bass guitar, centred on where we were connected, throbbing. My hips jerked back and forth, grinding down on him, and only his hands pinning my arms kept me upright.

Helpless, and expertly played like a fine instrument.

After the concert two nights and one state later, a roadie personally escorted me backstage.

He was in his dressing room, waiting for me, sitting in a brown-leather easy chair. He wore sunglasses, and his face was expressionless. Something about that, about the way he sat, casually but with a certain tautness, made me shiver – in a good way. If he was unhappy with me, I sensed we'd be working it out.

'Take off your clothes,' he said.

I complied, hands trembling with excitement.

Then he simply crooked his finger at me. Come closer. Come into my parlour, said the spider to the fly.

Every step I took on shaking legs was willing and eager. Nervous? A little. Nervous anticipation.

I was naked, and he was fully dressed. His leather pants were the same glossy brown as the chair, and I wondered fleetingly if he'd orchestrated that.

I knew what he wanted me to do before he even pointed. I draped myself across his lap, across the padded arms of the chair, my hair hanging down over my face. I even crossed my wrists behind me, and heard his soft chuckle as he trapped them against the small of my back.

Through the walls, I heard the dim voices and faint laughter of the backstage party. In the room, though, there was nothing except the rasp of my own breath as I waited.

The crack of his hand against my ass was like a rimshot.

I'd played at spanking games with various partners. Hasn't everyone? But they were silly, laughing, squirming-out-of-reach-before-it-got-too-intense games.

This wasn't a game. I was squirming, all right –

twitching as the heat and pain flooded me, pressing myself against him as the arousal crashed through me with every stinging slap.

This wasn't a game, and that was my last thought before the pain mutated into pleasure so strong that my sudden, sharp orgasm gripped me like a vice. It caught me unawares, stealing my breath.

Without waiting for permission (without knowing I should probably have asked for it), I squirmed off his lap on to my knees and unlaced his pants with my teeth. His cock sprang out, and I moaned as I took it in my mouth.

His hands threaded through my hair, guiding my motions. No, commanding them. I let him.

He told me I was doing good, and that fuelled my concentration. In fact, he kept up a litany of praise, and I lapped it up as I lapped at his cock. At some point he suggested something about inviting the rest of the band in, and I was lust-drugged enough to agree. He laughed, though, and said he wasn't ready to share me – not just yet.

He smelled of soap and musk, and soon he tasted salty-sweet.

Once, I got that awful song about the wheels on the bus stuck in my head. I'll never let *that* happen again.

The vibrator hums, and the bunk rocks, ever so gently. I had little idea, back then, of what I was getting myself into. A slow, steady climb to this.

Slow, steady climb. No ... relax. Don't come too soon, no matter how much you want to.

I hadn't initially planned on the third concert, two states later, but, as promised, a front-row ticket was waiting for me at Will Call, and the tour manager himself escorted me after the show was over.

Escorted me right on to the tour bus.

He had a private bus. Sometimes the other members

inches from my desperate eyes. I could
l, his musk, and hear him thrusting
her wetness.

e my own. My hips thrust uselessly off
se – so close! – but the vibrator wasn't
anted, what I craved, was just outside
y'd removed the gag, but I couldn't
up and run my tongue along him.
gain, and the staccato of his hips told
. In her. Of course. They'd warned me,

oned my decision when she lowered
y duty implied. But the taste of them
me, and there was something about
across the slick folds of another
a need in me I'd never known until
ease her, and thus please him.
n doing a good job. The noises she
the way she ground her wetness
as hint enough. When I felt strong
raps around me and slowly, oh, too
orator almost all of the way out of
n, I knew for sure. At the same time,
that my own pleasure was depend-
erformance and ability to make her

s stilling, but I knew she was close
ibrated against my tongue. I flicked
nd was rewarded with a frenzy of
sweet fluid.
dildo increasing its speed inside of
mistaken, the flick of his tongue
, driving me to the release I so

. Since then, each session has been
hed me further. Her inventiveness,
wicked combination.

rode with him, but he had the option of claiming it for
himself, and this time he did. I'd never been on a tour
bus before, and I revelled in the luxury of deep, cushioned
couches; cabinets of dark red, gleaming wood; the latest
technology in the form of plasma TV and DVR; the silk-
sheeted king-sized bed at the very back.

I'd brought my own nipple clamps – light, teasing
ones, all I'd ever played with – and his eyes lit up with
appreciation when, on my knees, I presented them to
him.

He used silk scarves that night to tie me down, teasing
me for a long time with his hands and mouth and the
clips. I twisted and writhed, helpless and pleading. And,
in the morning, he made me an offer.

I can never discuss the exact terms. Suffice to say there
was a contract, and it was a long one. It talked about
what I'd be willing to do (including other women, which
intrigued me), and made it clear that I couldn't tell
anyone, ever. My living expenses would be generously
compensated for. It also gave me an out: say the word,
and I was free to leave, no harm, no foul.

'It comes with a price,' he told me. I assumed that
meant the bondage, the spankings.

I was put in a private car to the airport, and my ticket
was paid for.

His last words to me were, 'Think about it.'

Of course I thought about it. I thought about it long and
hard. (No pun intended.) The real question was, would he
contact me? Or was it just a stupid game he played, to
get the silly groupies' hopes up? I'd never heard any other
fans talk about it, but I wouldn't share it with anyone if
it turned out not to be true.

I hoped, though. I made my decision, and I waited, and
a week later, he called. He flew me to the latest venue,
and I boarded the tour bus after the show to face him
and a lawyer across the table.

And I signed the contract without hesitation. Because I'd realised something: the overriding emotion I felt wasn't fear, or concern, or suspicion. It was anticipation.

The lawyer left, contract clutched in his hand, and I thought we were alone. I was wrong. His wife was waiting for us in the bedroom of the bus.

I'd seen her before, in pictures, on stage, but never face-to-face. She was petite, with a big smile and long, straight, silky blonde hair.

And, I'd soon learn, a wicked, twisted imagination.

Oh, I'd played around with my girlfriends before. I didn't have a problem with other women. I wasn't quite expecting this, but I thought I could roll with it. Hah.

There was a convenient hook on the ceiling, one I hadn't noticed the last time I was on the bus. My bound hands were fastened above me, not uncomfortably – my feet were still firmly on the ground, even if I couldn't free myself. Still, I felt my spine lengthen, my skin stretch, my nipples pucker.

She took advantage of that with nipple clamps – not the ones I'd brought, but ones she produced. These were stronger, more biting. My nipples throbbed in sympathetic time with my untouched, wanting clit.

The bus started, a low rumble beneath my feet and a jerk as it pulled out into traffic.

She curled up on the end of the bed, looking innocent and angelic, but I already understood that her looks were deceiving.

'On the road, when I'm not there, you can have him, to a degree,' she said. 'But, when I'm here, he's mine – and so are you. Do you have a problem with that?'

I shook my head. It was all I could do at that point, because she'd also fitted me with a leather ball gag.

'Excellent.' She got up and casually began stripping. 'He's got good taste, I'll give him that,' she added, giving me a studied look.

A strange co
without question
joint decision, a

Naked, she pl
nipples with he
through me, an
moved down, e
bars would com

'Well done,'
slick I was. He
and light to b
closer to her, s

That's whe

I realised t
watching? No
time, because
of me, filling
turned it on,
my moans
inside me, t

Still not

My frus
bed, buryi
twitched u
me off, b
drowned

Was th
to come s

They
my shak
was spr

'He's
unders
view f
sliding
appare

my lot to watch,
smell her arous
rhythmically into

I wished it wer
the bed. I was clo
enough. What I w
of my reach. The
stretch far enough

She screamed a
me he was coming
after all.

I almost questio
herself over me, m
together distracted
sliding my tongu
woman that fuelle
now. I wanted to pl

I must have be
was making, and
against my face, w
hands release the s
slowly, slide the vi
me, and then back i
I knew instinctively
ent on hers, on my
come again.

She froze, her hip
by the way her clit v
harder, deliberately,
motion and a gush of

As well as with th
me, and, if I wasn't
against my own cli
desperately craved.

That's how it bega
more intense, has pus
his skill – a dangerous

And now, over the relentless hum of the tormenting vibrator, I hear laughter. They're coming for me. I have no idea what they've planned. But I know it's going to be a long, hot night.

Pickup Girl A. D. R. Forte

It's that truck he has. That big, shiny metal and chrome monstrosity that purrs in diesel double-bass. It's a country-boy cowboy truck: dooley, off-road tyres, toolbox, even hunting lights. I've seen plenty like it around here and I know the type that drives them. Only thing is, he ain't a cowboy; not in the least, most generous stretch of the imagination. And maybe that's why.

Why I want him to drive me out into the warm wistful night of a Texan summer. Speed down an empty country road and turn off into a deserted field where only the stars watch. And there under the starlight, surrounded by nothing but night and open space, fuck me good and hard in the bed of that truck in true cowboy style.

Problem is, he wouldn't dare.

I know few people who make such a point of playing by the rules as Nathaniel David Marble. He's always on time. He always knows what to say. And his khakis never have a wrinkle. Sometimes I think his pants must be bewitched, goodness knows I find myself staring at them often enough, wishing they would just disappear.

I know it probably doesn't improve his opinion of me when I give in to sudden random fits of laughter, but it would probably be much worse if he knew I was picturing a band of twinkling, enchanted stars encircling his abruptly bare hard-on. Before I got down on my knees and started sucking him off with no regard to time or place or decent behaviour. I think the knowledge of that little fantasy would be more than he could handle.

Or maybe not. After all, he bought that damned truck.

Tony, my stylist and self-proclaimed expert on men of any orientation, would say he's compensating. But I venture to disagree. A man who's compensating doesn't have quiet confidence. He doesn't move through life with the air that he owns the world and never feels compelled to prove it. A man who doesn't have self-esteem doesn't have near-inhuman self-control.

Sure, he doesn't fuck casual acquaintances. Flirting isn't in his vocabulary. Yet, even so, I've caught a stray glance or a treacherous smile from time to time. And, even fewer and further between, I've brushed up against a temper simmering beneath that cool façade. I've faced Nate Marble down before and I've liked it. I'd like it even more if I had him twisting and arching under me, begging me to ride him harder. If only. But maybe . . . maybe he just needs direction.

I park my truck next to his. He knows it's mine and he'll know the black sandals and the suede bag on the passenger seat are mine. An edge of navy lace and silk peeks out of the open flap of the bag, part of some unknown garment. The sandals are black patent leather, four-inch heels.

Let his imagination come up with the reason for why they're tossed so carelessly when he knows I'm fanatically neat, neater than he is. Let his fantasy conjure up the picture of me wearing them and that lacy, silky something. I wonder what he'll think of, wonder what effect it'll have. There's a lot I would give to know. I'm grinning as I lock the door and leave the parking garage.

The next day I catch him looking at me despite his best pretence to be absorbed in the contents of the folder in his hand. So of course I walk right up to him.

'Hey, Nate.'

'Hi,' he replies, looking straight up and making eye contact. Sassy bastard.

'I didn't know you'd got a new truck.'

He starts to explain, to say something about when or where that I don't care about.

'I really like it.'

That cuts him off and the faintest trace of pink crosses his cheeks.

Embarrassment or pleasure?

'Thanks.'

He flips the folder closed and smiles. Not his polite smile – this smile reaches all the way to his clever, dark eyes, that are the colour of polished oak. Those eyes that have passed me over with cool indifference and blazed at me with impatience before. Today he cannot or will not look away, and the spark in his gaze is neither disgust nor anger.

'Take me for a ride in it sometime, OK?' I say as I smile and give his arm the lightest of squeezes. Then I walk away as if the whole conversation was just my attempt at being polite. As if I didn't really care. Oh, but I saw his face as I released his arm. Blazing red.

He comes to find me when the afternoon shadows lie in charcoal chunks and squares like giant tyre treads over my desk. He stands in the doorway and looks me over, weighing the plus-deltas. Doesn't he know that just by being there he's already sealed his fate?

Might be tonight, or next week, or six months from now. But he's as good as roped and hog-tied. He asks how my last meeting went. And I tell him 'great' and ask what's up. Why is he here? He tries to make up an answer, fumbles over it and gives in. Shrugs. He just came by to say hello.

I throw my head back and laugh and he stares at me, silent and smiling a secret smile as if to suggest he knows something I don't.

Oh, sweetheart, you don't know a thing. Pretend all

you want that this is not what it seems. You came to me. You're already mine.

We have a trip to a remote office. It's no coincidence that we elect to sync up responsibilities at that site on the same week. But he stops in twice at my office to mention that it 'really is a neat coincidence how that worked out'. Well. If it makes him feel better. I've got time for as long as he wants to play this game.

Oh, sweetheart, don't you know the waiting makes it hotter – so much hotter?

Goddamned hot. Desert heat the moment we step through the airport sliding glass doors onto baking-stone concrete and steaming blacktop. Heat that shimmers and moves on the executive taxis and stretch limos and beat-up four-doors crowding the concourse like a living, liquid thing. And the rental car doesn't fit either of us.

Yeah, there's plenty of room. But, by getting into that mulberry-coloured full-size sedan, we leave something else outside. We fit the image suddenly, and in those moments where we're reminded of who we ought to be, how we ought to behave, we don't know what to do.

I look out the window and fiddle with the air vent and my billfold while he adjusts the seat, the steering, turns up the air to an icy blast. And then I bless my carry-on bag as it falls over in the back seat. I lean back to shove it into place and my skirt slides up over the edges of my stockings.

I'm wearing stay-ups. Forget the garters. That strip of perfectly bare skin between French lace and cotton poly-ester promises that there's nothing else. No impediment of buttons or cloth to make fingers pause and fumble. Nothing to slow his speed.

He's turned to look at me, one hand on the steering wheel, one hand on the gear shift. His lips are parted.

Only when he realises a full three slow seconds have gone by and I'm doing nothing but looking at him with my eyebrows raised does he clamp them shut firmly. Refusal.

'Everything OK?' he asks.

I smile. Such control, my gorgeous Nate.

'Just peachy,' I say.

I wriggle back into place and make a token effort at pulling my skirt back down. It's not my fault if I can't get the hem quite back down to my knee – I've got my seatbelt on. I mean, really, how much squirming around can I possibly do in the interests of modesty? But he's got all his attention fixed on the road, not even sparing a glance my way. Iron-clad control. And by the time we hit the freeway he's doing nearly eighty.

I don't know how we get lost. But at some point I look out at the miles of sand and wind-stripped rock stretching out behind the telephone poles on either side of the road and realise we're nowhere near civilisation. I see him glance at the GPS console that confidently lets us know we're fifty miles north of the city. Never mind that we took the southbound freeway from the airport.

With an irritated grumble, he turns the console off.

'Well, this is fun.'

'Is it?' I put my notebook down and turn to him. I stick the end of my pen between my teeth and give him a considering look. 'I don't know about you but I could think of a lot more fun things than being lost in the back of nowhere.'

I tap the pen on my lips in mock thoughtful fashion until he gives in and laughs.

'I wonder what you'd consider fun.' He glances at me from the corner of his eyes and I pretend the question is as innocent as the tone it's delivered in.

'Right about now, a drink. Preferably with alcohol, but we'll take what we can get.'

I point ahead with the pen. The two lanes of the road have narrowed, with packed dust replacing what was paved shoulder ten miles back. Dust billows across the road and the distance shimmers behind a quicksilver curtain of heat, but out of the haze before us rise the ubiquitous white numerals of a gas-station sign.

'And maybe you can ask for directions.'

He gives me a look that could shred leather and I dissolve in laughter. The upholstery of the car seat is rough against the skin of my thighs where my skirt is well above my stockings, and, even on full blast, the air conditioning suddenly seems inadequate. First I think it's a blessing this material doesn't wrinkle much because my skirt is a hopeless crumple. And, second, that if I had my way it would be getting a helluva lot more crumpled right now. The sound of his voice at that moment feels like a hand sliding deftly between skin and cloth.

'Might as well get gas too since . . .'

It's hard as hell to keep up a façade of nonchalance right then, to manage a cool, smart-ass remark. But somehow I do, interrupting him mid-sentence.

'Since you might not be able to find the way back ever?'

We're parked at the single pump in what passes for a paved lot, although the desert is doing its best to reclaim the spot with the relentless scrubbing of sand and wind. A handwritten cardboard sign on the pump proclaims 'CASH/CHECK PAY INSIDE STORE FIRST!' I guess by that that it means the formerly whitewashed building sitting another thirty feet back from the pump and guarded by an ice freezer and a warped-iron bench outside. There's not a soul in sight.

He pauses in the act of getting out of the car and looks back. The pale-blue and white linen of his shirt is pulled tight across his shoulder. I should reach out and stroke the hard curve of muscle underneath, run my fingers up the back of his neck.

'You're asking for it,' he says, with a smile.

'Asking for what?' I want to goad him over that line, make him abandon propriety first.

'It.'

He's already out of the car.

Now it's my turn to feel my face burn. OK, sweetheart, so I underestimated you. You're playing with me too.

But I've got no problem throwing my hand.

Feeling silly, I grin anyway as I exit the car and walk towards the neon lottery sign struggling to make itself seen through a grimy windowpane. It doesn't matter how this plays out. Either way, I still win.

The 'store' is scarcely more than four sagging walls and a roof held together with a wish and a prayer. A rusty bell wrapped around the door handle with a length of wire jangles in fabulous discordance as I enter. At least the inside has the decency to boast a single humming refrigerator crammed into one corner. I head towards it with a nod to the ancient clerk sitting at the counter and half-snoozing over his porno mag.

There are plenty more where his came from under the dirty glass counter top. As I set bottles of wonderfully cold soda down on the counter I look the magazines over and contemplate getting one. Take it back to the car and tell Nate it's reading material for when I'm at the hotel.

I laugh aloud and the clerk wakes up abruptly, sending the magazine slithering off his lap.

It lands on the floor and flips open to reveal a blonde vixen in a fascinating pose involving two pillows, a table and an amazing sense of balance. I wonder if Nate would enjoy me like that, all pink and white lace and diamond-shimmer glossy lips. I can almost feel the pillows yielding to my weight, feel Nate's hands . . .

The clerk grunts and gives me a contemptuous look,

then bends to pick up the magazine with a mumbled apology. Evidently, he's mistaken my riveted fascination with the picture for embarrassment or outrage.

'No. It's OK really,' I mumble back, handing over my credit card. I'm amazed they even have a credit card machine in this place. As I wait the interminable age for the clerk to punch in the numbers with silver-ringed, wrinkled brown fingers, and then another aeon for the charge to authorise, my mind races.

I could ask for directions, but I don't want to know where we are. I don't want a set of clearly defined, helpful instructions on how to get to civilisation at eighty miles an hour. I'm right where I wanted to be: in the middle of nowhere, with him and only a couple thousand pounds of sheet metal and an engine to return us to sanity. When we want to return. If we want to.

I scribble my name on the credit-card slip and pick up the bottles with an absent-minded word of thanks to the clerk. He nods and shuffles away to disappear behind a bead curtain at the back of the store. It's like he's gone offstage intentionally, left me with free reign to do what I will.

Hot air rises up in a wave as I push the door open and, bottles in one hand, clumsily, nervously unbutton the top of my shirt. Two buttons only, just enough and not too much. I shake my hair back out of the way and head for the car – no, I *stalk* my way back to the car.

I've made up my mind. Here. And now.

The nozzle is still in the gas tank and he's leaning against the car looking at the map from the rental company.

He looks up and meets my gaze full on, and his eyebrows lift ever so slightly.

'So I think I know where we are now,' he says.

'Yeah? Well, good,' I reply in a tone that says I don't give a shit.

I step over the pump hose slowly, pausing an extra

half-heartbeat with one leg on either side, straddling the hose. Then I swing the other leg over. The movement puts me less than a foot from his chest. He breathes out slowly, steadily, looking at me with those marvellous eyes.

Dark eyes, dark hair. I notice his shirt sleeves are folded back once, baring his arms almost to the elbows. Damn. Give him a couple days in this desert sun and that golden-toned skin will darken to copper. I picture him: no shirt, jeans, headband, leaning against that cowboy truck of his and watching me just like he's watching me now. Willing me to come hither.

I've opened my own drink on the way to the car and I take a long sip from it now, tilting my head back and letting the condensation drip from the bottle on to the front of my white linen shirt. He makes a soft sound and reaches for the unopened bottle in my left hand. But, before his fingers can touch it, I whisk it from his grasp.

I swallow my own sip and smile, and then lean into him, chest to chest. Reaching behind him, I balance the second bottle on the top of the car, and then inch closer so that this time my legs straddle his. With one hand braced on the car doorframe and my Mary Jane pumps on either side of his loafers, I hold him captive. I bring my bottle to his mouth and brush the plastic edge along his lips.

'Uh-uh.' I pull the bottle back a little. 'Work for it.'

He looks at me and shakes his head, as if to say 'no way is she really doing this'. But his cheeks are flushed with more than the heat, and he obeys. And I get to see just what kind of knowledge prissy, perfect, good-boy Nate really has.

His tongue circles the rim of the bottle where my lips have been just a minute before. He licks each ridge where the cap screws on with the tip. His tongue darts into the mouth of the bottle and moves in sinuous, twisted precision. When he closes his eyes I feel the vibration of his chest-deep moan all the way through the bottle and into my hand. All the way into my skin. I stare in amazed, confused desire at the motion of his lips and his tongue on the clear plastic, and my pulse beats in matching harmony.

I'm still mesmerised, helpless like a charmed snake, when he lifts his mouth from the bottle and turns. When he proceeds to do to my mouth what he's just finished showing me he can. But there's so much more you can do with hot, resilient flesh than with plastic. And I'm a quick learner.

Be careful when you charm a snake. After the spell's over, she's a thousand times more vicious.

When we end that kiss I'm surprised we haven't created enough static electricity to set the pump on fire. But his pretty lips are bruised now, and I know for a fact that the truck wasn't compensating for anything.

Somehow I've managed not to drop the soda bottle through all this. I remember it when his hand closes over mine and he raises the bottle. My fingers slide through his and I let him have it. I've got better things to do with my hands while he's occupied. There's a certain fantasy I've wanted to fulfil for a long, long time.

I unbuckle his belt, and then the buttons on his no-longer perfectly pressed khakis. Smiling, I run my hands along his legs as I sink downwards.

'Oh hell!' he says, half laughing.

'Oh hell, yeah,' I correct him. He's still got the map in his other hand and I grab it, neatly sliding it into place beneath my knees and the rough concrete. It's far from an ideal solution, but then I pull down his khakis and boxers, and I'm totally distracted again. I think I've never seen a man look so utterly at ease with his pants and underwear around his ankles. He sips his soda pop and smiles.

'Don't tell me you're intimidated.'

I snort. 'Intimidated my ass.'

My voice gets softer and my fingers circle his cock, teasing. 'Impressed is more like it. But . . .' I let my tongue flicker along the underside of his length and just over the tip. He sucks in his breath.

'I can more than handle you . . .'

I spiral my tongue down his cock, almost enclosing him with my mouth – but not quite – and I feel his posture change, his body stiffen. I draw back and look up. At the naked, waiting lust in his face, my heart does a double flip. I love seeing that look, knowing it's all me. I close my teeth on the inner muscle at the top of his thigh, slowly, slowly add pressure until he groans aloud – a breathy, pleading, bite-me-harder-babe groan.

'. . . cowboy.'

I love the taste of him, the smell of him, the feel of him all the way into the back of my throat. There's nothing sexier than sucking a gorgeous guy off. The thought that it's nothing you should be doing anyway, that if Grandma saw you she'd faint, that it's damn hard to do on top of everything else, make it the hottest sexual act in the book. In any book.

And here on my knees at a gas-station pump in full view of the road and the whole damned world. With the smell of road dust and gasoline and engine oil in my nose; the hot metal of the car under my palms. With Nate – repressed, corporate, closet-cowboy Nate – moaning my name and fucking my mouth like it's the hottest piece of ass he's ever had. Yeah, this definitely counts as a Category 5 on the F-scale.

I'm torn between wanting to suck him until he comes and the slippery, aching friction between my legs. He makes the decision for me: his fingers tighten in my hair and he pushes me back. I lick my lips and stare at him hungrily, half displeased at having my pleasure taken away, half wild with lust.

'Up.'

I stand and he moves around behind me, sandwiching

my body between his and the car. He lifts my arms and begins to unbutton the rest of my shirt. His breath is like the touch of a brand on my neck, but his hands are unhurried, confident, sensual. He unhooks my bra. I hold my breath. He slides bra and shirt off my shoulders, halfway down my arms. I release my breath and gasp for another as his palms retrace their path up over my skin. By the time his knuckles graze my nipples I'm dizzy.

And still his hands don't stop. Now their path travels down to my long-suffering skirt, raising it, crumpling it delightfully over my hips as he nudges me forward. My breasts brush hot maroon chrome and steel and I gasp and arch, pushing my bare ass right up against his cock.

He stills and I glance over my shoulder, meet eyes full of concern.

'You OK?'

I can't answer, I just nod and plead with my gaze for him to keep going. Impulsively, he kisses my mouth again, softer than before, so soft you'd think we were making love instead of fucking. He circles his left arm around me and pulls my back into the curve of his torso, holding me where he can kiss me to his heart's content. But his other hand is busy between my spread legs. And he kisses me like a lover all the while he fingers me like a whore.

But, when the first sweet, intense bubble of pleasure rises in my clit and courses through every muscle from my hips right down to my toes, I have to tear my mouth away for air. His fingers never stop. And, bereft of my lips, he turns his passion to my neck and my shoulder, his teeth nipping the naked skin. Each bite a tiny, incredible torture.

But it's still not enough. I like big trucks and the bad boys that drive them. Fast and hard. I want all of him, in every way. I want his cock fucking my pussy. Fucking my ass. And damn it that I don't have lube here and now, but two out of three is good enough.

I reach back, struggling to keep my balance with one hand and to move my arm since my shirt is wrapped tight around my elbow. But I find him. I tug the head of his cock forward. And, after a moment's hesitation, a moment where I know prudent, anal-retentive Nate worries about whether this is a good idea or not, he follows my lead. And I know why we're here now, a thousand miles away from the safe confines of our world. He trusts me.

Ready as I am for him, he has to coax me, open me up bit by bit. And, oh hell, no, he wasn't compensating for a goddamned thing. But then he's inside of me, every last inch, and his fingers are tight on my hips as he fucks me. He sighs my name. He snarls it. Harder. And I'm coming again even though my mind is telling me this is insane and I should be far, far past the point of satiation. It tells me I'm going to be sore as hell tomorrow, but I don't fucking care. And then with a final thrust he stills, and I feel his heart pounding like a trip hammer against my shoulder blade.

Once again I can hear the sounds of the wind and the desert, the drone of a prop plane far overhead, the faint whirr of the ice freezer out in front of the store. The sound of his breathing as his head rests on mine. When it steadies at last, he raises himself on his arms, still bracing against the car for support, and I lever myself upright.

Some ingrained sense of prudishness makes me shrug my clothes up over my shoulders and hook my bra. To hell with buttoning the shirt, and my stockings are history. I think I'll just swap the shirt out for a long-sleeved T-shirt from my luggage. It won't take but a look to know the reason for the state of my clothing – or, on second thought, maybe not. I suddenly like the idea of walking into the hotel lobby with Nate Marble and every single stranger who looks at us knowing exactly what we've been doing.

The thought brings a grin to my face and he looks up from belting his pants and grins back. Damp strands of hair fall over his forehead. The starch of his shirt has long given up the ghost and his cheeks are still flushed. That's beauty right there.

'Remind me not to get lost with you any more,' he says.

'Oh?'

'Yeah. I might be too distracted to ever get back.'

I laugh and roll my eyes. 'Don't worry, cowboy, I'll club you over the head and drag you back.'

'Quite the charmer, aren't you?'

He gives me a long, long look.

Finally, he turns and takes the patient nozzle out of the tank, replaces it on the lever. The pump beeps uncertainly for a second or two before spitting out a receipt. I button my shirt halfway, collect the bottles from atop the car and dump them in the bagless trash can beside the pump. Then I strip off my stockings one by one and send them after the bottles.

'All ready?' he asks.

I nod. 'Yup. But Nate . . .?'

He turns in the act of walking around to open my car door and raises his eyebrows. A shadow of uneasiness crosses his face, like a little boy afraid of impending disappointment and trying his best to hide it.

I smile.

'Promise to take me for a ride in your truck.'

The shadow disappears. He smiles and my weary libido can't help but tingle in response. My heart can't help but flutter in anticipation.

'As many rides as you want, gorgeous,' he says.

'Good.' I brush my lips lightly against his as I get into the car and I hear his breath catch.

'And I promise not to let you get lost too often,' I add as he slides into his seat and closes the door. He laughs as he starts the engine.

Stage Four Maddie Mackeown

The girl sat and watched from a chair in the corner. Waiting. Then it happened. The door opened into a rush of light and warmth. The weary group pushed a way inside and the last person shoved the door closed behind them. An atmosphere of relief and dampness spread throughout the room.

'Come in! Come in and rest yourselves, good people.' The eyes of the innkeeper twinkled with a hospitality that was brought to life by the extra business delivered to him by the storm. Thank God for his mercies! His eyes flicked over the newcomers and coins rolled in plentiful expectation as he did an amazingly quick calculation that would impress the very chancellor himself.

'There, now, that's right. Get warm by the fire. My, my! What dreadful weather. Not good for travelling – but good for taking advantage of my humble hostelry. Sit down; rest easy and we'll bring you food and drink. Abby, where are you? Come on, girl, look lively! There's customers here need serving.'

The landlord bustled and prattled and fussed and fidgeted to the increasing inattention of the group to whom he spoke.

The tall man who huddled into his coat blatantly turned away from the fuss, detaching himself from the group. He stood near to the door in obvious refusal of the suggested comforts, removing his cloak to shake it free of clinging raindrops, while others were more inclined to take up the landlord's offer.

Drinks and food were duly ordered and the atmosphere began to relax at last while the shutters rattled as the rain was swept against them by the fierceness of the wind, and wooden beams were shrouded in smoke that had been puffed back down the chimney. People gathered close to the fire in a miasma of steaming garments as leaping flames began to chase out the chill, and the chattering of teeth eventually stopped. Voices began to bewail their sorry plight, as travellers will tend to do.

And, while they steamed and grumbled and shivered, nibbled and sipped, the girl sat alone in serene exclusion while she observed the noisy intrusion.

The oily landlord approached again, his darting eyes continually weighing up the situation to seek its advantage. 'Well, now, good people, can I be of any further assistance to you? It's terrible out there. Trust me, there'll be no end to it for a while yet. The stage continues as it must but there's a room here if you'd rather see the night out snug. I know for a fact that there'll be empty seats on the coaches tomorrow.'

Two of the company took up the suggestion as comfort tipped the scales against endurance. One traveller had already disappeared into the mist and it was journey's end for another two. So only the fate of the tall man near the door remained.

He spoke, his voice a deep richness that defied challenge. 'A tempting offer but I have business that cannot wait. I'll therefore leave with the coach.' He was already in the process of wrapping up again for the last stage of the journey. 'I see that I face the elements single-handed.'

'No, sir, you are mistaken, for I too have business.'

All eyes turned in surprise to the shadowy corner where wisps of smoke drifted around the girl who now stood, cloaked and ready for departure. She was slight and pale beneath a torrent of dark curls, her calm timidity and softness completely at odds with the roughness of the night.

The door opened and a piece of storm found its way

inside. A voice shouted, 'Stage ready to leave!' and the door was banged shut.

The girl crossed the room and many eyes followed her.

'My dear, it's wicked out there!' The kindly voice of a matronly body sought to protect the girl, who looked as if she might be wafted away by a single puff of the raging wind.

The girl simply smiled. 'I think that the bark is worse than the bite.' She pulled her hood well over and slipped one hand deeper into her muff, ready to do battle. She exuded an air of brave fragility.

The woman stepped nearer and placed a hand on the muff. 'Are you unaccompanied?' she asked.

The girl looked down at the touch and stepped back so the woman's hand slipped off. 'My maid is indisposed.' Well, dead, actually. 'But my guardian is to meet me at the next stop,' she lied sweetly.

'Allow me; take my arm,' said the man as the girl reached for the door handle. 'Never fear, madam.' He regarded the bustling body of concern. 'I'll see her safely into the coach.' He smiled down at the shaded face within the hood. 'I would not like you to be hurt.'

As if, she thought. 'Thank you, sir.' She delicately accepted his offer and they departed.

The breath of the storm gusted against them, buffeting their bodies as they leaned into its ferocity. The girl gripped on to the arm for support and it helped to steady her a little for the wind was certainly strong. She breathed in some of its force, feeling an energy surge up within her. She was ready for the challenge. After all the years of preparation, the time was right.

Billowing cloaks caught darts of rain as they hurried across slippery mud. He gripped the rim of his hat in an attempt to stop it from flying off into oblivion and she held on to her hood. It was quite a feat to stay upright but the man was well matched to the powerful gust. He shouted something close to her ear but she shook her head, unable to make out what he said as his words were carried away on the wind.

Across the courtyard the coach loomed out of the dusk, an early darkness brought on by the heavy cloud. A fork of lightning streaked across the sky and they both looked up, which was a mistake considering the puddles that needed to be dodged. The rumble of thunder followed a few seconds later, but sounded quite distant. Maybe the storm was beginning to die.

A thickly clad coachman huddled in readiness, turning to see when his passengers were safely aboard, while a groom was making final checks on luggage security.

The man held the door for the girl, but, as she climbed on to the step her foot slipped and she stumbled. Her hand flew out sideways in an attempt to regain balance and she struck him in the chest, meeting tough resilience. He grasped her arm.

Merde! she thought as a pain shot through her ankle. That's all I need.

She managed to pull herself up into the coach and he climbed in after her, nimbly efficient. The groom lifted the step in before slamming the door after them, and they were enclosed in the gloomy dampness.

'Stage-ho!' came the muffled call as fresh horses pranced into action. Wheels slithered, then gripped. The coach lurched forward and a dull thudding could be heard as hooves sank into sodden ground. The inn with its cheerful safety was soon left behind as the miles passed beneath them.

The man cleared his throat, 'Well, the sooner this miserable day finishes, the better. At least our driver appears to know his road.'

'Yes. He seems very skilful at dodging the mire, but then so are many.'

She peered at him through the gloom, feeling his gaze rather than seeing it. What an odd thing to say out of the blue just like that. She knew he'd be intrigued by the strange comment, but he turned away, making no further attempt at conversation.

Raindrops splashed on the windowpanes to mix with spattered mud from hoof and wheel. The trees by the wayside swayed in a wild storm dance, catching the wind and throwing it off again as golden leaves shivered to the ground. Then they too were left behind as the coach passed on to the moors.

Within the trapped space they sat in silence opposite to each other. She risked a glance in his direction. He was looking out of the window. She wondered why, since it was difficult to see much at all. Maybe he was giving her a few minutes of personal space in which to become settled.

She took a deep breath and closed her eyes. She was grateful for the bad weather that had thrown them into this fortunate seclusion. An unexpected bonus. She could not possibly have planned for that. All was going well as far as meeting was concerned but she needed to prepare herself mentally before she could take this any further.

She had thought about this man for nine years, throwing out childhood memories in place of her growing determination to catch up with him again. She had planned and succeeded to this point in time, only to be disturbed by unforeseen feelings.

It had been easy to select him from the group when the travellers came into the inn where she was waiting. His commanding height had been instantly recognisable. He hadn't changed much at all except that his beauty had aged in a dignified and striking manner. A ruthless strength simmered there beneath a calm poise, sending out an air of reassuring elegance and integrity.

She had sensed it all like a slap across the face.

What was worse was that she had slipped so easily into his protection when she'd felt his hands upon her. It was the warm and comfortable response of the trusting child. Yet here she was, a grown woman with dark purpose in her mind.

She had to shake off this paradox.

She risked another furtive glance and was shocked to find his eyes on her. A tingle crept along her spine. Her eyes flicked away and then back to his. He continued to look at her and she was unnerved by this audacity. Her skin prickled and the darkness bubbled up again within her. Both hands slipped deeper into her muff and she found a focus.

She deliberately moved her foot in search of pain to fuel her intentions but she was surprised by its severity. She gave an involuntary cry and tears welled in her eyes. *Don't let this happen! I must not lose control. I must not.*

He heard and saw the cry. 'What is it? Are you all right?'

His voice showed spontaneous concern and this upset her even more. She was losing it at the final stake. How dare he be so kind! It wasn't supposed to be like this. And yet in that moment she knew her self-deception, for she remembered at once his many kindnesses. She stared at him in perplexity.

'It's just my ankle. I twisted it when I slipped on the step.'

'Can I help at all?'

'Thank you but I doubt it. If I rest, it should be better by the end of the journey.'

'Forgive me, but that's probably not the case. The ankle might swell and then it'll be worse, I think, not better.' He gave her time to consider this. 'Perhaps you should remove your boot, or at least loosen it.'

He was right of course. She had suddenly found herself at a disadvantage. Pain has a certain tendency to divert one's concentration. *Merde encore!* What should she do? Quick thinking provided an answer. She would play on vulnerability. Pictures unfolded in her mind. Yes, she would attack him from a position of apparent weakness.

'That's what I should do. You're probably right.' A silence hung between them in the gloomy air. 'Excuse me.'

She made as if to bend towards her foot.

'Please, let me help.'

She considered the mucky boot. If the mud is still wet, which it's bound to be, it'll ruin his trousers. She smiled at the thought. Oh, well, this is unfortunate.

She sat back and he slid to the edge of his seat, reaching down to place a hand on her skirt. He removed his hat and put it on the seat next to him. He felt for her calf and at his firm touch she caught her lower lip with her teeth. He lifted her leg carefully and she allowed her knee to bend.

Slowly, she placed the raised foot on his thigh. A frisson sparked in the damp air.

'Forgive me if I hurt you.' His speech was direct but concerned, his accent skilfully erased. She watched him from beneath lowered lids as he took off his gloves and touched the falling fabric of her skirt. He briefly looked into her eyes – she noticed the whiteness in the dull light – and she pulled up the hem of the skirt.

His fingers pulled deftly at the buttons and her boot was soon loosened. Did he realise that he was handling dangerous material? He felt the ankle with surprising gentleness. No, actually, his gentleness didn't surprise her because she knew it of old. However, she winced in pain at the slight pressure.

'It's already quite swollen,' he said.

'Then remove the boot, but please be careful, monsieur.' His head jerked up. 'It hurts badly.'

He paused then continued to undo the buttons. She lifted the skirt a little higher. Gripping the heel of the boot, he slid his other hand up a little.

'Are you ready?'

She nodded. 'Yes.'

'How did you know that I am French?'

'I know many things about you.' Her nerves tingled and her gloveless fingers moved inside the muff.

He slid the boot smoothly from her foot with very little discomfort to her, a neat manoeuvre despite the jogging of the carriage.

'Who are you?'

She told him her name. He could only just hear the reply.

The storm seemed to be gathering a momentum as rain lashed the windows. She was taut with confrontation, wound up like a coiled spring.

He raised his eyes to hers and they stared at each other through the safety of poor light, pulses racing. The relevance of her name had registered immediately.

She suspected that already some realisation was clicking into place in his agile brain; that there was no lawyer with urgent business to meet him at the end of his journey; that this was no chance encounter and that he was facing a ghost from his past. But how did it all affect him?

Shifting further forward on his seat, he reached a hand to each side of her face and pushed back the hood of her cloak. Neither of them dared to move for long moments of time. Thoughts reeled and swirled in the space between them. Then, with soft fingertips, he smoothed a loose strand of hair and trailed gently across her cheek, over her mouth and down her chin.

She held herself stiff with alertness, tense with the challenge of her identity. She'd expected a rush of satisfaction to flood like a whitewash through her body, but it didn't happen. Instead, there was confusion as emotions tumbled in turmoil and she struggled to overcome them, to try to grasp some order from the muddle.

His fingers under her chin lifted her face into what little light there was. She looked at him steadily while he searched her face in the dimness. It was an inscrutable gaze. She realised that she'd been holding her breath and inhaled slowly and deeply, feeling a creeping heat despite the coolness of the day.

He was the first to break the silence. 'Sophie, little Sophie.'

After a moment or two longer, he dropped his hands. Nothing. Silence again. Her nerves stretched tighter like a cocked trigger. She felt his fingers at the sole of her stockinged foot as they began a firm, rhythmic massage. A tease of pleasure shot up her leg.

'I wondered what had happened to you in the madness. It was a crazy time. We were all caught up, trapped inside a ruthless political game.'

'No game. The Revolution was hardly that.' She paused to keep her voice even. 'My father was innocent. You knew, and yet you betrayed him.' It felt so good to be saying those words to this man. My father was innocent! It should be shouted, screamed aloud from the rooftops. You betrayed him!

But who would listen?

He was apparently calm and untroubled but, if the muted light had allowed, she would have seen the pain in his face. 'There were many innocents. But in the end it was everyone for himself in a bid for survival.' He shrugged and shook his head. There were no sufficient words. 'Each to his own. I was lucky.'

'You betrayed him and left him to his death!' She watched as she forced his mind back to those terrible times. Her father had been more than a business partner to this man, much more. He had been his mentor and friend, had always welcomed him into their home, especially after her mother had died.

'Let me tell you what happened. Please.' He touched a finger to her lips to forestall her as she tensed and opened her mouth to speak. 'Will you hear me out?'

She closed her lips, pulling away from his touch and reluctantly quelling the passion within. She nodded tersely. His relentless fingers at her foot continued and soothed her while she listened. She concentrated and struggled to superimpose his words on her preconceived ideas.

No! It all made sense, what he said: people, times and places, long-ago events, clicking together like a puzzle solved. No! But was it fabrication or fact? How could she sieve the truth from all her findings and now his rendering? Thoughts flitted, seemingly at random, through her mind.

But, unexpectedly, his voice calmed her. It also brought a rush of feelings from the past about this man with whom she had been infatuated, a god knocked from his pedestal. She recognised anew the power of his personality.

Her confusion split into a path of choices.

She had seen this whole process in stages, from the terrible events at the beginning, to a process of relentless research over the years and then on to planning his downfall. She had set up this encounter and had imagined the final stage of straightforward revenge.

But now? In all her thoughts she had not allowed for the substance of the real man. Hatred seemed to drain away from her. Maybe physical pain had stolen it.

In the Paris underworld it hadn't been easy to survive, yet she had managed exactly that, being passed along a line, from person to person en route to England and escape. She had been forced into an independence that came too soon. The young Sophie had been resilient and had not long remained an innocent.

She realised that he had stopped talking and was watching her. A single tear trickled down her cheek, unnoticed in the darkness. He was being gentle with her injury and gentle with her emotions, even though his words clearly stated facts that were so hard for her to hear. Maybe he understood.

'I don't...' Her words trailed away.

'We were all pawns, Sophie – little people in a vast happening.'

Little? You were huge to me. A giant magnet.

'We just have to let the nightmares slip into the past.' He paused to allow a silence in which swirling thoughts could settle. 'At least, let's sort out your ankle first.'

She felt his smile. His fingers traced a path up to her knee and then down a different path to the swelling. Her foot jerked in reaction to his touch.

'We should bind the ankle to hold it in a comfortable position and give it support.' She nodded and he continued, soothing her with his voice and his attention. An image flashed before her of his hands on a skittish colt, stroking and coaxing it into submission. 'We need something to bind it with, some sort of bandage.' He waited for her to speak.

She shook her head as if coming out of a daze, causing her curls to tremble charmingly around her face. She lifted her skirt slightly. 'We could tear a strip from my petticoat.'

She was amazed. Had she really said 'we'? Here she was chatting to this man as if nothing untoward had happened between them. But it helped at this moment to concentrate on something trivial and ordinary, something inconsequential.

'Your stocking might be better.'

Her eyebrows lifted in surprise but he would not see that. Suddenly, she wanted to feel his hands on her again. She recalled the young man that he'd been and the excitement on seeing him that had stirred in her, little Sophie on the verge of womanhood. Why had she forgotten? She remembered the smell of him and the touch of... Her eyes opened wide in recollection as abandoned memories were retrieved from hidden depths.

'Yes,' she said. Another solitary tear escaped.

He lifted her skirt to her knees and she lifted it higher still. The tension in the thickly moist air could almost be sliced. His fingers went to her garter and slid it up on to the skin of her thigh. He took hold of the stocking top and rolled it down and stretched it with care over the offending ankle.

She winced. 'Sorry,' he said.

He was in control and it felt so good to be mastered by him.

Her reeling emotions had steadied into a knot of pressure deep in her belly. She watched as he held the foot firmly in position and began to wrap the stocking around it, her eyes drawn to his busy fingers. She watched his face and scanned it in the dimness, searching for the man whom she had lusted after during girlish dreams. She now saw its mature version at her feet and yearned for the promise that had been so abruptly snatched from her. She wanted him still and she gasped as this awareness shocked through her.

He stopped, thinking that he was hurting her as he tucked in the end of the bandage. He looked up, knowing her desire, and could no longer ignore the subtle gleam of naked flesh when she inched her skirt even higher. He slipped from the seat to kneel before her and pressed his lips to the skin above the bandage.

Her body thrilled in its response.

Closing her eyes, she threw back her head until it hit the support behind and she flung her hands out to each side of her.

She slid further across the seat towards him and squirmed as his mouth worked its way inexorably upwards. As it reached mid-thigh she opened her eyes and looked down at the head that moved there. She buried her fingers in the sleek thickness of his hair and pressed his face more closely to her skin. She felt his teeth bite hard, the pain quickening her desire. She yelped and yanked his head upwards.

He jerked upright, his eyes locking on to hers. 'Sophie,' he whispered, 'my little Sophie.'

She was breathing fast. He caught the gleam of a tear streak and followed its path along her cheek. Leaning close, he moved against her and slowly licked the tear away. She caught her breath, wanting to cry out her sadness but stopping herself from doing so. His lips pressed roughly on to hers and she felt fingers touch high up between her thighs. She gasped beneath his mouth, tasting him, and flicked her tongue insistently against his, wanting it elsewhere.

She pulled at his hair and his head lowered once more to between her thighs. His fingers hardly fumbled as they moved her clothing aside to uncover her nakedness. He spread her open. His tongue found its mark and began to lick delightfully. Her breath came shorter as his mouth worked with greater insistence. He reached to pull at the other stocking, ripping it down while yet he sucked her. She kicked her other foot on to the seat opposite as she pushed against him. He pulled her thighs close so that he was surrounded by her, and dug his nails into her flesh.

She cried out, welcoming more pain, and turned her twisted ankle to enhance it. The bandage hung loose The momentum was building. She rocked her hips to rub herself against his mouth, pulling at his hair while he pressed in to make her come.

Turbulence climbed as the anger of the storm crashed around them in another flashing streak of light. Orgasm hit as brightness flared, suddenly intrusive, suddenly intense. Tears overspilled and she screamed his name. It was lost to all but him in the rumble of thunder. He raised his head and grabbed her wrists to ward off her nails, which went for his face. He pinned her arms down and pressed his body on to hers while she struggled beneath him and sobbed uncontrollably.

Gradually the raging calmed and he released her. He

pulled down her skirt and heaved himself up on to the seat beside her, touching shoulder to shoulder, with no words between them.

She felt stunned, exhausted and suddenly empty. Her plans were shattered. She entered a shadowland of raw emotion where nothing was clearly defined any more.

Her breathing slowed and she let her head rest on his shoulder. She was aware of the arrhythmic rise and fall of his chest as he struggled to remain in control. His fingers found hers and he took them in a loose grip. The warmth of his hand calmed her further. She felt protected, easy in his company and his dominance.

He shifted his arm to hold her, drawing his cloak over them both, and they snuggled into a recaptured intimacy. She breathed in their body warmth, turning to lay her head on his chest, and, as her hand moved across his body, she felt his erection. She took her hand away but he caught it and laid it on his hardness.

She wanted to finger him, to take him into her mouth, to take him to wild places under her lead. She slipped her other hand back into the muff, which lay crumpled between them, and felt for the cold hardness that was hidden there.

As she felt him beneath her fingers, hazy images flickered through her mind, of her mouth full of him and her loosened hair trailing over his nakedness. She wanted to undress while he watched and bend across his knees to be fondled. She saw him rearing up between her thighs and pushing into her body, which opened to his thrust.

It was tempting. It was exciting. Was that what she now wanted?

From inside a relationship it could be possible to decipher the truth. But maybe truth was no longer an imperative. Maybe its comprehension could never be total.

She hovered in a juxtaposed world of light and dark,

lost and found, love and hate, bouncing about in a shaky reality that had little to do with the jostling roughness of the ride.

Her fingers stroked the barrel of the small pistol that lay within the muff and she knew that she could be seconds away from revenge.

Her body started to tremble all over. He held her more tightly.

Something began to emerge from the confusion. A decision sparked and grew and her fingers began to move.

Outside, the storm was finally abating. The cloud cover cleared sufficiently at last so that some remaining daylight was able to make its way through, piercing the gloom and suffusing it with a softening glow. A final flash of lightning flew across the heavens to be followed moments later by a single crack of distant thunder.

Inside, the travellers headed onwards to their journey's end.

CC and Her Riding Machine
A Colorado Woman

Seven miles of red dirt and sagebrush south of the Colorado River, sex-laden moans drifted skyward. Eager bodies met with the intensity of flash floods and crackling thunder. Anonymous fate beckoned and there was no way either of them could not make love that day beside the cascading wall of water.

Christmas Candy Rider preferred to use her initials rather than the name her hippy-skippy parents dreamed up the morning of her birth. CC loved them; she just couldn't wrap her mind around their lifestyle and breathed a sigh of relief the day she left the rustic ski town in the Rocky Mountains for college in the city.

Early on the first morning of the spring break in her senior year, she packed her saddlebags and donned butter-soft riding leathers. The university in Los Angeles sent a preliminary approval for her application for graduate study in theatre. They scheduled an interview and an audition four days from now. The road trip signalled a transition: from practising her self-choreographed tap-dance routine to performing it for solid stakes.

Secure in knowing costume, music – and her laptop rested inside padded waterproof bags inside concha-studded saddlebags – she wriggled into the form-fitting leather jacket. Various zipper pockets held her cell phone, a pack of American Spirit cigarettes and a Zippo butane lighter. A sterling-silver chain connected her snakeskin wallet to a belt, cinching equally form-fitting pants below her exquisite bellybutton set into rock-hard abdomen muscles.

Hyped and expectant, CC lingered in the driveway of the condominium she rented with two other students. Dressed in fleece sweats and sleep crusting their eyes, they wished her farewell. After vision-checking the 350 Honda one last time, she bent forward and wrapped waist-length, strawberry-blonde hair in a messy bun. With one hand, she reached for the silver helmet with a black faceplate hanging on the handlebars and fitted it over her head.

'I don't understand,' the newest roommate whined, 'why you don't take your car. Driving a motorcycle to California is so-o-o dangerous.'

Ignoring the youngest, and the most ignorant, roomy that ever lived and actually enrolled in college, CC hugged them goodbye. Green eyes twinkled. 'See you in a week,' she said. 'Don't do anything I wouldn't do.' She winked, fastened the chinstrap, and smoothed on gloves that fitted like second skin.

'Break a leg,' the other roomy, her best friend, quipped in theatre language. 'Your routine bangs – accept the roses!' She slapped CC's butt and added, 'I'm trusting you to deliver that precious ass of yours back in one piece.'

Looking like something from a computer-simulated action scene, the heroine balanced on her left, black-heeled, steel-toed boot and swung her right leg up, out and over the rear tyre. She shifted the weight of the powerful machine, disengaged the kickstand and snuggled her 'precious ass' into the custom seat.

Then came the sequence she cherished – flick the key and, simultaneously, throttle and clutch the engine to life. Custom headers purred like a kitten and promised to roar like a lion when pressed. Sweet. Pale-pink glossed lips spread into a smile. 'It's you and me, baby,' she cooed. 'Let's see what we can do.'

CC's dad had encouraged her inclination for speed and

provided training on dirt bikes, quads and snowmobiles. High-altitude, subzero temperatures bred boredom and she whiled away many hours in their insulated, heated garage. During high school they rebuilt the Honda – her first and only true love. Part of her psyche, her persona and her self eclipsed when inclement weather forced her to drive her Toyota station wagon.

Astride the bike that morning, she skirted the foothills and reached the interstate west of the city. Eyes straight ahead and a song in her head, she relished the freedom of the open road. Right wrist flexed, left hand played out, and she accelerated on to the ramp.

Ah, she sighed, a blissful divided highway – sans stoplights and oncoming traffic with stupid dickheads turning left without warning.

Crouched like a racer defying wind flow, she banked curves and wound to the top of Vail Pass. Speed exhilarated her thoughts. Heat between her legs fuelled eroticism. Like the time after a Green Day concert, when she motored her love out of the parking lot. At the turning lane, the ultra-cool dude she met earlier in the evening revved beside her – on a Softail.

The light turned green; two riders burned pavement and negotiated one-way labyrinths into the seething, pulsing energy of lower downtown. A hundredth of a second before the next light turned, CC pulled the Honda's front wheel a foot off the ground. As soon as it touched down, she cut left and sped under a viaduct. He countered the daredevil trick, accelerated and moved in front.

Their cat-and-mouse game ended in a full stop in front of a club flanked by a string of bikes angled in an unmasked display of machismo. An intoxicating rhythm-and-blues band and a crowded dance floor absorbed the riders. They danced low and they danced dirty.

Dawn rose on two bikes parked in the driveway of her

condo. Panties joined jockeys in the deepest folds of sheets at the end of her bed. She straddled him high and he indulged her succulent, wanting pussy. Parts fitted like a manifold to head. Sweat mingled like lubricated, precision pistons in bored cylinders.

They did it again, drank brandy-laced coffee, and did it again. After saying goodbye, they never saw each other again. It wasn't a personal thing – just the kind of thing that happened when the heat of a bike ignited loins. Burning desires must be satisfied and safe anonymity works.

At two hundred and fifty trip miles, steep granite canyons laced with pine trees and budding aspens downsized into white limestone cliffs bordering the Colorado River flowing to the Baja. CC throttled down and exited the highway into the parking lot of a State Park on the river. She lit an American Spirit, wished it were a joint, and scrolled through her cell directory.

Just around the bend lay a city too small for her tastes – but she promised her cousin she'd visit. 'Katrina,' she said, 'what's up?'

'I'm cooking tofu rice balls with tamari sauce,' said the chirpy voice that duplicated their twin mothers. 'When will you arrive? The children and I prepared the guest room specially for you.'

Blue cigarette smoke lingered in the air and CC inhaled. 'Thanks for the invite,' she drawled. 'I made reservations at the Motor Inn. How about we meet up later?'

Sleeping over in a suburbia house with two kids, two dogs and a kitchen full of health food made her nervous. CC ate fast food – preferably microwaved. Tofu and rice slugged her system. Starbucks, doughnut gems, reefers and a bit of ma huang made her complete. End of story.

'What a coincidence,' Katrina exclaimed. 'Benny and I

are going to the Motor Inn after dinner. He's throwing a *bon voyage* party for his buddy on military leave. You'll like him.'

Doubt it, CC thought. A night of partying did not coincide with her plan to reach Las Vegas – a long ride. 'Call my cell and leave a message for the time,' she said. 'Got to go, my signal's futzing.'

It wasn't. The mobile connection displayed a robust five bars. She just couldn't hold a conversation with a granola-housewife cousin – let alone her husband, whose idea of a good time was watching *Seinfeld* reruns. How they ever got together was beyond her realm of imagination.

Meanwhile, a rugged man with more than a shadow of beard growth sat in a booth in the bar of the Motor Inn. It was one of those motels boasting a sport bar with tinted windows that faced the frontage road. The after-noon cocktail waitress, who was probably pretty in high school, batted mascara-overloaded eyelashes.

'Hey, handsome,' she trilled, and cocked a hand on her hip. 'What's your pleasure?'

'Bring me another Scotch and a Coors draft,' he said from under the brim of a baseball cap. Unblinking violet irises surrounding pitch-black pupils admired a Honda rolling to a neat stop under the awning. The rebuilt machine was lean and mean and fitted for someone who defied death on a daily basis. Nice, he thought, but the dude's heels are too high for riding.

The lithe figure dismounted, unsnapped the chin-strap, and pulled off the helmet. Approximately a ton of strawberry-blonde curls spilled around her shoulders and she strode into the lobby. The man with a beer in his hand stared. Room card clenched between her teeth, she re-emerged, engaged the bike and vanished around the corner of the stucco-covered rooms.

* * *

The Motor Inn offered an outdoor pool and hot tub. Tight, cramped muscles needed both, and CC's skin screamed for a bronze not sprayed or baked in a claustrophobic booth – a real tan under real sun. She also needed to think positive and think winner. Auditions require the extra mile.

The ground floor smoking room faced west. She hauled in her gear and straightaway packed a small brass pipe, lit up, and flipped on MTV. Gyrating to the strains of Joss Stone's 'Dirty Man', she yanked the black boots off her feet and wriggled out of the leathers. Dust caked the outside of the riding attire and sweat damped the inside. Underneath she wore cotton boy-shorts and a cotton cami.

A quick shower washed dirt and sweat from her hair and body. She hung the cotton undies on a towel rack and slid into a tangerine-coloured, string-tied thong bikini. Towel wrapped low, she strolled to the delightfully deserted courtyard and deposited sunglasses, reading material and towel on an umbrella table.

Salmon-polished toes grasped the diving board and tested the spring load. Satisfied and confident, the woman with the dancer's body arched into the pool. A few laps in fake-blue water later, she climbed the ladder on to the tiled patio.

Refreshed, and arranged on a lounge chair in the direct line of the sun, she cracked open a downloaded copy of the university's *Guide for Graduate Interviews*. Behind closed eyelids, she conceptualised intelligent and compelling answers to the questions listed under her area of study.

A voice intruded. 'Buy you a cocktail?'

CC's sunglasses slid down her nose and she looked up. 'Huh?' she murmured, and repositioned the shades.

A hulking figure blocked the sun, broke her concentration and generally pissed her off. 'A drink, a cold one?' he reiterated.

Head level with baggy surfer shorts, CC thanked the inventor of dark lenses. Her line of vision rose higher and she stifled a laugh at the ridiculous tropical shirt with wide lapels.

An amiable smile displayed white teeth. In spite of the ball cap jammed on his head, she noticed he needed a haircut – and a shave would help. 'No, thanks,' she answered, and resumed reading.

He, too, hid behind dark lenses. 'Humour me, babe,' he persisted, and eased his bulk into a plastic chair. She heard him pick up the poolside telephone and make a request. 'Two margaritas and an order of chips.'

'Seriously, *babe*,' she insisted, 'I'm not interested.'

He leaned into his spine and stretched his legs. 'That's quite the bike you rode in on,' he said with an admiring grin, and cracked his knuckles.

Before CC had time to gather her wits, the waitress wearing pants too tight in the wrong places delivered frosted drinks with straws. He flipped a twenty-dollar bill on the tray. 'Keep the change,' he said. She scowled, tossed ratted hair over her shoulder, and huffed out of the patio.

Eyes behind sunglasses met. CC sipped the lime-and-tequila drink. 'Find it difficult,' she taunted, 'to conceptualise a woman who handles both power and control?'

Robust laughter filled the still afternoon air and the man turned on the charm. 'When you wheeled in and I saw your boots, I seriously thought you were a gay dude.'

'I ride a machine in a style you're not privy to – get lost.'

'No call for rudeness,' he said. 'I get the drift. Enjoy the drink – and chips.'

'Thank you and good riddance,' she muttered, and absent-mindedly reached for a handful. The hunk with the disgusting attitude exited stage left – in the direction of the cocktail lounge.

* * *

Ponytail, cargo crops, a tissue tee and flip-flops comprised an adequate costume for an evening with no agenda, in particular, a hangover from Benny's gung-ho stint. A tinny rendition of the aria from *Cats* sounded. CC flipped open her cell. 'We're here!' chirped perfect, right-on-time Katrina. 'Come join us.'

Strolling pastel-washed hallways of numbered doors, CC pondered the possibility that her cousin ingested a homeopathic version of Prozac. Inside the lounge, her pupils adjusting to the dimness, a familiar voice called her name. 'Over here,' Benny yelled.

The throng of partiers obviously started imbibing much earlier. Perfect, straight-as-ever Katrina scooted and made space for her in the booth. 'Oh, you look so cute. How do you do it?'

'Hey, meet Katrina's cousin,' Benny said, and slapped the shoulder of a man flirting with the waitress whose tank top revealed sagging tits. 'CC, meet Roger.'

Shit, she thought, the player from the pool that undressed me with his mind – and the same slut who served us margaritas. No wonder she crusted.

The man spun in CC's direction. Deep violet eyes rimmed in black lashes made contact with emerald-green stamped with 'not interested' in neon letters. He looked her up and down. 'Fancy handle for a babe who controls three-hundred-fifty cubic centimetres of power,' he drawled. 'Or, should I say, "three-hundred-sixty degrees of control"?'

Hard, cold instincts surged. Spar. CC rose to her feet and leaned close to his ear – so close, in fact, her breath tickled. 'May your dick blow disease,' she whispered.

Katrina yanked her into a sitting position by the sash of her cargo pants. 'Don't take him serious. He's Benny's friend and he's drunk.'

'He's a jerk.' CC endured the festivities by studying character types. She prayed to the gods and goddesses above to never land a role as a flighty homemaker. She thanked them she'd never have to play the role of a testosterone-pumped military man.

Roger swaggered and reciprocated the cocktail slut's flirts. CC begged off early. 'Hon, do be careful on that motorcycle,' admonished perfect Katrina, sipping her umpteenth cranberry and club soda. 'Contrary to popular belief, you are not invincible.'

'Yes, mother.'

Perfect Katrina slipped, and she sniped. 'Pretty is as pretty says. Oh, I almost forgot.' She reached under the table. 'Here. I made a sandwich for your trip – vegetarian and complete protein.'

Weather dawned wet and the cotton undies failed to dry. What the fuck! CC thought. She tied on the bikini and stuffed the damp delicates in a side pocket of a saddlebag. Thinking positive, she braided her hair and prepared her gear for the long ride.

Rain drizzled and she checked out. 'Shit!' she murmured under her breath and wheeled the bike into the Conoco station adjacent to the motel. A black, Silverado King Cab truck hogged the pump.

Still wearing the baggy surfer shorts but with a hoody added and an unlit cigar hanging out of his mouth, Roger grinned. 'Shit!' she said loud enough for him to hear.

'Morning,' he said. 'Bad idea to ride in the rain – hydroplaning sucks.'

'Passing squall,' she replied. 'I don't need four tons of Detroit steel wrapped around me to feel virile.'

'Buy you a cup of coffee,' he said, and sauntered into the convenience store built around cash registers. CC rolled the bike under the awning, lifted her leg over the seat and pivoted on two-inch, black-heeled, steel-toed boots. Braid dangling down her back and wispy tendrils curling around her face like an angel's, she strode through the doors.

Styrofoam cups and chocolate-chip cookies balanced in

his hands, Roger claimed a window table and indicated for her to join him. A television set mounted on the wall played the weather channel. Prognosis dismal. 'What say we tie that bike in the back of my truck and I drive you down the highway?'

'And, how do you propose to load a bike into the bed of your truck?' she asked with a pained expression of superiority and intelligence.

'Two-by-six-by-eights kept in the back for a ramp for such occasions. I ride a Harley myself.'

'When you're not slutting with barmaids or playing soldier?' she snapped, and emptied six Amaretto creamers and as many sugar packets into her cup. 'Or are you good enough to do both at the same time?'

'Give me break,' he said with a pleading smile, and added the same amount of sweetness to his cup of coffee. He nodded towards the television. 'It's bound to get wetter.'

CC gulped the doctored brew and stuffed the cookie in a zipper pocket. 'Thanks for breakfast. The road's calling.' She pushed the Honda to the pumps and gassed up. Steady torrents of water poured from the corrugated awning, filled the dipped entrance to the frontage road and formed a large muddy pool.

Roger backed the King Cab alongside of her, rolled down the window and winked. 'Please,' he said.

A polite word, she thought. Didn't know it existed in a vocabulary of one-syllable grunts. 'OK,' she conceded. 'Just until the rain lifts.'

Wrangling a road bike into the bed of a truck requires muscles and team effort. CC pulled her weight and double-checked every tie-down. Dripping, she wedged her saddlebags in back of the seat, swung into the truck and dropped her helmet on the seat between them. It was too dark for sunglasses.

Wipers on high speed, Roger eased the truck through the potholes to the frontage road and turned on to the onramp. Traffic on the interstate was nonexistent and country music blared from a local radio station. 'Got any decent CDs?' she yelled. He handed her a flip case. One by one, she examined the music labels and nodded. 'Decent. I'm impressed.'

Miles spewed and CC stared out the window. Lightning flashed, thunder rumbled and rain drenched the ever-thirsting desert. The blessed event usurped expectations of a flawless ride. She yearned for the thrill of a throbbing engine and an eternity of speed.

Bored silly, she hummed along with the music. Wipers beat time to sideways rain. They reached the place where the interstate crossed a state highway. 'Mind if I take a southern route?' Roger asked. 'There's a chance we can get below this storm system.' CC shrugged.

His strategy worked. An hour later, the two-lane high-way emerged from cloud cover. Sunlight nearly blinded them. An endless vista of red dirt dotted with cactus and sagebrush surrounded them in all directions. 'Talk to me,' he said simply.

'Stop,' she said, and prepared to bolt. 'I'll unload my bike.'

He slowed and geared down on to the shoulder. 'Truce?' he asked. Tentative fingers reached across the helmet and touched the zipper of her cuff. 'If you can spare the time,' he continued in a strangely nice voice, 'there's a place I'd like to show you.'

'How long a detour?' she asked, and firmly flicked his hand off her wrist.

'An hour, maybe less,' he said.

She nodded. He engaged four wheels and manoeuvred on to an unmarked, rutted road. Presently, he nosed the enormous pickup to the edge of a white-limestone preci-pice. Gallons of flash-flood water dumped out of arroyos into the raging river below.

'Is this it?' she asked.

'No,' he said. 'Magnificent, isn't it?'

'Looks like red-mud soup.'

'The Spaniards named the river for its colour. Colorado means red.' He backed off the cliff and steered from the river. A box canyon loomed in front of them. 'Up for a short hike?'

'In these?' she asked and slapped the leathers with an open palm.

'The outfit you wore at the pool yesterday works for me.' He smiled a wicked smile.

'In your dreams, dude,' she sneered.

The walls of the canyon widened into an oasis. Roger parked under a cottonwood tree and turned off the ignition. Silence intermingled with rustling leaves. In a smooth sequence, he dismounted the driver's seat and pulled the hoody over his head. A threadbare T-shirt rose above his butt-slung shorts, revealed a dark hairline leading to forbidden fruits and dropped back into place. He threw his keys under the seat and jammed the ball cap low on his head.

Roger tilted and squinted into the sun. 'Near noon,' he said. 'Hungry?'

CC jumped off the running board, rummaged through a saddlebag and pulled out a pair of shorts and the flip-flops she'd worn the previous night. 'My inventory includes a disgustingly healthy sandwich and a crumbled chocolate-chip cookie.'

'Picnic time!' he exclaimed, and grabbed a mini-cooler from the rear of the cab. 'Pack-up. My inventory consists of two beers, a hunk of cheese and a Swiss Army knife.'

Finally, she laughed.

'Ready?' he asked.

'Go ahead, cowboy,' she said, and squelched a habitual urge to emit a cynical reply. 'I'll catch up when I get out of these sticky leathers.' Sitting on the running board, she pulled her feet out of the boots and wriggled free of the hot suit. Clad in three tangerine-coloured triangles, she stepped into the shorts and donned the damp cotton cami.

Animals, instinctively winding through sagebrush and cedar to water, rendered the narrow path easy to follow. When she caught up to him, he was on an incline. Calf muscles and hamstrings flexed and released. The dancer in CC appreciated muscles, tendons, sinews and strength.

Without warning, her pussy quickened. 'Be quiet, sweetheart,' she said inaudibly. 'He's not on our list.' Higher and higher they climbed across taluses. The sun peaked, shadows shortened and the heat of the day built. She followed his sure steps and her eyes wandered across a horizon resembling a diorama in the natural-history museum.

The trail flattened. Graceful as a doe, CC assumed the lead and brushed against him. Nipples under thin cotton grazed his chest. The hem of her shorts barely covered her butt. Each time she lifted a foot, he glimpsed darkness between her legs. Salmon-painted toenails matched blooming cactus.

Just beyond the curve of her shoulders, rock pillars supported an arch – their destination. The smell of water entered her nostrils. She heard an echoing rumble and squeezed through the slit. The setting took her breath away.

A wall of water cascaded into a crystalline pool. Back-splash filled the air and created humidity rarely found in a desert. An array of green-coloured ferns and delicate flowers sent an engraved invitation to relax and renew. 'This is it?' she whispered.

'Yes. You are the only other person who knows about this place. Can you keep a secret?' Dead-on serious, Roger resumed the lead and guided her to the base of the falls. He unfastened his sandals and pulled a shaver from the front pouch of his pack. 'Water clear enough for you?' he queried.

Eyes wide behind sunglasses, she pirouetted and revelled in his secret. 'Oh, yeah,' she said, 'and plenty hot.'

'Best remedy for heat is cool water,' he said, and entered the pool.

'Your clothes –' she warned.

'– need washed.' He dunked his entire body and vanished behind the waterfall. A few moments later, he re-emerged.

Amazing what water does for a person. For the first time, unguarded violet irises and black pupils twinkled. He shook like a puppy – hair splayed, streaks glistened, and slight waves flipped. Cute.

Munching on cookie crumbs, she watched him rub fine-grained silt over his skin – a cross between a mud mask and a pumice stone. He rinsed and stepped on the shore. 'The bath is all yours,' he said, and bowed low. His hand swung in front of her in a grandiose gesture.

She tried not to stare as he stroked the razor across the chin stubble. Dimples appeared at the sides of his mouth. A single droplet of water on the tip of his nose dared her to lick it off with her tongue. The threadbare T-shirt flew on to a rock. He dropped, stretched spread-eagled on the cool sand and let the sun's rays parch his body.

The awestruck woman kicked off flip-flops and pressed toes into the clear water. Unbraided hair hid her smile and bare feet waded to where water frothed. She ventured further and further until her feet lost touch and the waterfall pounded her head.

Canyon magic engulfed her mind and heightened her senses to the power of now. She surfaced and perched on an exposed granite rock. It seemed impossible to recall the date – or her name – or any of the other things that just seconds ago were so important.

Little snores intruded into her reflections; pussy jumped and nipples peaked. Ever so quietly, she stood and covered the distance to where he snoozed. She felt safe to appraise the situation with a ball cap covering his face.

Shirtless, on the carpet of sand and with his hands flung over his head, the buffed-to-the-max specimen of a man sported a tanned six-pack and just-right pecs. Whatever the dude did to maintain his corporeal body, she thought, he did to an extreme. Righteous.

She stifled a giggle. Below the carved abdomen muscles, a horny – or a wet – dream was transpiring. Generous balls enlarged and an endowed cock hardened under the flimsy shorts. Her own wetness oozed and her thighs tingled.

In a flash of inspiration, she removed her cami and wrapped it around his wrists. He jumped – a reflex. 'What the fuck?' he exclaimed.

Green eyes sparkled and full lips pouted a sultry smile. 'Behave,' she commanded. 'You are my captive.' She bent from the waist and silken ringlets caressed his thighs. Showing no mercy, she dragged the baggy surfer shorts to his ankles and tied the drawstring tight. His cock, with a majestic personality of its own, stood erect and seethed for attention. Backside to his line of vision, she straddled his chest and placed her weight on her forearms.

Butt raised high, the thong bikini divided her precious ass in equal portions. He tilted forward. White teeth gently clenched her bronzed cheek. He longed to see her face, but acquiesced to the feelings and the sounds of her passion. Breasts rubbed his abdomen and soft fingers rolled his balls.

Wetting the begging cock with saliva, she ran her tongue up and down the sides and sucked in and out with slick lips. Her mouth made popping noises. She swallowed the rimmed head deep, deep down her throat and drained him dry.

Filled with his world, she abruptly, and as though spring-loaded, bounced to her feet. Subtle spine towered over the handsomely rugged face. He gasped and sorrowed at the emptiness where lips and breath ceased reality. Tapping her heels to the rhythm of a song in her head, she untied the upper triangles and flung them on to the same rock as his shirt.

Tapping, gyrating and teasing, she glanced at him over her shoulder and loosened the strings of the bottoms. The thong caught in her crack. She tugged it free and the fragment of material slid to the carpet of sand. A ray of sun flashed as she turned towards him.

Velvet-lined pussy lowered and he drank in her beauty. Her perfume intoxicated him and his lips sought the fragrant flower. She moaned and her wetness increased. Hips undulating, she raised her spine and belly in an arch. Love lips vibrated and he tongued her to orgasm. Her body shuddered in ecstasy.

Servitude over, she frantically untangled the makeshift bonds and dropped on to the length of his stiff cock. He reached his hands around her waist and grabbed her ass. Searching fingers found the alluring crack of her butt. 'Need heat between your legs?' he whispered in her ear.

'Fire your hot engine,' she panted. 'Fuck me hard.'

Refusal not his to give, he paired her tempo with willing desire. She sat tall on his cock and cupped her breasts in her hands. Glazed eyes maintained contact. Sweat dripped. Pistons exploded. '*Yes!*' she screamed into the pristine air.

He flipped her over, raised her legs over her head and entered her from above. She wrapped her ankles around his neck, opened wider, and he plunged deeper. They rode each other like machines designed for endurance.

A naptime later they shared beer, cheese and a cigarette. Canyon swallows darted, circled and fed around them. 'Tell me,' she said. 'What kind of soldier are you?'

'The only kind there is,' he said grimly.

'What makes a person want to be a soldier?'

'Protect our country from bad guys.'

'Someday, somewhere, someone has to put the weapon down.'

'College addled your mind. Imagine for a moment that this is all that matters.' He wound his fingers into her hair and rolled her on to her spine. His thumb trailed the distance from her exquisite bellybutton to the hollow space above her ribcage – just to the left of her heart.

Encircling her breasts, he teased them to blushing, quivering tips. He pinched each one in turn, and sucked like they were the main course. 'How do I feel to you right now – if our truce holds?' he asked.

She wrangled from his embrace, rose above him on toned quads. Precious ass and precious pussy wide open above his face, she answered and countered. 'Strong, steadfast, and steady – and me?'

'Synchronistical softness and eager readiness.'

A last challenge from green to violet and she dropped on her knees. 'Anything else?'

'Wanton sexual desires ripe for satiation.'

'Takes one to know one,' she said, and playfully wrapped her cotton cami around his eyes. 'Are you good enough to do it blindfolded?' she asked.

'Anything you desire – it's bound to get better.'

The sounds of their lovemaking shattered the silence of the canyon beyond the rock pillars. However, the din of the waterfall drowned their wildest demands. Dawn rose on the empty bed of the King Cab.

Cockfosters Nuala Deuel

I have the most pointless job in the world. I'm an eraser on the London Underground. A walking rubber. I freeze discarded chewing gum on the tube seats and chip it away with a special chisel. I get rid of the graffiti on the District and Circle Line trains with a high-powered jet of water. I scrape off all the political stickers and club flyers stuck to the windows and grind away puerile messages etched into the glass. It's a pointless job for two reasons: one, it's never finished, and, two, there's always some twunt who will find it hilarious to spoil all your good work.

To combat the terrible surges of depression and boredom I experience down in the capital's bowels, I drink coffee laced with rum from a flask and I have regular sex with Natasha on and around the disused platforms at the long-defunct Down Street Station. Natasha is a supervisor on the Northern Line. She lives in a rented flat in Belsize Park that she shares with three other women. When I've got her breasts scooped out of one of her hot little bras and I've got my forefinger and middle finger wet, shaped in a V, fucking her bum and her pussy at the same time, and she's beginning that low, throaty moan that means she's about twenty seconds away from coming, she tells me she wants to take me home and throw me to those girls and see how I cope.

One of the most difficult parts of the job is staving off boredom. When you've been scrubbing at the word 'wanker' for half an hour with a piece of steel wool and most of a bottle of industrial-strength cleanser, your mind can be forgiven for wandering. There's little to distract you. You can try counting tube trains as they trundle through parallel tunnels; you can 'enjoy' the flash of electricity as it scatters across the dirty arcs of tiling. Sometimes, long after the trains have stopped running, you can holler a greeting and see if anyone will reply, and then play 'Guess Where I Am'. Sometimes I've had replies from as far as sixteen stations away. Actually, that's not a bad game. But, on the whole, it's grim, unrewarding, uninspiring grind. If it weren't for Natasha I'd have to think hard about my options. Jump under a Northern Line train, or something a bit flashier: the Jubilee, say.

After the shift has finished, whoever's staggered off duty will try to rekindle the fires of life with a couple of drinks in a Camden pub, the usual location we all gravitate to once we stagger back out into the real world. This particular day, I thought, consisted of a good crowd, and by that I mean colleagues who I wouldn't mind finding in my bed at some time during my life. There was Natasha of course, and Lou, a fellow cleaner who was a real tomboy despite her amazing 36-26-36 figure. Patti had only been in London for a short time, newly delivered from some industrial backwater in the north, and was a little bit shy, but she was cute, looked a little bit like Gwyneth Paltrow, same sad eyes, but not as polished, not as aware of herself. She was involved with escalator maintenance. And then there was Mute, not his real name – nobody knew his real name – but you can guess why we called him what we called him. He was a Nigerian with skin like the night-times you get above remote countryside: solid, clean, immanent. He was a rock, in more ways than one. One hundred per cent attendance record, clocked in five minutes before up-tools, clocked off five minutes after down-tools. Always available for overtime. Never a problem. And he was built like something that needed chisels to construct. We'd tease him while he drank his Malibu and pineapple juice,

playing 'Shredded Wheat', some stupid little game someone remembered from school.

You started by placing one hand on his knee and if he
didn't react, someone shortened the distance by one hand
width, and on and on until either he freaked or you
ended up with a hand full of cock. Not that any of us had
gone that far. Mute, no matter if he was wearing the
baggiest overalls ever constructed, always managed to fill
them out, especially when he sat down. The sight of his
tight thighs, and that coil of hot dong resting against
them, always made my heart patter a little bit harder,
brought a little layer of sweat out in the gulley between
my tits. Mute never chickened out of the game, but we
did. I always made a point of brushing his tip with my
fingers though, just to let him know I wasn't scared
either, and that if we weren't in a busy pub, with
company . . .

Lou saw our little game and played on the other thigh.
Mute sat and sipped and stared into the middle distance.
I gave him the usual little tickle and Lou went so far as
to pinch his balls. He might have arched an eyebrow,
nothing more. I went to the bar to refresh our drinks and
Lou followed me.

'What a gorgeous big hunk,' she said. 'I wish I could
get his motor started.'

'I know,' I said, enjoying the view down the front of
her blouse. 'I've done everything but open my legs to him
but he's so laid-back he could pass for comatose.'

'Well, I went a little further than that.'

'You did?' I said, with more astonishment than Lou
deserved. She seemed affronted, but went on to tell me
what had happened on the escalator at Angel after the
tube station had closed the previous Wednesday.

'We'd shut off the power along a section of the District
Line and he was down in the tunnels with a couple of arc
lights, struggling with a mass of hair and dust and God
knows what that had become entangled in the tracks.

There was a slight possibility of fire, you know. So he was trying to get this horrible, ancient human tumbleweed out of the tracks and I decided I'd take him a flask of tea. It was hellish warm down there and he had taken off his jacket, rolled his overalls down to his waist. He was gleaming under the lights like some dark, beautiful stone you'd find at the beach, polished, still wet from the sea.

'I decided, heck, show some solidarity, and did the same. I peeled off and strode up to him, breathed in, shoulders back, chest out, nearly poked him in the eye. But he just took the flask off me, nodded thanks and went back to it. I asked him if he wanted a rest, use a couple of other muscles for a change, but he either didn't hear me, or was ignoring me ... so ...'

Here, Lou leaned in further towards me and looked around her to make sure nobody else was listening. She loves her theatre, that Lou.

She said, 'I took my overalls off, leaned back against the wall, put one arm around the back of my head to lift my left boob – my best one – and fingered myself in front of him.'

'You did *what*?'

'I masturbated. I really gave him a great show. Spreading myself, grinding my hips into my knuckles, Jesus, I was so wet – I mean, wanking in front of a beast like that, it's some turn-on, I can tell you.'

I must have been standing there with my mouth open, unable to get much further beyond the idea of Lou approaching Mute with a flask and her huge breasts swinging gently in the warm, subterranean breeze.

'I was lost to it, after a while, as if I wasn't there any more but back at home in my armchair finger-fucking myself to a George Clooney film, or relaxing in the bath with the loofah gently slipping over my puss while I slide the soap around my arsehole –'

'Lou!'

'Oh, Jeez, sorry. Anyway, I was losing it, you know, five

seconds till lift-off, and I opened my eyes, ready to beg him to help me on my way with his tongue or his prick or, God, the flask even – by then I didn't care. And I'm coming, yapping like a dog, and the lights are off, he's slowly plodding back to the platform. It was as if I wasn't there any more. I finished myself off and got dressed and headed back to the platform, my face turning red as a tube sign. But he didn't even look my way in the staff room. No wink, no shake of the head as if to say *you naughty girl*. I was starting to believe that I hadn't actually done anything.'

I took a drink. My mouth was dry as underground air. 'Maybe he's gay,' I said. But I didn't really believe it. I was sure he flinched, thickened slightly, got a little hot under the collar whenever I gave his meat a little tickle at the end of our games of Shredded Wheat. I was bizarrely jealous of Lou, despite Mute's unwillingness to pick up on her overt flirtations. We went back to the table with the round of drinks and I sat down and swung my attention between Lou's enormous cleavage and Mute's impervious expression. Maybe he wasn't gay. Maybe he was just asexual. Maybe he was so dim he didn't understand a pass when it was thrown his way. Maybe he didn't know what being horny meant. I couldn't believe that either.

A couple of drinks later, I needed the loo. I went off to the ladies', my mind filled with plots and plans and hopes and needs, all of which I suspected would be in tatters before too long. Mute was as immovable as a boulder, and about as emotionally charged. But the heart wants what the heart wants. I wanted him. At least to try. If he gave me the brush-off as he did Lou, then fair enough. But I had to know where I stood.

Patti came into the toilet as I was straightening my hair, reapplying my lipstick, about to return to the gang. She smiled at me and quietly asked me how I was. I like Patti a lot, perhaps because she's so shy. I don't perceive

her as a threat, in any sense. Not where men are concerned, or attention, or looks. I mean, she's all right in the
facial department, a bit plain. If you were to pass her on
the street you wouldn't really give her another look, but
she does have this amazing arse that rocks and rolls as
she walks as if it were independent of the rest of her
body. Firm, smooth, round, tanned but with a hot little
white whale tail where her thong has been in place.
Thing is, she's always cladding it in baggy trousers, or
voluminous skirts. She's not one to promote her best bits,
dear Patti. I asked her if she wanted a refill and she said
yes please, Australian Chardonnay. And then, as I was
reaching for the door, she said, 'I won't step on your toes,
you know, where Mute's concerned.'

'Excuse me?'

'Mute. I . . . well, I know you like him.'

'Oh, you do, do you?'

She nodded. 'You should see your face when he enters
a room. It's like someone's brought you in a massive
birthday cake, blazing with candles.'

I was about to protest, weakly, when she said, 'I won't
make a play for him again.'

I felt my mouth drop open again. I was going to have
to be careful. Tonight was proving to be deleterious to
my jaw hinges. Despite having heard her with crystal
clarity, I asked her to repeat herself, just so I could have
the time to fully recover.

'Yes,' she confirmed. 'It was a couple of weeks ago. I
was just finishing up with the down escalator at Angel,
you know, the big one, and it had been a hard day. I had
grease and dirt and dust impacted into every crease of
my body. I looked like a miner coming up from the pits
after an eight-hour shift. But I have a membership with a
spa at one of the boutique hotels – a present from my old
man – and I had a couple of comp vouchers that you're
allowed to use throughout the year.

'I wasn't planning on using one, I just fancied a shower

and a sauna and a long lie-down in the steam room, but Mute came out of the ticket barriers same time as me and he looked dog-tired. I asked him if he fancied a spruce-up, maybe a massage or a swim, and he said yes. Well, you know Mute, he didn't actually say yes, he just widened his eyes a little and started following me.'

Patti leaned her beautiful tush against the bank of sinks and put her head back, closed her eyes for a second. Her flat, northern vowels lingered over her description of seeing Mute pad down to the swimming pool in his white Speedos, wet from a long, hot shower. The way he limbered up at the poolside, stretching, twisting, bending, his chocolate muscles coiling and smoothing out like something made of padded silk. His abs like big, chunky buttons to press.

'I was watching him from one of the loungers, wrapped up in a soft towelling robe. I'd scrubbed myself clean and had a good sweat in the steam room. I was feeling sleepy and fresh and minty clean. And horny as a fucker.' I was momentarily stunned by this outburst. This was Patti. This was someone who blushed if someone said 'bottom', outside of the anatomical context. 'He dived in, did twenty lengths, front crawl. His pace did not waver. He was quick. He moved through the water like something born to it. By the end of it, when he got out, and his Speedos were slicked to his skin and I could see everything in them, I was so wet I needed another shower. He was barely out of breath. I thought of him on top of me, spending that much time and energy on me. And then –'

She closed her eyes, as if imagining the moment, perhaps convincing herself that it really happened. I wanted to back out before she said it. I was lost. I was out of touch. Here was a shrinking violet. A shrunken violet. And she was about to tell me she fucked the man I wanted while menthol steam rushed around them in a dripping room filled with tiny blue tiles and soft light.

'I took my robe off. I just ... shrugged it right off. I was standing there, naked, anybody could have come in. And I got to my knees and I said, "Mute, I would really like to fellate you."'

'You said "fellate"?'

'Yes. I was being ... polite.'

'And ... what?'

'He continued to dry himself, he smiled at me in a kind of shy way, and then he left.'

'You didn't –'

'No. Nothing. I went back up to the changing rooms, got dressed, but he was gone when I came out. He'd left a message with reception. "See you at work."'

I felt elated, but at the same time sorry for Patti, and also warned. *This was somebody you thought you knew*, the warning went. *This is someone you know not one iota*.

We went back to the table. Mute was steadily sipping at his sweet liquors, and seemed unfazed by the fact that two women in his present company had made explicit their desire for him. I went cold, and glanced quickly at Natasha. Had she also made a play for him? I thought she was mine alone to fiddle with. Of course I couldn't stop her if she was interested. I wanted his cake and to eat her too. But in the way she looked at him I could see that there was something there. She was flirting, but in a kind of low-key way. From that I could tell that she had been knocked back at some point. My God. Who did this man think he was? Did he get off on teasing everyone around him and then blowing them out? Was it some kind of power kink? I almost got up and let him have an earful. How dare he never say a word and yet mess around with my colleagues' – my friends' – emotions like that? They probably took his silence as a green light. They shouldn't have done that, but they were acting in good faith. And he was leading them on like some tuneless Pied Piper. Why are you here? I wanted to ask Lou, Patti, Natasha. Why don't we leave him on his own to practise speechlessness and love up all the women in the bar with his eyes.

But I didn't. I sat down next to him, took a big swallow of my lager, and Shredded Wheated him all the way up to his nuts and bolt.

Work. What do you do when you find a train spray-painted with a thousand words from the Bible? It's like reading a big book. You don't think you'll ever make it through, but you start at the beginning and take it one word at a time.

I worked it with solvents and cloth, brushes and water. I wore a surgical mask and goggles. I listened to music on my iPod. Kristin Hersh, Manic Street Preachers, Jeff Buckley. I thought of Natasha. Her hot little items of lingerie that never looked quite the same when I tried them on. It was something in her skin, something incandescent that set off the patterns and textures and colours. When the battery on the MP3 player died, I listened to the song of the trains as they chuntered through the tunnels, squealing and shrieking as if in pain that they would never see anything but this peculiar kind of darkness.

Ten minutes before shift's end, I was smearing a little elbow grease into something like the twentieth 'thy' I'd encountered, when I felt a hand snake between my legs and squeeze my pussy through my overalls. I turned quickly, my breath in my throat, thinking, *Mute?* but it was Natasha, grinning wildly, more than a little drunk. She was brandishing something that looked like a policeman's truncheon and for one panicky moment I thought it *was* a truncheon, and that she was about to brain me with it for what I'd done to Mute the other night. But then I saw that it was made of silicone, as black as the tunnels, and sculpted into the shape of an erect penis.

'What,' I said, 'is that?'

Excitement spilled from her eyes like diamonds from a smuggler's purse. 'It's a cast,' she said.

And I was suddenly going, 'No. No. No. No. No.'

She'd spent an evening with Mute and a couple of pounds of plaster, creating a mould of his hard-on and then spending a fortune on a silicone reproduction. 'He won't fuck me, but now, in a way, he will,' she said.

'He won't fuck you, but he'll happily let you wank him to attention so you could smear him in concrete?'

'Plaster,' she corrected. 'But, yes, he was happy to do it. When he was *big* . . .' And at the use of this word she brandished the dildo, which jiggled alarmingly, emerging from both ends of her tiny fist like a hot dog that doesn't fit its bun.

'So,' I said, feeling tired and unwanted and unsexy. A thousand words of 'Thou shalt not' will do that to you. That and an ache for someone who looks through you. That and the girl you like to get naked with telling you that she's so desperate for a fuck she'll become a brick-layer for an evening. 'So, what now? You going home to fill yourself up all night or did you actually want me for something?'

She leaned into me and kissed me hard on the lips. I felt her tongue mash into mine. Her eyes were open. A comma of light on each one, the pupils large, drinking me in. She tasted of Pernod and bubblegum.

'I want you, honey,' she said. Her long dark hair seemed to drag away the darkness from everything else so that she was this figure of black amid pale surroundings. 'I want to play.' She pressed the dildo to the gulley between my breasts and for a moment it was Mute standing there, offering me his cock, a giant seemingly formed from the shadows where he did his work.

I said yes. I asked where. Here?

'No. There's a train waiting at Platform 2. Mike D is taking it to the terminus at Cockfosters in twenty minutes.

He said we could hitch a ride. The carriages will be empty. We could fool around. I could introduce you to another kind of Mute, one who couldn't speak back even if he wanted to.'

The last few minutes of my shift went by as if viewed through scratched glass. I couldn't focus. I was ashamed about it, but, hell, was I excited about the chance to feel Mute deep inside me, even though it was by proxy. I dumped my kitbag and my dirty overalls in the cabin and trudged the hundred metres or so to Platform 2. I needed a shower, a drink and bed, but I was energised by the sight of Natasha leaning out of the rear carriage, dressed in a white halter top that revealed her swollen nipples. When I reached her, I fell upon her and kissed her for an age. By the time we'd finished, the train had left the station. We had about twenty minutes before we reached the terminus. The lights throughout the carriage were out, as they always are when a decommissioned train is being shunted from one location to another, to ensure nobody accidentally boards it. I felt Natasha's thin fingers on my belt buckle. She flipped me over once it was loose and tugged my jeans free. My bottom tightened in the sudden chill. My face was pressed into the seat next to the glass divide by the doors. My breasts were exposed and I could feel my nipples rub a little bit on the coarse upholstery. The sensations there fed the heat that was building in my cunt. I bit my lip and closed my eyes to the moment. Natasha was kissing the puckered flesh of my bum and teasing me by pretending to pull aside the gusset of my thong. At the last moment she'd let go and the elastic would flick back and mildly sting my pussy lips. She gently scratched the area around my clit through my knickers and I pushed back, trying to capture more contact with her fingers.

'Do it,' I said, and she lightly smacked my arse, as if to punish me for being impatient. I felt my flesh jiggle at the blow, and a bloom of heat work its way south from the surface to my mons. I wanted to touch myself but I was afraid of more retribution. I thought instead of Mute and the slabs of muscle and flesh that made him who he was. I thought of him swimming in tight trunks, or submitting himself to Natasha's hands as she worked his cock into a state where it could be slathered with wet plaster. I couldn't understand his self-control. These were attractive women throwing themselves at him. I couldn't think of anybody, other than the Pope maybe, with that level of self-control.

Suddenly I heard an alarm blaring through the carriage as it rocked and buffeted through the tunnels, gathering pace. But it wasn't an alarm, it was me, howling as Natasha gently slid that demon dildo deep between my sodden cleft. I tried to move against her fingers, to take as much as I could, but the pain was too great. Great in the best sense of the word. So intense as to become some unimaginable facet of pleasure. I was kept there as she gently seesawed it into me, on this terrific borderland between hurt and honey, loving the pain and fearing it, loving the depth of the pleasure and fearing how deep it might reach. I came three times almost without knowing, the sensations so great as to mask the greatest one of all. I felt myself collapse, my hands pressing against my breasts and my belly to somehow check that I was still there, still the same person, that the experience hadn't triggered some amazing metamorphosis. By degrees, I recovered. The train was slowing. The station scrolled across the windows.

The lights came on.

Natasha was sitting with a broad grin on her face, twenty feet away in a seat on the other side of the carriage. Opposite me sat Mute, his smile threatening to out dazzle the harsh sodium glare.

'I hope you have a valid ticket,' he said.

WICKED WORDS ANTHOLOGIES –

THE BEST IN WOMEN'S EROTIC WRITING FROM THE UK AND USA

Really do live up to their title of 'wicked' – Forum

Deliciously sexy and explicitly erotic, *Wicked Words* collections are guaranteed to excite. This immensely popular series is perfect for those who enjoy lust-filled, wildly indulgent sexy stories. The series is a showcase of writing by women at the cutting edge of the genre, pushing the boundaries of unashamed, explicit writing.

The first ten *Wicked Words* collections are now available in eye-catching illustrative covers and, as of 2005, we will be publishing themed collections beginning with *Sex in the Office*. If you never got the chance to buy all the books when they were first published, you can now complete your collection and be the envy of your friends! Look out for the colourful covers – guaranteed to stand out from everything else on the erotica shelves – or alternatively order from us direct on our website at www.blacklace-books.co.uk

Full of action and attitude, humour and hedonism, they are a wonderful contribution to any erotic book collection. Each book contains 15–20 stories. Here's a sampler of what's on offer:

Wicked Words

ISBN 0 352 33363 4
£6.99

- In an elegant, exclusive ladies club, *fin de siècle* fantasies come to life.
- In a dark, primeval forest, a mysterious young woman shapeshifts into a creature of the night.
- In a sleazy midwest motel room, a fetishistic female patrol cop gets dressed for work.

More Wicked Words

ISBN O 352 33487 8
£6.99

- Tasha's in lust with a celebrity chef – it's his temper that drives her wild.
- Reverend Billy Washburn needs salvation from Sister Julie – a teenage temptress who's set him on fire.
- Pearl doesn't want to get married; she just wants sex and blueberry smoothies on her LA poolside patio.

Wicked Words 3

ISBN O 352 33522 X
£6.99

- The seductive dentist – Nick's encounter with sexy Dr May turns into a pretty unorthodox check-up.
- The gender-playing journalist – Kat lusts after male strangers whilst cruising as a gay man.
- The submissive PA – Mandy's new job fulfils her fantasies and reveals her boss's fetish for all things leather.

Wicked Words 4

ISBN O 352 33603 X
£6.99

- Alexia has always fantasised about being Marilyn Monroe. One day a surprise package arrives with a sexy courier.
- Bridget is tired of being a chef. Maybe a little experimentation with a colleague is all she needs to get back her love of food.
- A mysterious woman prowls the back streets of New York, seeking pleasure from the sleaziest corners of the city.

Wicked Words 5

ISBN 0 352 33642 0
£6.99

- Connor the tax auditor gets a shocking surprise when he investigates a client's expenses claim for strap-on sex toys.
- Kate the sexy museum curator allows a buff young graduate to make a thorough excavation of her hidden treasures.
- Melanie the interior designer and porn fan swaps blokes with her best mate and gets up to nasty fun with the builders.

Wicked Words 6

ISBN 0 352 33690 0
£6.99

- Maxine gets turned on selling exquisite lingerie to gentlemen customers.
- Jules is stripped naked and covered in cream when she becomes the birthday cake for her brother's best mate's 30th.
- Elle wears handcuffs for an indecent liaison with a stranger in a motel room.

Wicked Words 7

ISBN 0 352 33743 5
£6.99

- An artist's model wants to be more than just painted, and things get pretty steamy in the studio.
- A bride-to-be pays a clandestine visit to the bathroom with her future father-in-law, and gets much more than she bargained for.
- An uptight MP has his mind (and something else!) blown by a charming young woman of devious intentions.

Wicked Words 8

ISBN 0 352 33787 7
£6.99

- Adam the young supermarket assistant cannot believe his luck when a saucy female customer needs his help.
- Lauren's first night at a fetish club brings out the sexy show-off in her when she is required to wear an outrageously daring rubber outfit.
- Cat's fantasies about hunky construction workers come true when they start work opposite her Santa Monica beach house.

Wicked Words 9

ISBN 0 352 33860 1

- Sarah gets a surprise when she and her husband go dogging in the local car park.
- The Wytchfinder interrogates a pagan wild woman and finds himself aroused to bursting point.
- Miss Charmond's charm school relies on old-fashioned discipline to keep wayward girls in line.

Wicked Words 10 – The Best of Wicked Words

- An editor's choice of the best, most original stories of the past five years.

Sex in the Office

ISBN 0 352 33944 6

- A lady boss with a foot fetish
- A security guard who's a CCTV voyeur
- An office cleaner with a crush on the MD

Explores the forbidden – and sometimes blatant – lusts that abound in the workplace where characters get up to something they shouldn't, with someone they shouldn't – someone who works in the office.

Sex on Holiday

ISBN 0 352 33961 6

- Spanking in Prague
- Domination in Switzerland
- Sexy salsa in Cuba

Holidays always bring a certain frisson. There's a naughty holiday fling to suit every taste in this X-rated collection. With a rich sensuality and an eye on the exotic, this makes the perfect beach read!

Sex at the Sports Club

ISBN 0 352 33991 8

- A young cricketer is seduced by his mate's mum
- A couple swap partners on the golf course
- An athletic female polo player sorts out the opposition

Everyone loves a good sport – especially if he has fantastic thighs and a great bod! Whether in the showers after a rugby match, or proving his all at the tennis court, there's something about a man working his body to the limit that really gets a girl going. In this latest themed collection we explore the sexual tensions that go on at various sports clubs.

Sex in Uniform

ISBN 0 352 34002 9

- A tourist meets a mysterious usherette in a Parisian cinema
- A nun seduces an unusual confirmation from a priest
- A chauffeur sees it all via the rear view mirror

Once again, our writers new and old have risen to the challenge and produced so many steamy and memorable stories for fans of men and women in uniform. Polished buttons and peaked caps will never look the same again.

Sex in the Kitchen

ISBN 0 352 34018 5

- Dusty's got a sweet tooth and the pastry chef is making her mouth water...
- Honey's crazy enough about Jamie to be prepared and served as his main course...
- Milly is a wine buyer who gets a big surprise in a French cellar...

Whether it's a fiery chef cooking up a storm in a Michelin restaurant or the minimal calm of sushi for two, there's nothing like the promise of fine feasting to get in the mood for love. From lavish banquets to a packed lunch at a motorway service station, this Wicked Words collection guarantees to serve up a good portion!